(Aaron

Other books by Alex Ander:

Special Agent Cruz Crime Dramas:
Vengeance Is Mine (Book #1)
Defense of Innocents (Book #2)
Plea for Justice (Book #3)

Aaron Hardy Patriotic Thrillers:
The Unsanctioned Patriot (Book #1)
American Influence (Book #2)
The London Operation (Book #2.5 – FREE – Details in every Aaron Hardy ebook)
Deadly Assignment (Book #3)
Patriot Assassin (Book #4)
The Nemesis Protocol (Book #5)
Necessary Means (Book #6)
Foreign Soil (Book #7)

Standalone:
The President's Man: Aaron Hardy Vol. 1-3
The President's Man 2: Aaron Hardy Vol. 4-6
Special Agent Cruz Crime Series
The First Agents

The President's Man

Patriotic
Action & Adventure

Alex Ander

The UNSANCTIONED PATRIOT

Aaron Hardy Series
Book #1

Chapter 1: Nigeria

June 30th, 9:55 p.m. (local time); somewhere in the foothills of the mountains in Nigeria

"Team one in position—over."

"Copy that. Team two—report—over."

"Team two is in position—over."

"Copy that. Team three, what's your status—over?"

"Team three—thirty seconds to ready—over."

Hidden high above the compound below, Sergeant Aaron Hardy moved his legs and body as much as he could. He had been in the prone position for the last seventeen hours and his muscles were cramping. In two days, he would celebrate his thirtieth birthday. At this moment, however, his body felt much older.

Hardy had enlisted in the United States Marine Corps as soon as he graduated from high school. He spent the first four years of his career serving overseas, primarily in Iraq before becoming a member of the Second Marine Special Operations Battalion, headquartered at Camp Lejeune, North Carolina. For the next five years, he was involved in numerous direct-action, special reconnaissance and counter-terrorism missions, until Colonel Franklin

Ludlum asked him to command a team of his own to conduct top-secret missions all over the world.

Lately, Hardy had been considering a new line of work. During the last five years, his body had been under an extreme amount of stress and it did not recover as quickly as it once did. He was still in great physical shape, but he knew if he maintained this break-neck speed, his body would fail much quicker. He still wanted to be part of the special operations community, just in a little less intense setting that did not require so much reconnaissance. The countless hours spent waiting for the action were making him grow restless and sometimes took a greater toll on his body than the gunfights. He wanted to see more action and he wanted more control over it. He wanted to take the fight to the enemy instead of waiting for the enemy to dictate the terms.

Hardy peered through his binoculars and scanned the compound. The main building was located in the center and was dark and quiet. Two sentries guarded the main gate and appeared tired and bored, eager to be relieved of their duties. The two buildings that served as living quarters for the soldiers were located fifty meters to the rear of the main building and were only ten meters apart from each other. Both were alive with activity. The men inside were raucous, engaged in a card game. Music blasted from one of the buildings. 80's punk rock, Hardy thought, twisting the binoculars and glancing at his watch. He raised the binoculars to his eyes. His earpiece crackled.

"Squad leader, this is team three. We are in position, awaiting your orders—over."

"Copy that." Hardy slowly swung the binoculars to the right. "All teams standby—over."

Hardy checked his watch three times in the next few minutes. This was exactly what was making him grow restless—the waiting. His team was in place ready to carry out their tasks, but everything hinged on the target.

The voice of team leader one filled the airwaves. "Inbound vehicles eight hundred meters out and closing fast."

Finally. Hardy caught sight of the approaching headlights to his left. He watched two SUV's speed toward the compound and come to a stop outside the main gate. The lead vehicle slid forward, when the tires locked. The guards opened the gate and waved them through. Once at the main building, the second SUV's occupants jumped out and took defensive positions around the first SUV. Four men, dressed in black suits, white shirts and black ties, armed with AK-47 rifles stood guard, their heads rotating left and right, searching for security threats. The driver and the front passenger of the first SUV, similarly dressed, hurried inside the main building. After a few moments, they re-emerged and stood on either side of the front door, looking all around the immediate area. The one to the left raised his wrist to his mouth. The left-rear door of the first SUV opened and another man carrying a rifle came around to the right-rear passenger door and opened it. Two feet swung around and landed on the ground. The man inside lunged his upper body forward, giving him the momentum needed to get out of the vehicle. The man, a Nigerian warlord, was the most powerful drug dealer in the country. He stood six-feet, two inches tall and weighed at least three hundred pounds. His alias was simply, The Nigerian.

Using his middle finger, Hardy spun the wheel on the binoculars, zooming in on the man's face. He needed visual confirmation to proceed with the mission. The man had his back to Hardy, examining his surroundings. He watched the man button his suit coat and take a few steps toward the main building before stopping. "Show me your face," Hardy said under his breath. When the man continued his gait, he turned his head to the right and Hardy had positive identification. "All teams, this is squad leader. We are a go. I repeat—all teams, we are a go on my command—over."

"Copy that," replied all three team leaders.

Hardy dropped his binoculars, wrapped his right hand around the stock of the M40A5 sniper rifle in front of him and shouldered the weapon. He closed his left eye and acquired the two guards at the main gate through the rifle's scope. Swinging the rifle to the right, he placed The Nigerian in his crosshairs. When the man was two steps away from the front door of the building, Hardy gave his teams the 'GO' command.

In less than five seconds, all the men with rifles from both SUV's were on the ground, shot by Hardy's teammates. After giving the 'GO' command,

Hardy had the two guards in his sights and eased back his weapon's trigger. He heard two muffled 'pops' from his rifle and confirmed they were both down, the 7.62x51mm NATO bullets hitting their targets.

"This is team leader one. All tangos are down. I repeat—all tangos are down—over."

Seconds later, Hardy heard two massive explosions. Both of the buildings to the rear of the main building blew apart. One huge fireball rose from the remains and lit up the night sky. In the distance, Hardy heard small arms fire before his earpiece came alive.

"This is team leader two. All tangos have been neutralized—over."

Hardy held his breath, waiting for team three's situation report. Team three had the most delicate part of the mission. Their orders were to secure The Nigerian. They were to engage him only if he returned fire. Even then, they were to shoot to incapacitate him. Unable to wait any longer, Hardy called for a situation report.

"Team three, I need a sitrep—over." All he heard was silence. Sporadic weapon's fire came from the main building. His team members were shouting. It sounded like a struggle was taking place inside. The commotion stopped as soon as it had begun. Silence ensued. Hardy repeated his command. "What's your sitrep, team three?" There was no response. "Team two, advance on the main building—I repeat—team two—"

"Squad leader, this is team leader three—"

Hardy squinted through the binoculars. "Team two, stand down and await further orders. Go ahead, team three."

Team leader three: "We have your birthday present...all wrapped up and ready for delivery—over."

Hardy sighed. "Copy that, team three. All teams rendezvous for evac." Hardy paused before letting a grin form on his face. "Good work, gentlemen. Let's go home."

Thirty minutes later, with all of his men safely aboard two Bell UH-1Y Venom (Super Huey) helicopters, Hardy felt the tension leave his shoulders. His head fell back and he let out a slow, long breath of relief. He had brought his team to the completion of another mission without any casualties. In twelve hours, everyone would be stateside, enjoying some much needed rest and relaxation. He shut his eyes. *A good day.*

Chapter 2: Jack

Jack Darling took another long drag on his cigarette before tapping it on the ashtray in front of him. As his fingers spun the glass of straight Scotch whisky on the counter, he adjusted his weight on the barstool. He checked his watch again. He did not like waiting. He saw himself as a busy man and every minute he wasted waiting on someone else was a minute lost in his constant pursuit of the next big story.

As an investigative reporter for The Washington Post, Jack Darling had spent the past twenty years building his reputation in journalism on integrity, making sure his sources were legit before any story went to publication. His attention to detail was next to paramount. His perfection caused him to work long hours, tracking down leads and verifying sources for each story.

Jack loved journalism, but he had been thinking about a career change for some time. He was almost fifty-years-old; however, the eighteen-hour days made it seem as if he was approaching, if not beyond, retirement. He wanted one last big story before he put away his pen and paper. He wanted to go out on top, remembered as the reporter who broke that *big* story wide open. Maybe, he was dreaming. Maybe, he was already over the hill. He glanced at his watch. The man he was supposed to meet tonight was late—probably would not even show.

A waste of time, Jack thought, downing the rest of his Scotch before motioning for the bartender to get him another drink. Jack loved to drink and smoke. With the hours he put in at his job, these two guilty pleasures helped him relax. He always knew his limit though and never crossed the line, especially when he was working a lead. After mashing his cigarette butt in the ashtray, he reached for the half-full pack of cancer sticks, popped one out and stuck it between his lips. He thumbed his cigarette lighter twice. Before he could get a flame, his antiquated flip phone rang—the number was blocked. He thumbed open the device and pushed a button. "Jack Darling," he said, the unlit cigarette flopping up and down when he spoke.

"Are you alone?"

"What? Who's this?"

The voice repeated the question, louder the second time. "Are you alone?"

Jack thought he recognized the speech pattern. "Adam?" The man Jack was meeting at the bar only identified himself as Adam. "Where the hell are you? You're late. I've been waiting here for fifteen minutes."

"I know. I've been here for forty-five minutes. Now, are...you...alone?"

13

Jack sat straight and whipped his head back and forth, trying to find the man. "Of course, I'm alone. Where are you?"

"Have the bartender send your second drink to the table in the back corner."

Jack started to speak, but stopped when the line went dead. He told the bartender to send his drink to the back corner and slid off the barstool. He did not like games. Games fell under the umbrella of wasting time. The frown on Jack's face transitioned into a scowl. Adam had been in the bar for forty minutes and never made contact. *This guy has some serious trust issues.* Jack had had two conversations with the man. Both times, he was cocky and rude. There was also an underlying nervousness in his voice.

As Jack approached the booth in the back corner, the man's features became visible. He had short, dark hair, parted on the side. His dark-colored eyes were darting back and forth as if he was searching for someone. He wore a blue sport coat over a white shirt, his tie was loosened a bit and the first button of his shirt was undone. The man seemed to be in his mid-twenties. Even though he appeared to be physically fit and quite attractive, the first word that came to Jack's mind was 'nerd.' When Jack stopped at the booth, the man stood and extended his hand. The man was well over six-feet tall, but slim. Jack shook the hand and they sat.

Jack was the first to break the initial silence. "So, why all the cloak and dagger stuff and what do I call you?"

"Adam is just fine. I don't want my real name associated with any of this, not—" he stopped talking when the waitress appeared.

Not acknowledging Jack, she placed his drink on the table and stared at Adam. "Can I get you another?" She was not trying to hide her interest in him.

"No, thanks, I'm fine for now."

After she left, Jack put a small tape recorder on the table and pressed 'play.' Not wanting to waste any more time, he started the interview. "Adam, it is. So, Adam, why am I here? What do you have for me?"

Adam shook his head. "No tape recorders. In fact, I want your word I will be left out of your story."

Jack pushed the 'stop' button and retrieved a note pad and pen from his pocket. He motioned with the items in his hands and looked at Adam. "Is it all right if I take a few notes?"

Adam nodded and spied the people in the bar as if someone was listening to their conversation.

Jack opened the note pad to a blank page. "You look scared."

"You would be, too, if you'd seen what I've seen. So, where do you want me to begin?"

"Let's start at the top." Jack straightened and leaned forward, clicking the pen and scribbling to verify it worked.

Adam squirmed in his seat and took a last glance around the bar before telling his story.

Adam was a low-level information analyst at The Tucker Group, a company providing security for high-ranking officials of large multi-national corporations and Chief Executive Officers, travelling outside of the United States.

A week ago, Adam discovered he had computer access to information way above his security clearance. He did not know why, but being a techie and curious by nature, he snooped around some of the files. He found the information so vast that he grabbed a flash drive and downloaded the information. Halfway through the download, the data transfer stopped and his security clearance returned to level one. He tossed the drive into his bag and turned his attention to his workload.

When he arrived at work the next day, two men in suits met him at the front door and escorted him to the top floor, where he waited in a conference room. Fifteen minutes later, a man came into the room and proceeded to ask Adam questions regarding the information he had viewed the previous day. Knowing they had caught him, he admitted to viewing the information, but told them he did not know what it was and continued working on his projects. The man questioned Adam for two hours before dismissing him.

At noon, Adam's boss, accompanied by the same two men, who met him at the front door in the morning, showed up at his cubicle. The man handed Adam an envelope and told him his services were no longer needed. Adam gathered his personal belongings and the two men in suits escorted him out of the building.

Jack flipped a page in his notebook. "What was in the envelope?"

Adam took a long drink of his beer, raised his eyebrows and swallowed. "There was termination paperwork, a paycheck for the remainder of the week and another check...for *ten...thousand...dollars.*"

Jack stopped writing. "They gave you ten thousand dollars *after* firing you?"

Adam nodded before bringing the beer bottle to his lips.

"For what?"

Adam shrugged his shoulders and tipped the bottle back.

"Is it standard policy for the company to give such large checks to employees that have been terminated?"

Adam shook his head. "Not to my knowledge."

Jack licked his finger and flipped back several pages. "Did you tell the man in the conference room you had downloaded information to the flash drive?"

"Are you nuts? I was already in a deep hole. I wasn't about to give him a shovel too." He checked his watch and peeked at their waitress. She had stolen several glimpses of him.

"So, what was on the flash drive?"

Adam reached into his pocket and produced a small USB flash drive. He placed it on the table and pushed it toward Jack, making a big show of the motion. "I started going through it when I got home that afternoon. There's some serious messed up—" he stopped and waved his hands in front of his face. "I don't want anything to do with this."

Jack picked up the flash drive and examined it.

Adam slid to the end of the seat and stood. He gestured toward the three empty beer bottles on the table. "This is on you."

Jack nodded, but said nothing. He studied the flash drive. He was dying to know what was on it.

"Now, if you'll excuse me..." Adam pointed at the flirtatious waitress. "Either I'm going home with her, or she's coming home with me."

"I've got one last question." Jack squinted at the man towering above him. "Why me—why give this to me? Why not take it to the police?"

Adam laughed. "You should know the answer to that question better than *me*. If you want something done in D.C., you don't go to the police. You go to the press."

Chapter 3: Flash Drive

9:21 p.m.

Jack Darling sat on the edge of the black faux leather couch in his living room and leaned forward, moving the mouse attached to his laptop computer. His eyes glued to the screen, he could not believe what he was reading. After his meeting with Adam, Jack had gone straight home. He plugged the flash drive into his computer and pored over the information it contained. Halfway through he realized his hopes and dreams of having one last story that would forever immortalize him as one of the best investigative reporters Washington, D.C., maybe even the nation, has ever seen, was about to come true. He was getting ahead of himself. He had to verify the authenticity of the data on the drive.

Without looking away from the screen, he reached for the glass of whisky to his left, brought the glass to his mouth and tipped it all the way back. When none of the liquid touched his lips, his concentration was broken. He lowered the glass and saw it was empty. Setting the glass on the coffee table, he reached for the bottle of Jack Daniels and started to pour himself another glass, but stopped.

He needed his mind to be sharp. He had to formulate a plan to get this story to print.

Jack stood, rolled up his sleeves and walked across the living room to a small table cluttered with sheets of paper, a phone book and several pens. He shuffled through the papers. Not finding what he was looking for, he opened the wide drawer beneath the tabletop. Pushing items out of the way, he found the business card of an agent of the Federal Bureau of Investigation—Special Agent Raychel E. DelaCruz.

Jack had spoken with her a year ago when he was investigating Congresswoman Hayes, caught in a sex scandal involving one of her male staffers. The staffer was providing her with top-secret information in exchange for a future position in her cabinet, if she won her race for United States Senator. Special Agent DelaCruz had been the lead agent on the case, credited for bringing down Congresswoman Hayes. She had only been an agent for a couple of years, but she impressed Jack. He liked her ten seconds into their conversation. She was extremely professional, and he had a sense she was an honest, no-nonsense kind of person. Jack valued integrity and he had a knack for seeing that quality in others.

Flicking the business card between his fingers, he stared at the pile of papers on the table in front of him, not looking at anything in particular. After almost a minute, he reached into his pocket and took out his cell phone. After typing in the numbers from the business card, he put the phone to his ear. Several rings later, he heard the agent's pre-recorded voicemail message.

"Special Agent DelaCruz, this is Jack Darling. I'm a reporter for the Washington Post. We met a year ago when you were leading the investigation into the case against Congresswoman Hayes. Anyway, I have recently come into the possession of some information I think you'll find interesting. I'd like us to meet..."

Chapter 4: Peanuts

July 1st, 11:57 a.m.

Jack Darling tossed a handful of peanuts into his mouth, while he waited for Special Agent DelaCruz to arrive. They had arranged to meet at noon at a restaurant on 'H' Street NW. He loved the establishment's hot dogs with bacon and cheese. Plus, the restaurant provided free peanuts. Jack checked his watch and saw it was a couple minutes until noon. No sooner had he reached for more peanuts than he looked up and saw a woman enter the restaurant. She scanned the patrons, stopping when her eyes settled on him. If this was Special Agent DelaCruz, then she was even more attractive than he remembered. The woman wore a typical outfit for someone in her position, black slacks and a blazer with a white blouse. As she removed her sunglasses and put them in her blazer pocket, Jack recognized her face. The real giveaway, however, was the badge and gun.

"Mister Darling, I presume."

Jack stood and extended his hand. "Special Agent DelaCruz, I'm glad you were able to meet with me on such short notice. Please, have a seat."

Jack gestured toward the chair on the other side of the table.

"Thank you." She shook Jack's hand and sat. "Please, call me Cruz."

DelaCruz was her full name, but when she joined the Army, her fellow soldiers eventually dropped the Dela part of her name and called her Cruz. They would joke with her and say it was too long and too difficult to pronounce. To this day, her shortened name had stuck with her.

When she was seated, Jack got the attention of the waitress and said to Cruz, "I know you're busy, so I took the liberty of ordering you a burger and fries. It should be out soon."

"Thank you." She took a couple of deep breaths and settled into her chair.

"If you don't mind me asking, you seem a little winded. Are you okay?"

"I'm fine. The office is not far from here, so I decided to powerwalk it and get some exercise."

The waitress set two plates of food on the table. "Can I get you something to drink?"

Cruz smiled. "I'll just have water, please."

When the woman left, Cruz ate a couple fries. Fast food was not her favorite; however, not wanting to be rude, she felt obligated to eat some of the meal. "I don't mean to rush you, but I have a long day ahead of me. So, if we could get down to business, I'd really appreciate it."

"Of course. I understand." With one hand firmly holding the hot dog he ordered, Jack stuck the other hand into the bag next to him, pulled out a manila folder and handed it to the federal agent.

Cruz opened the folder and perused the contents. Taking small bites of her burger, she chewed and read.

Jack gave her time to process the information.

Minutes later, she put down her burger. "Have you verified any of this?"

Jack wiped his mouth with a napkin and swallowed his last bite of food. "I'm in the process of doing that now, but I wanted to bring you in on it as soon as possible. I was hoping you could use the resources at your disposal to check on those areas to which I would not have access.

Cruz nodded her head. "I can do that." She closed the folder. "Is this all of it?"

"That's only about half of what was given to me." Jack motioned toward the folder. "I made copies. You can keep that."

"What about your source?" Cruz grabbed a few more fries.

"He wants nothing to do with it. He worked for a private security company called..." Jack retrieved his notepad and flipped through a few pages, "The Tucker Group before they fired him." Jack leaned closer to her. "Get this—the day they fired him, they gave him his regular paycheck along with a $10,000 bonus."

Cruz tilted her head and raised her eyebrows.

"Yeah, I know. I've never heard of a bonus for getting canned, either."

Cruz checked her cell phone—it was 12:30. "Do you have anything else I should see, Mr. Darling?"

"I have plenty more for you, but I need to check into it first. So, what do you say? Are you in?"

Cruz stood. She held up the folder. "If this checks out...yes, I'm in."

"Great," said Jack, standing and shaking the agent's hand. "You have my number." He watched Cruz pull a ten-dollar bill from her pocket. "The bill's already been paid." He smiled. "You can get the next one."

She returned the gesture. "Thank you. I'm sorry to have to eat and run, but now that you've given me more work to do, I really must be going."

Jack laughed. "I understand."

She hesitated and stared at the folder. "If you don't mind me asking, why did you contact *me* about this, Mr. Darling?"

"I like your looks." Jack realized the implications of his words when he saw Cruz's body stiffen and her eyes narrow. He quickly raised a hand. "Let me clarify. You *looked* like a person I could trust. I was impressed with how you handled the case against Congresswoman Hayes and something told me I should contact you."

Cruz's shoulders relaxed. "Thank you. I'll be in touch, Mr. Darling. Have a good day."

Chapter 5: Ole Town Tavern

8:46 p.m.

Aaron Hardy walked down 41st Street, admiring the Federal Reserve Building on his left. It was good to be back on American soil, taking in the sights of Washington D.C. He was on his way to the restaurant to meet his entire team for drinks. In a few hours, Hardy would turn thirty and his team was determined to celebrate this birthday milestone. After the mission in Nigeria, everyone was excited to get out and blow off a little steam. The restaurant of choice was The Ole Town Tavern, a small well-known tavern in the Downtown District of D.C. Its roots went back to the turn of the twentieth century. Arguably, the restaurant had the best-fried shrimp on the East Coast.

Hardy tugged on the handle of the heavy glass door and stepped inside. The noise of a raucous crowd greeted him. He was immersed in the atmosphere of patrons mixing food, alcohol and sports. The place was packed with people cheering for their favorite team and downing a few too many beers. Hardy sidestepped servers and squeezed between tables, heading for the back of the building, where his team had reserved a small room.

Hardy entered and an ovation of applause erupted from his men. He saw several empty beer bottles on the table. They had a head start on him. He took off his jacket and placed it on the back of an open chair. After listening to several good-natured comments about his age and being told the next round of drinks was on him, he left to find the men's room. Halfway down a narrow and dimly lit hallway, he stepped aside and let two young women pass. He nodded his head and both women gave him a flirtatious smile. His cell phone rang. Connecting the call, he watched the women, who had cranked their heads around for another glance.

"Hello, this is Hardy. Hello?" The voice on the line was barely audible. Something happened with the game on the television and the people clapped and screamed. "Hold on a second." He found a nearby door at the back of the restaurant and slipped outside. As the door was shutting behind him, he went back to the caller. "Okay, this is Hardy. Who's—" Hardy never finished his sentence. The restaurant behind him blew apart, sending fragments of glass and brick flying through the air. The force of the explosion threw open the closing door, which slammed into his back. His head rocked backwards and bounced off the door before his body was thrown more than ten feet, landing near a metal dumpster. Rolling onto his side, he saw flames shooting out of the upper windows. The heat from the fire singed the hairs on his arms. He crawled behind the dumpster, which gave him some protection. Lying on his back, the last thing he saw was the night sky and a full moon before a secondary explosion pushed the dumpster—and Hardy—further away from the building.

Chapter 6: Shower

Special Agent Cruz stood in the shower. As the hot water pelted her head and cascaded down her back, her mind wandered. She had put in a long day at work. Since her meeting with the reporter, she had worked another eight hours and was physically and emotionally tired. All she wanted to do was unwind and get some sleep.

A few moments later, she felt a few tears mixing in with the droplets on her face. Long days like today brought her to the brink of exhaustion and she was too tired to fight her feelings of loneliness. She allowed herself to fantasize about what it would have been like to have someone to come home to, someone she could talk to about her day. At times like these, the solitude that came from living alone seemed to permeate every pore of her body.

At twenty-nine years of age, Cruz was by no means old, but she was approaching thirty, a number that had forced her to think about her life and what she wanted. When she was younger, she focused on her career, telling herself there would be time for a family later. She had dated a few men, but the relationships fizzled. Once they realized that beneath her good looks lay an intelligent and competent person with a strong drive for excellence, they became intimidated and fled. Rinsing the shampoo from her hair, she tried to remember the last time she was on an actual date. Unable to answer her question, she chuckled. *Has it really been that long?*

Cruz threw the shower handle to the right and stepped out of the tub, her feet landing on a soft floor mat. She yanked a towel off the rack near the shower and patted her hair. She was an extremely attractive woman. Her slim, but well-toned five-foot, eight-inch body was the envy of women ten years younger. Her dark brown hair fell well below her shoulders, paired with an equally beautiful set of dark brown eyes. She had a long face with high cheekbones and a flawless complexion. Having competed in beauty pageants since she was a teenager, winning her state competition and placing second in the Miss America Pageant, she had always taken care of herself.

After drying her body and blow-drying her hair, she took a black satin teddy off the hook on the back of the bathroom door. Raising the slinky garment above her head, she let it slide over her body. As the spaghetti straps touched her shoulders, the hem of the teddy came to rest above the knee. She picked up her hairbrush, shut off the light and shuffled into the bedroom.

Approaching her bed, she ran the brush through the full length of her hair several times before gathering her hair into a ponytail and securing it with a pink elastic ribbon.

Setting the hairbrush on the nightstand, she knelt by her bed, put her elbows on the mattress and folded her hands. She always prayed this way before going to bed. She knew it was childish, but this was how her mother had taught her. Mentally exhausted, she was not able to find the words she wanted. She made the sign of the cross by touching her forehead, chest, left and right shoulder with the fingers of her right hand and prayed, "Our Father, Who art in heaven..." After a few seconds of reciting the prayer in her head, she concluded aloud, "Deliver us from evil. Amen." Again, she made the sign of the cross and stood.

Throwing back the bed covers, she climbed into bed and slid back against the headboard of the bed. She propped her pillow behind her before reaching to her right for a book on the nightstand—a romance novel.

Cruz's job required her to be around many tough men. Most of them had military experience. If she wanted their respect, she had to be tough as well, oftentimes going toe to toe with men twice her size. She never wanted her toughness, however, to consume her femininity. When she was on her own time, she could let her hair down, literally *and* figuratively. Reading romance novels, as cliché as it sounded, allowed her to get away from her life as an FBI agent and get lost in another world, another life. It also allowed her to dream of a life, one day, with a man who saw her true self and loved her for who she was as a person.

Reading only a couple of pages, her eyelids drooped and she found herself re-reading the same sentence two and three times. She placed the book on the nightstand on the other side of her badge and holstered Glock 23 handgun. She pulled the chain on the bedside lamp and the whole room was dark, except for a faint light coming through the window from a full moon outside. Cruz slid her body further under the covers and plopped her head onto the pillow. After a few minutes of watching the moon cast shadows of swaying tree branches on her bedroom wall, she fell asleep.

....

Two hours later, Cruz's eyes fluttered. In the distance, she heard an intermittent buzzing sound, but could not place the source. She had been in a deep sleep and was not sure if she was dreaming. The buzzing sound stopped. She closed her eyes. Seconds later, the sound returned. Rotating her head to the right, she located the origin of the noise. She dropped a lazy left arm over her body and fumbled for the phone. Her hand came to rest on the holstered Glock. She slid her hand off the weapon, picked up the phone and swiped a finger across the screen. "This is Cruz." Her voice was barely audible and slightly raspy.

"Cruz, its Harper. Where are you?" Agent Christopher Harper was five-feet, ten inches tall with an average build and rugged facial features, sporting a nicely trimmed goatee mustache. He was a recent graduate of the FBI Academy at Quantico. The director assigned him to be Cruz's partner. He was five years younger than she was, but he brought a level of maturity to the partnership that made up for the age difference. They had only been working together for a couple of months, but they had formed a good working relationship. Their skills complemented each other well.

Looking at the clock on her nightstand—11:23—Cruz was going to tell her partner how stupid his question was, but she bit her tongue. Before she could answer, Harper continued.

"There's been an explosion. Preliminary evidence says it may be terrorism. The director wants all hands on deck on this one."

Hearing the words 'explosion' and 'terrorism', Cruz propped herself onto her elbow. "Where was the explosion?" She leaned to her right and rubbed her eyes with her thumb and forefinger.

"A restaurant in the Downtown District...Everyone in the place was killed, except for one person. He's been taken to the hospital. The director wants us there when he wakes up to have him answer some questions."

"Which hospital," asked Cruz, throwing the covers off and swinging her legs over the side of the bed?

"Washington...I'm almost to your place. Are you ready?"

Standing, she lifted the hem of her teddy with her free hand. "I'll be out in five minutes."

Chapter 7: Captivated

11:51 p.m.

"How...are...injuries?"

"...nasty bump on his head, but...fine."

"How soon will he...answer questions?"

"As soon as he feels...overnight for observation..."

Hardy's eyes were heavy. He struggled to open them. Voices faded in and out of recognition. He did not know where he was or what was happening to him. *Am I dead? Is this heaven...or is this*— He did not want to consider the alternative. Pressure built on his right arm. To his right, he heard a familiar 'whirring' sound followed by a series of beeps. When the beeping stopped, the pressure on his arm ceased and he heard a whoosh of air. Putting the pieces together in his mind, he had a good idea of where he was, unless heaven had blood pressure machines, too. His eyes fluttered open ever so slightly and he saw the fuzzy images of two people standing to the right. One appeared to be a man, while the other was definitely a woman.

The man: "It looks like he's starting to open his eyes. I'll give you five minutes. He really does need to rest."

After opening and closing his eyes several times, images came into focus. The first thing he saw was the overhead light. His eyes moved left. He saw a reclining chair in the corner next to a bank of windows. The shades were drawn and no light escaped from around the edges. Rolling his head to the right, he saw a woman standing at the side of his bed. When he looked at her, Heaven came to his mind again. She was so beautiful she could have been an angel. As soon as the thought came to his mind, he felt his face getting warm. *What am I saying?* He had no idea what an angel would have looked like if he *had* seen one. *I must be on some good drugs.*

The woman leaned over him. Her long dark hair, tied in a ponytail, fell forward over her left shoulder. The tips of the shiny strands almost touched Hardy's bicep. Staring into her dark brown eyes, he was captivated by her appearance—she was both attractive and all business at the same time. He did not know why she was standing over him, or whom she was; however, his pounding heart and the tingling sensations in his stomach were clear signs he wanted that to change. *Wow, these must be top-shelf drugs.*

Hardy blinked his eyes, hoping to clear his mind. A man in his line of work did not let people get too close. Doing so could cost him his life. This woman, however, had disarmed him without even saying a word. Hardy pushed his feelings deeper inside and willed his mind to remember how he had gotten here. *My teammates—are they alive?*

Special Agent Cruz smiled. "How are you feeling, Mr. Hardy? The doctor says you have a bad bump on your head, but you should be fine."

Hardy did not respond. He was still scolding himself for being taken off-guard by this woman.

"Are you feeling up to answering a few questions?" She checked the screen on her vibrating phone before silencing the device.

"Who...who are you?" Hardy coughed and felt a sharp pain in his back.

"I'm sorry. Forgive me for not introducing myself. My name is Special Agent Cruz of the FBI." She held her credentials for him to see. "I'm here to ask you a few questions about what happened at the restaurant. Do you remember what happened, Mr. Hardy?"

Hardy's mind recalled the blast and he had a good idea what had happened. He was more concerned about the welfare of his teammates, however. "What about the other people in the tavern?" Images of the burning building rushed to greet him, and he knew the answer to the question.

Cruz lowered her head before lifting her eyes toward him. "As far as we know, you're the only one to survive the explosion. Did you have family or friends in there?"

Hardy shut his eyes so tight he saw spots. He saw the faces of each team member. They were good men and now they were dead. The thought was almost too much to bear. He had lost good friends in combat, but not to this extent.

Seeing his twisted face, Cruz frowned and touched his arm. "I'm sorry for your loss."

Out of the corner of his eye, Hardy glimpsed her and noticed the tone of her voice. She truly was sorry for his loss, not only saying what everyone was expected to say in such a situation. "Thank you." He pinched the bridge of his nose between his thumb and forefinger. "Has anyone claimed responsibility yet?"

Cruz tilted her head. "What do you mean?"

Hardy rolled his head toward her. His eyebrows shot upward. "I think you know what I mean, Special Agent Cruz. If the explosion were caused by...oh, I don't know...a gas leak, the FBI would not have sent over an agent to interrogate me. There must be more to it. The FBI must have reason to believe this incident is related to terrorism. So...has anyone claimed responsibility?"

Dodging his question, Cruz opened her note pad and flipped pages. "What is it exactly that you do for a living, Mr. Hardy?" Most people in his current condition did not ask such questions, unless they had experience with explosions, bombings, violence, terrorism or a background in the military or police.

Hardy was not going to get answers. She was in charge of the investigation and accustomed to asking, not answering, questions. He decided to drop the inquiry.

The doctor came into the room. He was a black man in his mid-thirties, dressed in a white lab coat. Under the coat, he wore a light blue dress shirt and a muted red striped tie. With Hardy's chart in his hand, he walked around to the left of the bed. His black eyeglasses rested further toward the end of his narrow nose. He was reading the chart through the eyeglasses, until he shifted his eyes upward, toward his patient. "How do you feel, Mr. Hardy?"

"Tired," Hardy said flatly, staring at the ceiling. "I'd like to get some sleep." He hoped the response would put an end to the questions from Cruz. He could not answer her questions without compromising his position in the military. He needed time to think about what had happened and what he was going to do next.

"That sounds like a good idea." The doctor scribbled on the top piece of paper. "We're going to keep you overnight, while we run some tests; however, unless something bad comes back, you should be released in the morning." He clicked his pen and tucked it into the pocket of his lab coat before getting Cruz's attention and motioning toward the door. "Special Agent Cruz, if you don't mind..."

Cruz fixed her eyes on Hardy. Multiple questions were lined up in her brain. Her instincts were telling her there was more to Aaron Hardy than a simple man who was in the wrong place at the wrong time. Realizing her interview was finished, she politely smiled. "We can talk more in the morning, Mr. Hardy. Get some rest."

The doctor walked to the door and held it open for Cruz. As she left the room, her mind was still mulling over her last query. Over her shoulder, she said, "I'm guessing, military—possibly Special Forces."

Once they had left the room, Hardy's lips formed a slight smile and he said under his breath, "Attractive, professional *and* smart."

Chapter 8: Terror-Related

July 2nd, 7:01 a.m.

Hardy was awakened by loud voices outside his
room. His last dream had been a nightmare. He saw
the faces of his teammates gathered around the table
at the tavern. Everyone was laughing, drinking and
having a good time. Their faces became distorted,
while they tried to tell him something. He could not
hear anything. Their mouths were moving, but no
sounds could be heard. He felt the back door to the
tavern hit him, throwing him to the pavement.
Everything went black.

Hardy sat up in bed, leaning on his elbows. The
bed sheets were damp and his skin was perspiring.
He saw the clock on the wall—seven o'clock. The
light coming from around the window curtains told
him it was morning. Ruffling the bed covers, he
found the call button for the nurse's station and
activated the device. As soon as his head hit the
pillow again, the door swung open. Three men in
varying shades of dark suits rushed in and
surrounded Hardy. A fourth man pushed a wheel
chair. The first one to reach his bedside flashed a
badge—Department of Homeland Security. The man
was of average height, but wide and heavily muscled.

His suit coat was too small for his frame. He had no discernible neck. His head looked as if it was setting on his shoulders. His hair was styled in a military crew cut. When he spoke, his voice was deep and coarse. It was easy to see he was in charge of this crew.

"Hardy, I'm Becker with DHS. We're here to get you to a more secure location." Becker undid the blood pressure cuff from Hardy's arm and threw back the bed covers. He offered his hand, while positioning the wheel chair.

Not fully awake, Hardy struggled to catch up with the action. "I don't understand. I thought the FBI was in charge of—"

Becker interrupted. "Not anymore. We have reason to believe the attack on the tavern is terror-related. We have orders from the Deputy Secretary to get you out of here...*immediately*. Now, please, Mr. Hardy, we need to move." Becker grabbed Hardy's arm and shoulder, helped him up and eased him into the wheel chair.

Hardy craned his head over Becker's shoulder and saw the FBI agent, who was with Special Agent Cruz, talking on a mobile phone. He was waving his free hand in all directions, stealing glances at the men from DHS. Hardy recognized the makings of a peeing match between the FBI and DHS.

Spinning the wheel chair around, Becker leaned into Hardy and whispered, "Colonel Ludlum wants to see you."

Colonel Franklin Ludlum was Hardy's commanding officer. He planned and coordinated every mission carried out by Hardy and his team. Upon hearing those words from Becker, Hardy relaxed. Ludlum must have found out he was alive and arranged to have him picked up and brought back to the base.

Being wheeled out of the room, Hardy nodded and smiled at the FBI agent, who was pacing back and forth, visibly upset. Unsympathetic, and with a touch of sarcasm in his voice, Hardy addressed the man over his shoulder. "Have a nice day." He was glad to be getting out of the hospital and back to the base, where he and Ludlum would figure out who killed his men. From there, Hardy would take over and do what he did best.

Chapter 9: The Chase

7:09 a.m.

Special Agent Cruz took a sip from her coffee mug before guiding it back into the cup holder on the console of her black Dodge Charger. She nearly spilled the coffee when a black Chevy Tahoe barreled onto First Street. Thinking the SUV was going to sideswipe her car, she swerved to the right to avoid a collision. "Jerk." She navigated her way up First Street toward Washington Hospital, watching the Tahoe in her side view mirror. She pressed a button on the dashboard, placing a call from her cell phone through her vehicle's onboard computer.

Agent Harper answered after the first ring. He had remained at the hospital, so Cruz could get a few hours of sleep. "Cruz, I just left you a message. Four guys from DHS were here and they took Hardy."

"What?" Cruz turned left onto Hospital Circle NW and accelerated toward the front doors to Washington Hospital. Her voice grew louder. "And you just let them?"

"They said it was a matter of national security, and that they had orders from the Deputy Secretary of DHS to transfer Hardy."

"When did they take him?" Cruz jammed her foot on the brake pedal and brought her vehicle to a stop, tires skidding and screeching.

"They just left. Where are you now?"

"I'm out front." She rolled out of the vehicle. "I'll be right in."

"Stay there. I'm on my way out." A few moments later, he rushed out the front door.

Cruz stuffed her phone into her pocket. "What did they look like?"

"Four men in dark suits—Hardy was in a wheel chair."

There were a couple parked vehicles nearby, but neither one contained Hardy. They were about to search the building when Cruz stopped and stared at the sidewalk.

Harper whirled around. "What is it?"

She moved her open hand an inch above her head as if she was rubbing it. "Did one of them have a crew cut and a thick neck?"

"Yeah, he appeared to be the one in charge."

"Come on, let's go." She darted toward the Charger. "I think I saw them."

Harper barely got his second foot inside the vehicle before the Charger squealed its tires, fishtailed around the circle and headed toward First Street. The rapid forward movement shut the door for him.

Cruz's vehicle accelerated down First Street, heading south. She pointed at the windshield. "Look for a four-door black Chevy Tahoe. It was moving in this direction."

Driving along First Street, Harper scanned the area to the right, while Cruz took turns watching the road ahead and the area to the left. When they came to Michigan Avenue, she saw a black SUV on Michigan, veering to the right onto Franklin Street. She cranked the steering wheel to the left and sped toward Franklin, passing slower vehicles. Once on Franklin, she noticed the SUV stopped at a red light on Franklin and Fourth Street. "This is our chance to catch them." Cruz rocked her right foot forward and steered the Charger into oncoming traffic.

Harper's eyes moved in all directions, trying to find anything solid to grab, while his partner sped past Glenwood Cemetery. They almost crashed with an oncoming car that had turned onto Franklin. He clutched the console and gritted his teeth. "Hey, Cruz, how about we try not to die today?"

The muscle car raced toward the intersection of Franklin and Fourth. Cruz glanced at the traffic light. "Stay red, stay red." A white truck turned left from Fourth Street and headed straight for them. Stepping on the brake pedal, she spun the steering wheel to the left to avoid another head-on crash. Out of the corner of her eye, she saw Harper's dress shoe planted on the glove box, his leg pushing his torso deeper into the seat. The Charger went over the curb. She yanked the steering wheel back to the right and punched the gas pedal. Cruz brought her Charger to a halt on an angle, directly in front of the SUV. Harper disengaged his seat belt and was on his feet before the tires stopped rolling. Relieved to be upright and in one piece, he approached the driver's side of the Tahoe with his right hand on the butt of his service weapon. Cruz hurried around the front bumper and closed the distance between her and the SUV. She had thrown back the right half of her blazer, the fingers of her hand tickling the weapon on her belt.

Chapter 10: Franklin & Fourth

"What...the...hell...is going on?" The driver of the black Chevy Tahoe, watching through his side view mirror, saw a Dodge Charger leave the road, go over the curb and come to a stop in front of his SUV. The door nearest to him swung open. A man jumped out and approached his side of the vehicle. The man's hand was on his weapon. "That's the FBI agent from the hospital."

Sitting in the passenger seat, Becker noticed his driver had slipped his hand inside his sport coat. Becker's voice was calm and steady. "Take it easy. Remember, we're agents from the Department of Homeland Security. We have authorization to move Hardy. Just play it cool." Becker cranked his head around and gave his fellow agent, seated to Hardy's left, a slight nod.

Special Agent Cruz held out her badge. "I'm Special Agent Cruz of the FBI. Under what authority do you think you have the right to take *my* witness?"

"Settle down, Sweetheart. I'm with the Department of the Homeland Security."

Sweetheart? Did he just call me, Sweetheart? Cruz growled, "I'd like to see some identification."

Becker's right eye twitched once. "I don't answer to you, Miss—Agent Cruz. I'm operating on orders from the Deputy Secretary." He stuck his hand out the window and poked a finger at the Charger. "If you'll kindly move your vehicle, we'll be on our way."

Cruz tightened her grip on her service weapon. "You're not going anywhere."

Agent Harper stared at the driver. He leaned left, flicked his eyes toward the back seat and spied Hardy sitting between two men.

Hardy analyzed the scene unfolding before him. Cruz was determined she was not going to give up her witness. While the exchange between her and Becker grew more intense, Hardy put his hands on the back of the front seats and adjusted his position. He was only wearing an open-back gown and a pair of hospital socks that came just above his heel. The DHS agents had not given him time to put on street clothes. When he settled back against his seat, he felt something hard jab him in the side. Looking down, he saw the agent on his left had a gun, the muzzle pressed against Hardy's ribs.

The agent grunted. "Sit back and keep your mouth shut."

Hardy felt the hairs stand up on the back of his neck. He wheeled his head around to the right. The agent seated there touched his forefinger to his lips. Hardy's stomach churned, his pulse quickened and he felt his blood pressure skyrocketing, all signs that his body was preparing for a fight.

His bare butt cheeks and back sweating against the leather seat, Hardy was unarmed and surrounded by four DHS agents. One of them was pointing a gun at him. *What the hell do they want?*

Are these men really DHS agents? Hardy remained motionless, his mind spinning to come up with answers, more importantly, a way out of this mess. He was sure of only one thing. He did not like having a gun pointed at him. The man on the other end of that gun—and his friends—were not *Hardy's* friends. *All right, Special Agent Cruz, I choose you.* He thought about calling out for help to the FBI agents, but that might start a gunfight. And, he would be in the middle of that gunfight with no way to defend himself and a slim chance at disarming his adversaries, especially when one of them already had the advantage. No, he needed a distraction. Cruz's voice broke his concentration.

"I don't care what your orders say." Cruz shot a finger toward Hardy. "That is *my* witness and he's coming with *me*."

Becker shook his head. "That's not happening, Agent—" Becker reached for the driver's arm, "No, don't." It was too late.

Agent Harper yelled 'Gun' and drew his weapon, but the driver had the jump on him. The FBI agent was struck by a bullet and he dropped to the ground. Cruz yanked her weapon from its holster, took a few steps backward and fired at Becker, who was going for his gun.

The man to Hardy's left removed his pistol from Hardy's side and rolled down the window, preparing to join the fight. Hardy saw his opportunity. He drove his right elbow into the bridge of the man's nose to his right. Blood spurted out and his head rolled backward. Hardy put one hand on top of the man's head and the other under his chin and violently twisted. The man's head slumped forward against his chest.

The man to Hardy's left brought his weapon back toward Hardy. With both hands, Hardy grabbed the man's gun hand and rammed it against the partially open window. The gun discharged, sending a bullet into the driver's headrest. Particles of foam and debris floated back toward them. Hardy swung his left elbow into the man's groin, rolled the gun's muzzle under the man's chin and pressed the trigger. The report was deafening, made even worse by the weapon's close proximity to Hardy's ear. The bullet exited out the top of the man's head. Brain matter mixed with blood sprayed the left side of the SUV's storage area.

Taking control of the pistol, Hardy saw an empty brass case caught between the slide and the rear of the barrel. The weapon had malfunctioned. He dropped the magazine into his lap, moved the slide back and forth a few times, re-inserted the magazine and operated the slide again to chamber a live round. He looked toward the front of the SUV. Both the driver and the passenger were motionless, their heads lying on their chest. Neither FBI agent was in sight.

Hardy opened the left-rear door, pushed the dead man out of the vehicle and climbed over him. Shutting the door, he saw one FBI agent lying in the street, blood coming from a wound in his right thigh. Moving forward, Hardy paused to look inside the SUV. The driver had been struck in the back of the head. The passenger had two bullet wounds in his chest. Both men were dead. He peeked over the hood and saw Cruz lying on the ground. She was not moving.

Hardy approached the male FBI agent and knelt in front of him. The agent lifted his weapon, but Hardy disarmed him and tossed the gun under the Charger. He removed the hospital gown and ripped the drawstring from it. Using the gown as a bandage and the drawstring as a tourniquet, he stopped the flow of blood coming from the leg wound. "Keep pressure on that. Help will be here soon."

Moving toward Cruz, Hardy was buck naked, except for the hospital socks on his feet. Squatting in front of Cruz, he checked her body for bullet wounds—there were none. He felt her neck. She had a strong pulse. He ran his fingers along the back of her head and came across a small knot. *She must have hit her head.* He pulled out her mobile and dialed 9-1-1. "Officer down, officer down...Franklin and..." He read a street sign to his right. "Franklin and Fourth—I repeat—officer down on Franklin and Fourth. Send an ambulance." He left the phone on and placed it on Cruz's stomach. Hardy bolted back to the SUV. Dragging the driver from the vehicle, he hopped inside and eased the Tahoe between the Charger and Cruz. Once he was clear, he pressed down on the gas pedal and sped east on Franklin.

Chapter 11: Re-Group

Hardy had heard sirens before he left the scene. The police would be there soon, and witnesses were sure to describe the vehicle he used to get away. He needed to get out of sight and re-group. Houses lined both sides of Franklin. Most were too close to the house next door for his entrance to go unnoticed. He spotted an open garage door attached to a secluded house set back from the road. No cars were parked in the garage or the driveway. The owner must have forgotten to close the door after leaving for work. Someone could still be home, but he had to take the chance. Trying not to draw any attention, he made a textbook left turn, steered the Tahoe into the driveway and drove into the garage.

Hardy slid out of the vehicle and found the button to shut the overhead door. As the door closed, he made sure no one had seen him enter the garage. A naked man peeking out from a garage was guaranteed to warrant a 9-1-1 call. He opened the right-rear passenger door and stripped the dead man, who was close to Hardy's size, of his suit. Plus, the clothes were not as bloody as the clothes of the other man. Fully clothed, Hardy relieved the man of his weapon, a Sig Sauer P229, a paddle holster, magazine pouch and spare magazines.

Conducting a thorough search of both men, Hardy found nothing on them that explained who they were, or who their employer might be. They were clean, except for their hardware and a roll of cash wrapped with a thick rubber band. He estimated each man had a thousand dollars, which Hardy pocketed.

Moving around to the rear of the SUV, he lifted the rear door and saw four black duffle bags and four MP5 rifles, complete with two-point slings, red dot lasers and Surefire flashlights. Hardy dragged one of the duffle bags closer and unzipped it, revealing its contents. Judging from what he saw, these men could have been a tactical assault team. Hardy and his team had used much of the same equipment on their missions. He picked up one of the MP5's along with the several magazines from the other rifles and stuffed everything inside the open bag. Before zipping it shut, he found a sound suppressor for the Sig Sauer and attached it to the pistol.

Hardy moved past the driver's side of the SUV and opened the door leading to the house. He scanned for any signs that the homeowner may have a dog, and crept inside. Directly in front of him was the dining room, the kitchen was to the left. He advanced to where the dining room joined a large living room. From here, he could see into the back yard through a set of sliding glass doors. No one was on the first floor or in the back yard. He crossed the living room and ascended the stairs leading to the second level, his eyes darting back and forth, searching for homeowners. At the top of the stairs, he turned and moved down the hall. Two open doors were on each side. He cleared each room, ending with the master bedroom. He was all alone in the house. After detaching his pistol's sound suppressor, he holstered the weapon and stowed the sound suppressor. Leaving the bedroom, he saw his reflection in the mirror attached to a beautiful antique armoire. The shirt was bloodied. He rummaged through the dresser drawers and closets, finding a red Washington Redskins t-shirt with the team's logo emblazoned on the chest and a pair of blue jeans. The jeans were a little big, but he found a belt in the back of the closet. After adding a pair of white socks and some basketball shoes, he grabbed a light jacket nearby and went downstairs.

In the living room, Hardy picked up the television remote and hit the power button. He channel surfed, until he found the news stations. He wanted to see if the media had reported on the story of the shooting. He scooped a laptop computer from a coffee table, but put it down when he noticed a smaller tablet with attached keyboard on the couch. Hurrying to the dining room table, he powered-up the tablet before plugging the charging cord into a nearby electrical outlet.

While the boot-up process commenced, Hardy felt his stomach growl. He had not eaten anything in over twelve hours. Grabbing a frying pan from the dish drainer next to the sink, he put it on the stove and turned on the burner. Opening the refrigerator, he retrieved a carton of eggs, a tub of butter and a plastic container of milk. Dropping a mound of butter into the frying pan, he spotted a loaf of bread.

Ten minutes later, Hardy was shoveling the eggs and toast into his mouth, while studying the information on the tablet's screen. He had done a simple Google search for Special Agent Cruz. The query provided quite a bit of information about her. He was amazed at what one could learn about people through the Internet, especially a Miss America Pageant runner-up. Her full name was Raychel Elisa DelaCruz, born in 1986 in Dalhart, Texas, a small city of less than ten-thousand people, located at the Northwest tip of the state. At age eighteen, she had won the beauty pageant for her home state before placing second at the Miss America Pageant. Reading her bio, he came across a statement she had made during the Miss America Pageant. She was quoted as saying, 'I feel a special calling to serve my country, possibly something in the military.' He read the quote again, tapping his finger on the table.

Hardy stood and used the telephone hanging on the wall to place a call to a friend who worked for the Central Intelligence Agency—Kevin Hernandez. Hardy had not spoken to Hernandez in more than three years. The two men had served together in Iraq for more than a year before Hernandez left the military and started working for the CIA. The two of them remained close for several years, until Hardy's career took a different path. Halfway through the third ring, Hernandez picked up the phone.

"Kevin, its Hardy...Aaron Hardy."

55

"Aaron Hardy, as I live and breathe," said Hernandez. "What the hell have you been up to, you son-of-a-"

Hardy interrupted him. "I've been good, Kevin, but I need your help and I don't have much time. Do you still have access to personnel files for military members?"

"I don't hear from you in three years and the first thing you say is 'I need your help.' That's not very polite, you know. But, then again you always were more of a hammer than a glass of fine wine." Hernandez chuckled.

Hardy played along. "Hi Kevin, it's good to talk to you. How's the wife and kids? Is the job going well?"

"Smart ass," said Hernandez. "All right, what can I do for you?"

Hardy spelled out a name. "Raychel Elisa DelaCruz...I need whatever you can get on her and I need it *yesterday.*"

"What's the rush?"

"I'm really short on time and I can't get into it. I wouldn't be asking if it wasn't important, Kevin. I owe you one for this."

"Yeah, yeah, I'm still waiting for you to make good on those other I-O-U's. I should have something for you in fifteen minutes."

"Thanks, Kevin. Call me back on this number." Hardy returned the phone to the cradle and went back to the tablet.

For the next fifteen minutes, Hardy recalled the events of the past twelve hours. He should contact

Ludlum, but he remembered what Becker had whispered in his ear, as they left the hospital room— 'Colonel Ludlum wants to see you.' *Was Ludlum part of the operation to abduct me, or were those men using my connection with Ludlum to get me to let my guard down?* He was unsure if Ludlum could be trusted, but the man was Hardy's only lead. Still considering his options, he sprang from the chair when the phone rang. The caller ID showed it was the number he had used to contact Hernandez.

Hardy plucked the handset from the cradle. "Talk to me, Kevin. What've you got?"

"Do you still have the same email address from three years ago?"

"Yes." There were a few moments of silence. Hardy could hear Hernandez typing.

"I just sent you a couple of files. This DelaCruz woman is quite a looker. Are you thinking of dating her and wanted to run a background check on her first?" Before Hardy could answer, Hernandez continued. "If you're not dating her, you could always give her *my* number."

"No, we're not dating." Hardy typed in his user name and password. "Besides, you wouldn't be her type—she likes *attractive* men." Hardy grinned, appreciating the light-hearted moment in the midst of chaos and dead bodies.

"Wow! Three years go by and all you have for me are demands and insults. I guess it's true what they say about not needing enemies when you have friends like—"

"Listen, I appreciate your help on this, and I really do owe you one."

The humor left Hernandez's voice. "Don't worry about that. Are you in some sort of trouble? If there's anything I can do, just say the word."

"Thanks, Kevin. I appreciate that. You've already helped me a great deal. I have to go."

"Okay. Take care of yourself, my friend. Next time don't wait three years to call, you got it?"

"I won't." Hardy hung up the phone and focused his attention to the tablet's screen, reading the information Hernandez was able to provide on the special agent from Texas.

She joined the Army at age twenty-three after earning a Bachelor of Science degree in Criminology from Texas A&M University—San Antonio. She spent two years, serving in a couple of support roles in the areas of intelligence and computer information systems. She never came close to the action overseas. When she was honorably discharged, her rank was that of corporal. Hardy read everything a second time. *Not much here...Still, her presence in the hospital and the way she handled herself with the fake DHS agents...tells me there's more to her than what I'm seeing from her military file.*

Hernandez had also attached another file. Hardy clicked on the icon and he had access to her career at the Federal Bureau of Investigation. Skimming the screen, a better outline of her started to form, one that fit the image he had in his mind.

After being discharged from the Army, she started a career as a police officer for her hometown of Dalhart, Texas. Two years into her career, she made a routine traffic stop that resulted in a shootout with a Mexican drug trafficker who was on the FBI's Most Wanted List. She received minor injuries in the shootout that ended with the capture and the arrest of the fugitive. She received special recognition from the FBI, and she was promoted to the rank of sergeant in the Dalhart P.D.

One year later, at age twenty-seven, she was accepted into the FBI and graduated at the top of her class. At twenty-nine years of age, following a lengthy investigation, she arrested Congresswoman Hayes and received a commendation from FBI Director Phillip Jameson. Six months later, she was directly responsible for exposing another corrupt Washington government official, who resigned his position. He was arrested on charges related to his actions, while serving in the United States Senate. She was promoted to a supervisory special agent position in the Fraud and Public Corruption Division.

At this rate, she's on the fast track to becoming director. Hardy shut down the tablet and unplugged it from the wall outlet. Staring at the phone on the wall, He had a difficult decision to make. Actually, it was not that difficult. He had no other options, but to contact Colonel Ludlum and find out what he knew. Picking up the phone, he paused before dialing the phone number for his boss.

Chapter 12: The Director

9:19 a.m., Washington Hospital

FBI Director Phillip Jameson advanced in his career by following orders and making sure his superiors got all of the credit. As a rookie agent, he learned that making life difficult for your bosses might help them overlook people for promotions. As a result, he worked hard and never expected anything more than his paycheck at the end of the week. The people above him took note of his work ethic and wanted someone like him on their team; thus, Jameson became FBI Director very early in his career. As the head of the Federal Bureau of Investigation, he demanded the same integrity from those who worked for him.

Fifty-years-old, Jameson was physically fit, regularly lifting weights and jogging. He was one inch short of six feet in height and weighed one hundred and ninety pounds. He was bald and wore rounded, rectangular eyeglasses with thick black frames. His work attire was always the same—black suit, white shirt with a red tie. He changed the shade and print of the tie, but the color was always red. His shoes were black and shined—absolutely no smudges. Although no one knew, he had a separate closet at home for his business attire. His clothing was a projection of what you could expect from him. He was a man who brought to bear rock-steady leadership and decision-making skills and always backed up his agents.

Director Jameson strode down the hallway of the hospital. Two junior agents were one-step behind him, one on either side. His long strides carried him forward at a pace that those walking with him found difficult to maintain. The other agents alternated between walking and jogging to keep up with him. Jameson turned left at the end of the hallway. He made an immediate right turn before entering the hospital room where one of his finest agents was lying in a bed, having been involved in a gunfight two hours ago.

"Cruz, I'm glad to see you're awake." Jameson gestured for the two agents to wait outside and closed the door. "How are you feeling?"

"My head feels like Tank has been sitting on it for an hour, but other than that, I feel good to go, sir."

Tank was the nickname for one of the agents who had accompanied the Director. Tank had received his nickname because of his size. The man was six-feet, six-inches tall and tipped the scales at 250 pounds of solid muscle. He had only been with the FBI for a little over a year, but had made a name for himself as someone you definitely wanted on your side if you ever got into a fight.

"Good to hear," said Jameson, through a thin smile on his lips. He came closer to the bed.

"When can I get out of here...I've got a lot of work to do?"

"Soon, but first I'd like to talk to you about what happened out there. What do you remember?" He shook his head and held up his hand. "First, let me say you did one hell of a job patching up Harper. That field dressing saved his life. He's in surgery now, but the doctors say he's going to make it. If you hadn't done that before dialing 9-1-1, the doctors said he would have bled out in a matter of minutes. Nice work."

Cruz was silent. Her mind was searching for the details of the incident. "Excuse me, sir, but I'm not sure what you're talking about. I don't recall applying a field dressing to anyone, let alone calling 9-1-1. The last thing I remember before waking up here is seeing a naked man running toward the SUV."

"So, if you didn't do it, then who did? No average person could have done that, unless he or she had military or medical training." After a few moments of silence, he continued. "Anyway, what *do* you remember?"

Holding a cup of water in her hand and taking small sips, Cruz filled in the director on the events leading up to the shootout. She grabbed a pitcher and filled her empty cup.

"So, there were four men inside the Tahoe with Hardy?"

Cruz nodded.

"There were only two bodies at the scene. What happened to the other three men?" Jameson let the question hang in the air, while he made a call from his cell phone.

"This is Director Jameson. I need you to find out if there are any security cameras near Franklin and Fourth and get me any footage from this morning between seven and nine...Thank you." He put the phone in his pocket. "Get some rest, Cruz and I'll see what I can do to get you released." He reeled around and was out the door before she could reply.

Cruz picked up her mobile from the tray table and scrolled down her list of contacts. When she had found the name she was looking for, she pressed the 'dial' button. After a few rings, a good friend of hers at the FBI answered.

"Hey, Cruz, it's good to hear from you. Are you out of the hospital already?" Martin O'Neal was an FBI computer specialist in his mid-twenties. He and Cruz had gotten to know each other throughout the years. His help was crucial to Cruz getting the evidence she needed in the case against Congresswoman Hayes.

"No, I'm still here, Marty. Can you do me a favor? I need all the information you can get on one Aaron L. Hardy."

"Would that be the same Aaron L. Hardy who survived the tavern blast last night?"

"Yeah," said Cruz, her mind re-playing the events since the explosion.

"Am I looking for anything in particular?"

"I'm not sure. My gut tells me he's ex-military, possibly Special Forces. You can start there."

"Will do, Cruz." O'Neal changed the subject. "On that other matter you wanted me to investigate..."

Cruz remembered she had given O'Neal the file folder from Jack Darling.

"I found something. I did some digging and it turns out that seven of those eight names you gave me either have turned up dead or have disappeared completely in the last year. As you know, those were all high-profile names—known drug lords, heads of state, even an ambassador."

"Did you find any details on their deaths?"

"In one case, there was a witness who stated he saw several men, dressed in black military clothing in the area at about the same time the drug lord was gunned down. In another case, a hotel cleaning lady was asked to use her key card to open a room by several men—"

"Let me guess...all dressed in black military clothing."

"That's right. Interesting, isn't it? Anyway, that's all I have so far, but I'll let you know if I find anything else."

"Thanks, Marty. Let me know as soon as you have something on Hardy, too." She disconnected the call and set her phone on the tray table. She stared at the ceiling. *Who were those men in the SUV and why did they want Hardy? Who called 9-1-1 with my phone? Who saved Harper's life?* Cruz doubted it would have been any of the DHS imposters. *Perhaps it was a passing civilian. Or...*She let her mind contemplate another option. The door opened and a nurse entered.

"Hi, dearie," said the smiling nurse. "I have your discharge papers for you to sign."

Chapter 13: We Need to Talk

9:47 a.m.

Colonel Ludlum's voice gave away the shock he was feeling. "Hardy, thank God you're alive. When I heard about the explosion, I thought for sure everyone was dead. How did you survive?"

"I got a phone call." Hardy switched the phone to his left ear before picking up a remote control and shutting off the television.

"What do you mean?"

Hardy waved his hand. "It doesn't matter. We need to talk, but I don't want to do it over the phone. When can we meet?"

"I'm in meetings for most of the afternoon." Ludlum checked the time on his wristwatch. "I can leave early and meet you at my house around four."

"That'll work. I'll see you there." Hardy slowly lowered the receiver onto the handset's hook, his mind making a checklist of the things he was going to need. He took a step toward the dining room table and shoved his hand into his front pocket.

Chapter 14: Ranger

Hardy took one of the rolls of cash from his pocket, peeled back five one hundred-dollar bills and left them on the dining room table. He scooped up the tablet and charging cable and went to the garage. Slipping the tablet inside the duffle bag in the back of the SUV, he left the garage through a side door.

Walking down Franklin Street with the duffle bag over his shoulder, Hardy scanned the houses on either side of the street, searching for signs the homeowner was not home. He had been trained to see tiny details ordinary people never noticed. The skill had served him well, saving his life and the lives of his men on numerous occasions.

A block ahead, he spotted a modest house with four or five rolled up newspapers on the front porch. The lawn, higher in length than the neighbors, was beginning to dry out in the July heat, despite the presence of a water sprinkler in the middle of the brown lawn. Strolling up the driveway, he went to the front door, rang the doorbell and picked up the newspapers, waiting to see if anyone answered the door. Turning around he ambled over to the water faucet and twisted the knob—the hiss of water and air mixed, and the sprinkler rotated back and forth. Hardy moved to the back of the residence, carefully stacking the newspapers. If people saw him, they would think he was there to pick up the newspapers and take care of the house, while the owners were away.

Standing by the back door, Hardy checked the nearby houses to see if anyone was watching before breaking the glass on the door with his elbow. Snaking his arm around the jagged glass attached to the frame, he unlocked and opened the door before stepping inside the garage; an older model Ford Ranger was parked inside, facing the street. Dark blue with an extended cab and a flat fiberglass topper covering the bed, the truck would be perfect. Hardy twisted the handle of the topper before lifting it and throwing his duffle bag inside. When the topper was secured, he went to the door leading to the living space of the house. Sneaking inside, he saw he was in the kitchen. Behind the door, a coat rack on the wall held two light jackets. Next to them was a set of keys. Swiping the key ring, he went to the Ranger—they were a match.

Inside the Ranger, Hardy pressed the button on the garage door opener, clipped to the visor. The large chain attached to the overhead door strained, lifting the overhead garage door. He started the engine and eased the truck out of the garage and into traffic.

On his way to Ludlum's house, Hardy made a couple of stops to pick up supplies and fill the gas tank on the Ranger. Driving away from the gas station, he checked the digital clock—11:21. He wanted to get to Ludlum's house early and conduct reconnaissance of the surrounding area.

The forty-minute drive to Kent Island had been smooth. Hardy was able to avoid the heavy lunch-hour traffic. He had used the time to review the events leading up to this moment. He had initially thought terrorists were responsible for the explosion at the tavern; however, since the failed kidnapping attempt at the hospital, he was certain that was not the case. No, the two were definitely related. The big question was 'how?'

Hardy's thoughts turned to Special Agent Cruz. He checked the side-view mirror, pushed down on the turn-signal lever and passed a slow-moving vehicle. He smiled, remembering what Kevin Hernandez had said to him on the phone, 'Are you thinking of dating her and wanted to run a background check on her first?' Hardy had been so focused on obtaining as much information on her as he could, he did not realize he had developed feelings for her.

Hardy's job for the past three years had made it nearly impossible to have any kind of serious relationship with a woman. He never knew when he was going to leave for a mission or how long he was going to be gone. Women were not waiting in line for a man with those qualities. Cruz may have been different, however. One did not advance to her professional level in such a short time by spending time with family. She may have been someone who would understand him and his unconventional working hours. With his left elbow on the door, he rested his head on his fist and let a breath of air slip past his pursed lips. Had the circumstances been different, he would have asked Cruz out on a date. The scenery on either side of the Ranger changed from water to tall trees and green grass. Hardy's thoughts returned to the mission.

Colonel Ludlum lived in a one-story home at the end of Chesapeake Drive on Kent Island. On the other side of the Chesapeake Bay Bridge, Hardy turned right onto Romancoke Road and drove past Chesapeake Drive, parking the Ranger on Camp Wright Lane, a secluded road surrounded by trees, located behind Ludlum's house. Not knowing if he could trust his boss, Hardy wanted to park out of view from the man's house.

With the Ranger parked in the woods, Hardy double-checked the status of his Sig Sauer, grabbed a pair of binoculars and a set of lock picks from the duffle bag in the truck bed, and disappeared into the forest.

Chapter 15: Nice Work, Marty

"It's close to noon. Call me as soon as you get this." Special Agent Cruz had left three messages for Jack Darling. Each call went straight to voicemail. With O'Neal's help, she was able to verify the information Darling had given her, and she wanted to know what progress the reporter had made on his end. Every detail she had led back to The Tucker Group. She had placed calls to the organization, but no one of importance had returned her calls, only secretaries, who gave her scripted responses. The Tucker Group was somehow involved. She could sense it, but could not prove it.

During her career with the FBI, Cruz had developed a keen sense for detecting when people were not being honest with her. This talent had been her greatest asset when she investigated those who were suspected of criminal wrongdoing. She dissected a person's words and examined them against the person's body language, tone of voice and facial expressions. She knew if she was getting the truth or that person's *version* of the truth. She was good at this part of her tradecraft, sometimes too good.

She had often considered her penchant for detecting lies had been part of the reason for her failure with men. She had never caught any of them cheating or lying to her, but once that familiar feeling of distrust swept over her, she could not recover. Cruz sat behind her desk and stared out the window. Large and puffy clouds sporadically intercepted the sun's rays. *Maybe they didn't leave because I intimidated them. Maybe I pushed them away.*

Thoughts of Hardy forced their way through her lamentations over past relationships. The first time she had seen him in the hospital, he had seemed different from most of the men she had known. Even in his then current and somewhat vulnerable condition, he had seemed...dangerous. She had worked with many men during her time in the military and law enforcement, but none of them had conveyed that quality to her. What seemed peculiar, however, was not the aura of danger that emanated from Hardy. No, it was the way he made her feel, a feeling of *trust—a sense of safety.* Cruz recalled the incident on Franklin and Fourth Street. Her face flushed and she smiled when her mind's eye saw the butt of the naked man—it was firm and cute. *It had to belong to Hardy.* She remembered seeing him in the back seat of the SUV, wearing a hospital gown. *He must have used the gown to dress Harper's wound.* Lost in thought, she flinched when someone knocked on her office door. The door opened a crack and Martin O'Neal's head appeared.

"You got a minute, Cruz?"

"Come on in, Marty." She pinched the front of her blouse between her thumb and forefinger and fanned her chest. Her cheeks were warm and she felt as if she had been caught looking at dirty pictures. Standing, she met O'Neal at the small conference table, located to the side of her desk, halfway to the office door. "What's up?"

O'Neal was wearing a blue suit, white shirt and blue tie. Gold-rimmed, oval-shaped eyeglasses sat on his narrow nose. His light-colored hair was short, almost in a crew cut style. The two sat at the table and faced the window. O'Neal placed a file folder in front of her. "Take a look at this."

She skimmed the contents of the folder. "What am I looking at here?"

"Remember how everything we had pointed toward The Tucker Group being involved, but we just couldn't find the lynch pin tying them to the deaths and disappearances of the people on that list?"

Cruz lifted her head and nodded.

"I found that pin." O'Neal leaned forward and pointed out several lines on the papers. "These here are sizable monthly deposits to The Tucker Group on the first of every month like clockwork. Now, it doesn't show where the money is coming from, but I used my contacts and was able to find out the money originated from a Swiss bank account."

"Whose name is on the account?" Cruz peeled back a sheet of paper and glanced at the page beneath it.

"The Swiss won't divulge that information—confidential."

"So, it's a dead end." She let go of the piece of paper.

O'Neal leaned back before sitting erect and pointing at the file folder. "Ordinarily, yes, but I noticed the amounts were exactly the same every month, right down to the penny."

Cruz whirled her head around toward O'Neal, hearing the excitement in his voice.

"So, I dug a little deeper and discovered the amount matches with a line item buried deep in the operating budget for the Department of Defense." He raised his hands. "Let me back up a bit. The *exact* amount is not there; however, there are several smaller amounts listed that, when added together, equal the amount that was deposited into the account of The Tucker Group on a monthly basis. The dates even match."

Cruz squinted and tilted her head. "The DOD is regularly giving money to a private security company...in exchange for what?"

O'Neal shook his head. "That's just it, Cruz. They aren't giving money *directly* to The Tucker Group.

"I don't understand."

"To the untrained eye, it looks like several small random amounts are being expensed on the usual types of items the military would need—bullets, bombs, guns, etc. They are so small that no one would think twice about it. In actuality, the money is being transferred to the Swiss account, which acts as a holding account, if you will, until the figure hits this specified amount." O'Neal pointed to the line items on the papers. "Then, the transfer is made to

The Tucker Group, and the process starts all over again."

Cruz was putting together a picture in her mind and she did not like the image. Somewhere, someone in the government was channeling money to a private corporation. When things like that happened, top-secret covert black-ops programs usually were at the heart of it. Those involved did not want American taxpayers to find out how their tax dollars were being spent.

"Are you ready for the next piece of the puzzle?"

Cruz faced O'Neal. "What, there's more?"

He pursed his lips and nodded his head. "Senator Chuck Hastings personally made the request for every one of those smaller expense items."

She shrugged. "He's Chairman of the Armed Services Committee. He's involved with the budget."

"That's true. It may be nothing or it may be part of something bigger. I don't know. All I know is that he does not normally make requests of this nature. It's a little odd and might be worth investigating."

Cruz stood. "Nice work, Marty."

O'Neal nodded. "I also have some information on Hardy."

Cruz had walked away and picked up her desk phone. Hearing his words, she held the phone in mid-air and looked back at the computer guru.

O'Neal glimpsed his watch. "How about I tell you over lunch?"

Her breakfast had consisted of a cup of coffee. She had not even taken one bite of her bagel before

Agent Harper called and informed her of the hospital episode with the fake DHS agents. Her free hand went to her stomach and she felt a hunger pang. "Give me a minute." She contacted her secretary. "Get me the office of Senator Chuck Hastings, immediately."

Chapter 16: Tahoe

Special Agent Cruz tossed two pills into her mouth and took a swig of her soft drink. Her head throbbed. "So, that's it. He just disappears from the radar and after three years suddenly shows up outside a bombed-out tavern in D.C."

"It's weird, I know." O'Neal finished the last of his French fries after swirling them in catsup.

Cruz started to speak, but stopped when her cell phone rang. She answered it. "Cruz...Uh-huh...Don't touch anything. I'll be there in ten minutes."

"What's going on, Cruz?"

She dug a twenty-dollar bill out of her pocket and threw it on the table. "They found the SUV from this morning. Let's go."

She dropped O'Neal at the office and sped toward the house where the D.C. police had found the SUV. She parked her Charger in the driveway behind two police cars, hurried to the garage and flashed her credentials to an officer. "What do you have?" She put on a pair of rubber gloves, given to her by another officer.

The first officer read from his notepad, summarizing his notes. "The homeowner came home for lunch to find the SUV parked in his garage. When he saw the bodies, he backed out and called the police." The officer pointed toward the three duffle bags in the back of the SUV. "That's some heavy hardware. What do you think was going on here?"

"I'm not sure." Cruz searched the vehicle for clues. She discovered the shots she had fired at the scene made contact with the man in the front passenger seat and killed him. The man in the back seat had his neck snapped, presumably by Hardy. Cruz was impressed. He had been surrounded by four armed men and he killed three of them. After examining their gear and clothing, she could see these men were highly trained. It would have required superior hand-to-hand fighting skills for someone to do what Hardy had done.

She spent the next two hours talking to the homeowner, investigating the scene and knocking on doors in the neighborhood to find out if anyone had seen anything. She discovered Hardy had taken clothes and a computer tablet from the house and left $500 on the table. He was most likely armed, since there were four men in the SUV and only three duffle bags.

Cruz checked her phone—it was close to 3:30. She wrapped up everything with the responding officers and thanked them before leaving for her meeting with Senator Hastings. En route, she got a call from O'Neal. "What is it, Marty?"

"We got an ID on one of the dead DHS agents from the shooting. Are you ready for this? He's ex-military and employed by...The Tucker Group."

Cruz checked her side view mirror. "The same Tucker Group that's receiving the money transfers from the Swiss bank account?"

"That's right. We also found out that twelve of the people killed in the tavern blast were ex-Marines. Like Hardy, their service records stop three years ago."

Cruz had another piece of the puzzle. Her mind was in overdrive, trying to put the pieces together. Hardy must have known and served with those Marines. She pushed her foot down on the accelerator to make it through a traffic light. *That blast was no act of terror. It's too much of a coincidence.* Four men posing as DHS agents, one of whom was working for The Tucker Group, kidnapped Hardy less than twelve hours after he survived an explosion that killed a dozen other Marines. Her mind was a million miles away when O'Neal spoke to her.

"Cruz, are you still there?"

She blinked her eyes. "Yeah, I'm here."

O'Neal knew she had not heard him. "I said I think I may have a connection between The Tucker Group and Hardy. Right before they went dark, Hardy and those Marines were under the command of a Colonel Franklin Ludlum. He's now high up on the food chain over at the Department of Defense."

"I'm going to need to talk to him." Cruz found a parking spot and shut off the engine to the Charger.

"I thought you might say that, so I took the liberty of contacting the DOD. Ludlum's secretary said he left early for the day and was heading home.

79

He has a place on Kent Island. I sent you a text with all the information."

"Thanks, Marty." Cruz slammed the car door and hurried toward the building. "I'll head over there after I'm done with Senator Hastings. I owe you one." She ended her call and hustled through the front door.

Chapter 17: Hastings

Senator Chuck Hastings was the Chairman of the Armed Services Committee and had served several consecutive terms in the United States Senate, representing the state of Massachusetts. His political power stretched everywhere in Congress and he was not above using that power to get what he wanted, politically and personally.

At age fifty-five, he was bald, except for a small layer of hair around the back of his head, just above the neck. He had a thick, puffy nose below two deeply set eyes. His bushy eyebrows almost came together to form a single brow. He was overweight and reeked of stale cigar smoke. He had never married. Women found it difficult to be in his presence for a few minutes. The thought of spending a lifetime with the man would have discouraged any woman. The absence of a wife did not mean Senator Hastings had been without female companionship over the years. His sexual exploits were known on Capitol Hill. Hastings' money and power were enough to purchase women whenever he wanted them, sometimes two and three at a time. Although senators, members of Congress and staffers knew about the actions of Chuck Hastings, no one said anything, since Hastings was a friend of the President of the United States, James Conklin.

Hastings and Conklin had roomed together during their four years at Harvard University. After graduation, Hastings started a career in politics. His cunning intellect and connections from his days at Harvard helped him win a senate seat and rise in seniority. Hastings had helped his friend Conklin win two terms as Governor of Massachusetts after the latter had served his country.

Conklin was a marine with the First Battalion 8th Marines and stationed in Beirut, Lebanon in 1983, and was among the 128 who were wounded when a suicide bomber detonated a truck bomb near the building serving as the barracks. Two-hundred forty one American service members were killed. Hastings suggested to Conklin that he use his hero status in the election and it paid off. Conklin won in a landslide victory.

Hastings sat in his office chair, puffing on a Cuban cigar. He heard a knock on the door. He plucked the cigar from his lips. "Come in."

His secretary leaned halfway into the room. "Senator Hastings, Special Agent Cruz of the FBI is here to see you. Shall I send her in?"

Stamping out the cigar in a nearby ashtray, he motioned with his other hand. "Please." Hastings had refused Cruz's repeated calls to meet with him. When he got a call from FBI Director Jameson, he agreed to the meeting out of respect for Jameson, whom the President held in high regard. One thing Hastings had learned during his time in politics was not to upset the President or anyone who held favor with the man.

Hastings stood and clasped his hands behind his back. He strolled around his desk to greet his visitor. On the other side of his desk was a large circular rug, emblazoned with an image of an American bald eagle. He stopped short of stepping on the eagle and waited. The office door swung inward and he watched Cruz enter the office and approach him. *She's gorgeous.* The words were so prominent in his mind that he wondered if he had uttered them aloud.

"Thank you for seeing me on such short notice, Senator Hastings." Cruz extended her hand.

Her beauty stunned Hastings. He had not heard a word she had said. He stood there with his hands behind his back, his mind envisioning her naked. She said his name a second time and he responded.

Hastings stuck his hand out and the two shook. "It's nice to meet you, Agent Cruz. Please have a seat." He motioned toward the two chairs facing his desk before walking around them and sitting. "What can I do for you? I'm afraid I don't have much time." He gestured toward the clock above his office door—it read 3:55. "I'm scheduled to be at a committee meeting in five minutes."

"I understand, Senator. I'll get right to the point." Cruz spent the next few minutes outlining what she had discovered from Martin O'Neal. She finished by asking the senator a question. "Senator, do you have any knowledge of or involvement in any of this?"

Any ideas Hastings had entertained about what this woman would be like in bed had been replaced with utter contempt for her. His head went from white to crimson, in color. "How dare you come in here and accuse me of having anything to do with this." The muscles in his neck strained, causing the rolls of fat above his shirt collar to flap up and down. "I am a United States Senator who has served his country proudly for nearly three decades." He pointed a pudgy finger at Cruz. "I agreed to this meeting as a courtesy to your boss. Does Director Jameson know what you're accusing me of doing?"

"Senator, he was the one who arranged this meeting. I had credible information that public corruption was taking place at a high level in our government. Any information you can provide will help me find those responsible and bring them to justice. No one is accusing you of anything, Senator." Cruz remained calm, unaffected by Hastings' outburst. She had constructed her question to elicit a response from Hastings. She did not expect the response to be so damning. No one in Hastings' position would have reacted the way he did, if innocent. A normal reaction would have been anger, but anger over the criminal activity happening in Washington. An innocent person would have been eager to cooperate with Cruz and the FBI.

"This meeting is over, Agent Cruz." Hastings stood, walked to the door and opened it. "Rest assured I will be speaking with Director Jameson."

Cruz stood and followed him to the door. She stopped when she was even with the Senator. She turned her head and gave him the most attractive and seductive smile she could muster, knowing his proclivities toward women and how he had stared at her when they first met. "Thank you for your time, Senator. You've been more helpful than you know." She left his office and strode down the hallway.

When Cruz had disappeared from sight, Hastings returned to his desk and used his personal mobile phone to make a call. After a few seconds, he heard a voice on the other end of the line.

"Senator Hastings, to what do I owe the pleasure?"

"Save it, Robert." Hastings rolled his eyes toward his office door. "We've got a problem."

Chapter 18: Kent Island

Hidden among the trees behind Colonel Ludlum's house, Hardy checked the clock on the prepaid cell phone he had purchased earlier—4:07. He held the binoculars to his face. The Colonel had been home for twenty minutes, but Hardy did not know *where* the man was in the house. Hardy's surveillance had shown the neighborhood around the house was quiet. He had not spotted any vehicles loitering on the street, and no one appeared to be waiting in the house. *I'll give it five more minutes.*

As Hardy watched through the binoculars, his mind slipped to other missions he had been on over the years that required a lot of the same type of surveillance. Most everyone who joined the military only thought about the action—the running and gunning, shooting, explosions. There was more time spent in preparing for a mission. The action was over in minutes. The planning and preparation could take hours or days. One mistake could cost you your life or the life of one of your team members. That was unacceptable.

He recalled his first encounter with the military. He was a senior in high school. One day at lunch, he walked over to the recruiter for the Marine Corps and struck up a conversation. Fifteen minutes later, he knew he had found his purpose. It was the slogan, 'The Few, The Proud, The Marines,' that captured his attention. The slogan had appealed to Hardy at his core. Being a loner, he saw himself as one of the few kids who stood out from the crowd. He was never ashamed of who he was or what he did. He was proud, even though all his teachers had repeatedly told his parents he never applied himself to anything, despite his intelligence. Hardy smiled. The Marine Corps had given him an opportunity to apply his skills and he had served his country well for the last twelve years. His smile disappeared when the faces of his men flashed in front of his eyes. He was determined to find who was responsible for their deaths and bring them to justice.

Out of the corner of his eye, he saw movement at the far right end of the house. The curtains in the corner window opened a crack before closing. With a possible fix on Ludlum's location, Hardy could now move to his entry point and access the structure. He stowed the binoculars and readied his set of lock picks.

Hardy moved parallel to the back of the house. Using the tree line for cover, he turned right and came to the side of the house, opposite of where he had seen the curtains move. When he was even with the house, he sprinted across the side yard and past the garage, stopping at the back door, next to the garage. He thrust the lock pick gun into the door handle and within seconds had unlocked the door and gained entry.

The laundry room was on the other side of the door. Hardy drew his pistol and let his eyes adjust to the darkened room. He cleared every room between the entry point and the other end of the house. Keeping low and close to the right wall, he took slow steps, feeling for objects in his path.

Approaching the last room, he heard a 'clinking' sound. *Ice cubes.* With his body pressed against the wall, Hardy leaned away from the wall, peeked inside the room and stood erect. He repeated this motion two times. The Colonel was alone, sitting behind a desk, pouring himself a drink. His uniform coat lay over his chair. His tie was hanging loosely around his neck and the top button of his shirt was unfastened. Hardy could see sweat on Ludlum's forehead. The man had taken two sips of his drink, jerking his head toward the window between sips. Hardy watched him pull on his tie, cranking his head back and forth. Hardy holstered his weapon and sauntered through the doorway.

Startled by his unannounced visitor, Ludlum's right hand instinctively reached to his right before stopping when he saw Hardy. "Damn it, Hardy. You almost gave me a heart attack, sneaking up on me like that. What the hell is wrong with you? You could have just knocked on the door."

Hardy did not respond. He looked around as if expecting to see someone else in the room.

Ludlum came around the desk and gave Hardy a hug. "It's good to see you my friend. I'm still in shock that you're alive. How did you make it out?"

"I told you, I got a phone call. I couldn't hear the caller, so I slipped outside just as the bomb went," Hardy threw his hands into the air, "*boom.*"

Ludlum stood in front of Hardy, gawking. He half-turned around. "Can I get you a drink?"

Hardy shook his head, *no*. If he wanted to get information from Ludlum, he needed his wits.

Ludlum pointed to the single chair facing his desk. "Have a seat."

Hardy sat, while Ludlum went behind his desk and plopped into his chair. The two men sat in silence for several long moments. They seemed like boxers, sizing each other up before a fight. Judging from their body language, no one would have known they had worked together on dozens of top-secret missions all around the world. Ludlum was the first to break the silence.

"So, what is it that you wanted to talk to me about?" He took a sip of his drink and set it next to the nearly empty bottle of bourbon.

Hardy shifted in the chair. "What do you know about what happened in that tavern?"

Ludlum shrugged, holding the position for a few seconds. "I only know what the media has been saying. It was an act of terrorism. Everyone was killed." He avoided making eye contact with Hardy. "It's a damn shame, all those men being killed." He lowered and shook his head.

"Well, almost all of them." Hardy kept his eyes on Ludlum.

"Yeah, that's true. *You* made it out."

"I made it...so did Ruiz and Carlton." Hardy waited for the man to take the bait.

Ludlum raised his head and stared at Hardy. "What? Ruiz and Carlton are alive, too?"

"They went to the bathroom right before I stepped outside. I was able to go back in and drag them out before losing consciousness."

Ludlum's jaw was slack. If he had been smoking, his cigar would have fallen onto the desk. "Well, how are they are? *Where* are they?"

"They're fine. They've got a few scratches like me." Hardy set the hook a little deeper. "They're in the woods right now, armed to the teeth and watching my back." Hardy needed to know if Ludlum was involved and he knew he was not going to get answers by asking. Colonel Ludlum was a highly decorated military veteran, a shrewd tactician. No, Hardy needed to bait him.

The Colonel's gaze went to the window, beyond which were the woods behind his house. Ludlum's cell phone rang and he flinched. After he saw the caller, he tapped the screen and the phone stopped ringing.

Hardy gestured with his head. "Go ahead, take it."

"That's all right." Ludlum flicked his eyes downward. "It's just the office... I'll call them later."

"So, you don't have any information about the bombing. Nobody you know has any idea who would want to take out my team."

Ludlum's mind was somewhere else. "You know, I think I will call the office. It might be something important. Do you mind?"

Hardy shook his head. "No, go right ahead."

"I'll be right back." Ludlum rose from his chair and left the room.

Hardy stared straight at the clock on the wall, watching the second hand move. When thirty seconds had passed, he stood and moved to the door. Ludlum was in the next room, talking behind the closed door. Hardy put his ear to the door and listened.

"That's not enough men...Ruiz and Carlton are in the woods. Next to Hardy, they're the best...I'll try, but he's not stupid. He's going to know something is wrong...All right. How far out are they? I'll try to keep him here for as long as I can. This damn thing is out of control...Don't tell me to calm down. My career is at stake...I should have never agreed to this..." Ludlum listened for a few seconds before jamming his forefinger against the phone's screen several times, ending the call with no formalities.

Ludlum strolled into his office and saw Hardy had not moved. Ludlum came around his desk and sat.

"Is everything all right at the office, Colonel?"

Ludlum tossed his phone onto the desk. "What? Oh yeah, everything's fine. Shirley just couldn't find some paperwork for her...*reports*."

Liar. Hardy stared at Ludlum. There was a brief moment when Ludlum's expression showed he knew Hardy did not believe him.

"So, what were we talking about again?"

Hardy thought about shooting Ludlum where he sat. *Not yet. Be patient*, he told himself. "We were talking about your involvement in the deaths of my teammates." Hardy was done playing games.

"What are you talking about? I didn't have anything to do with their deaths. They were killed in an explosion." Ludlum's eyes shifted to the window again and back.

Hardy leaned back, never taking his eyes off his commanding officer. He may have been nervous earlier, but he was crossing into the realm of agitation. Ludlum looked at the window again.

Hardy's hands lay on the chair's armrests. He moved his right forefinger toward the window. "Are you expecting someone?"

Ludlum locked eyes with his guest. *What does he know? Has he figured it out? Is he here to kill me? Just a little longer and the tactical team will be here.* Ludlum's eyes moved toward the top desk drawer to his right, where he stored his handgun, a Colt 1911.

When Ludlum's eyes came back on him, Hardy saw a change in the man's face. Sweat beads had formed on Ludlum's brow and he had lost the color in his cheeks. Hardy's muscles tensed and his right hand opened. This standoff had all the makings of an old western movie, two men standing in the street, waiting for the other to make a move. When Ludlum's eyes went back to his right, Hardy knew the moment had come.

A split-second later, both men were standing, their weapons pointed at each other. "That wasn't your office secretary on the phone." Hardy shook his head. "Why? Why did you kill my men, *your* men?"

Ludlum's mind raced through his options. If the tactical team arrived in time, they would kill Hardy, but Hardy would see to it he took Ludlum with him.

"Answer me," growled Hardy.

"All I wanted to do was serve my country, not live a lie. I never wanted to betray her, or those men." Ludlum had grown weary of the lies and deceit. Putting a voice to his thoughts gave him relief. His actions were in the open. He chuckled to himself. Talking with Hardy seemed like counseling. *The first step is admitting you have a problem.*

Hardy had two hands wrapped around his firearm. He was staring at Ludlum over the top of the sights. "What are you talking about?"

Ludlum let out a puff of air and grunted. "You still haven't figured it out yet, have you?"

"Enlighten me. What haven't I figured out?"

"You don't work for the Marines or the military or the United States Government, Hardy. You work for me and I work for The Tucker Group. As far as the military is concerned, you and your entire team were honorably discharged three years ago when I recruited you. All of our missions over that time were unsanctioned operations, given to us by The Tucker Group—a private corporation, having nothing to do with the U.S. Government. In fact, if Uncle Sam had ever discovered what we were doing, we would have been tried and convicted for a whole host of crimes, maybe even treason."

Hardy repeated Ludlum's words in his mind— *Unsanctioned operations, private corporation, treason.* He thought he was serving his country, not a private company. "I don't believe you."

"It's true. Our government, the American people, they have no idea what we've been doing." He paused. "Do you remember the mission in Russia six months ago, the one where we took out the man working for the Russian mafia?"

"What about it?"

"He had no connection to the mafia, whatsoever. He was a Russian ambassador, making things difficult for outside companies that wanted to do business with Russia, and we killed him. Can you imagine the fallout if the Kremlin discovered the United States was involved in the assassination of one of their ambassadors? We'd be looking at world war three."

"How?" said Hardy. "You said it yourself. We didn't work for the U.S. Government."

"Do you think that will hold up in the eyes of world leaders? They would all be questioning what else we had done. Our reputation around the globe would be forever tarnished. Anyway, what difference does it make? The people at the top decided to shut the whole program down, and burn all evidence of its existence."

Hardy's body tensed. He tightened the grip on his handgun and gritted his teeth. "What difference does it make? You had my team murdered." He was shouting when he finished his sentence.

Ludlum shook his head. "That wasn't me. The people at the top made that decision. I had a choice to make. I was either in or out. I chose to be *in.*"

94

Ludlum lowered his gun a little, thinking of his words. His shoulders slumped and the gun in his hands felt heavy. He was tired of the lies and the deception. He wanted it to be over, done. His voice articulated his surrender. "Believe me, it's a decision I regret."

Hardy had his finger on the trigger of his pistol, ready to put two rounds into the traitor's chest. After three years of deceit, culminating in the outright killing of his team, Hardy felt justified in ending the man's life. He had it coming. Hardy raised his pistol, putting the front sight between Ludlum's eyes. He slowly pulled the trigger rearward, but stopped.

Ludlum sighed. "Like I said, Aaron, all I ever wanted to do was serve my country."

Hardy watched Ludlum's body drop into the chair. The man slouched and gaped at the gun in his hand.

"Instead, I betrayed her...and those men." Colonel Ludlum studied Hardy, his protégé. "I'm sorry, son. You deserved better." He pressed the gun to his right temple and pulled the trigger.

Chapter 19: Escape

Hardy stared at the lifeless body of his former commanding officer, slumped in the chair. Blood was streaming from the entry wound. Hardy's world had been shattered. His mind went back to the missions he had conducted in the last three years. He thought he had given his life to his country. He had believed he was part of something bigger. Sure, he killed, but he had thought those men deserved what they got. They were enemies of his country, men who sought the destruction of America. *Were they?* He was not sure. He was not sure of anything.

Hardy picked up Ludlum's glass of bourbon. He brought the glass to his mouth, but stopped. He examined the amber alcohol. Regardless of how he felt, he had a mission to complete. Ludlum had given him a clue in finding who was responsible for the deaths of his men. Finding their killer, or killers, was all that mattered. He could drown his sorrows later. He set the glass on the desk and walked away.

Before he had taken a step, Hardy heard a creaking sound come from the hallway. It was faint, but he had heard it. The floor in the hallway was made from hardwood boards. No one else was supposed to be in the house. He had cleared it. Hardy stood still and slowed his breathing. He closed his eyes, so he could focus on his hearing.

The noise came again. With his Sig Sauer pistol in his hand, he glided across the room and stood behind the open door. He peered through the gap between the door and the frame and saw a figure, a gun. Advancing, the person cleared every room, as Hardy had done. Passing by the last open door, the person was illuminated by the light shining through the doorway. *Special Agent Cruz.* He holstered his pistol and waited.

As Cruz entered the room, the gun in her hand emerged from behind the door, above the doorknob. Hardy grabbed the gun with his left hand and her right wrist with his right hand. He pushed both downward and the gun discharged, sending a bullet into the carpeted floor. He twisted the gun out of her hand and tossed it behind him. With her back to him, she thrust her right elbow backward and connected with his stomach. He doubled over. The blow was weak, but strong enough to make him gasp for air. Out of the corner of his eye, he saw another elbow strike coming toward his head. He ducked under it and Cruz's momentum spun her body around. She was facing him. He wrapped his arms around her waist and drove her backward toward a bookshelf that extended to the ceiling. He felt her body go limp, giving him the time he needed to grab and pin both of her wrists to the bookshelf and drive his left leg between her legs. He shoved his body against hers, so she could not move.

Cruz fought back. She twisted her wrists to break free of his grip. When that failed, she tried to knee him in the groin, but her leg barely moved. His body was pressed against her torso, forcing her to draw in her stomach and rise to her tiptoes. The back of her head was aching, having hit the bookshelf in the same spot that had smacked the concrete during the shootout. She tried to push her captor backwards. He was too strong. She relaxed her body and glared at him. "I'm an agent of the United States Government. I order you to release me."

Their faces inches apart, Hardy gazed into Cruz's eyes. She was even prettier than when he had seen her in the hospital room. He could see his reflection in her eyes. "We don't have time for this." He glanced at her full lips. "You need to trust me. We have to get out of here. They'll be here any minute."

Pinned against the bookshelf, Cruz was out of options. She scolded herself for having been disarmed so easily. She knew better than to walk into a room, leading with her firearm. Staring into Hardy's eyes, she saw the same aura of danger she had noticed at the hospital. This was a man who could kill with his bare hands. She had seen firsthand what he was capable of doing and she was not scared. She stole a quick look at his lips. "Who's coming?"

"Ludlum sent a team to kill me." Hardy caught the scent of her perfume. Her chest and neck were perspiring. "They won't care that you're an FBI agent. After I'm dead, they'll put a bullet in you, too."

Cruz found it difficult to avert her stare from his deep blue eyes. When she did, she saw the slumped body. "Did you kill him?"

Hardy shook his head. "He shot himself with his own gun." With her attention focused on Ludlum, Hardy admired her features. Above her buttoned blouse, he glimpsed a gold chain and the top part of a gold crucifix. His eyes moved to her slender neck and jawline. A gold studded earring was centered on her earlobe. He finished at the top of her head, where her hair was drawn tightly into a high ponytail. When he dropped his eyes, she was staring at him. He could not tell if she believed him or not. They were running out of time. He needed to make a move, so he decided to take a chance. "We don't have time for this, Agent Cruz. I'm going to let you go and we're going to get out of here." His body did not budge. Professionally, his mind was telling him to release her. Personally, his mind—more accurately his heart—was screaming *never let her go.*

"Well," she said. "Are you going to let go of me?"

Hardy relaxed his grip and backed away from her. He half-expected her to mount another assault.

She lowered her arms and straightened her blazer. Maintaining eye contact, she moved to where her gun was lying on the floor.

Hardy's eyes flicked toward the weapon. *Moment-of-truth.*

She bent over and picked up the weapon, racked the slide to eject the empty case and chamber a new round. She paused for a moment.

Hardy could see she was contemplating her options.

After a few seconds, she holstered her weapon.

Inwardly, he breathed a sigh of relief.

Cruz pointed at the dead man. "Now, tell me what happened here."

Hardy brushed past her and into the hallway. "Let's go."

"I'm not going anywhere, until you give me some answers." She followed him down the hall and past the living room. "Why did Colonel Ludlum shoot himself? What happened in that SUV? Who are you? What—" her barrage of questions were interrupted when Hardy turned on her.

"When we get out of here, I'll tell you whatever you want to know." They were really pushing their luck at this point. He wanted to get out of the house. The desperation was apparent in his voice. "Right now, we really need to—" Hardy saw a red dot appear on her groin and move to her chest. He charged Cruz and tackled her. They landed behind a leather sofa. Cruz was on her back. Hardy was lying on top of her.

Cruz pushed his chest and tried to roll him to her left. "Get off me," she shouted before the wall behind the sofa was riddled with bullets, sending pieces of wallboard, wood and dust toward them. Hardy dropped his upper body on her, trapping her hands between their bodies, while he raised his hands to cover her head. They jerked their heads away when another round of incoming fire strafed the wall.

Hardy got to his knees. Straddling Cruz, he twisted his upper body, brought up his gun and fired several rounds toward the front door. Cruz wiggled out from under him, drew her pistol and prepared to return fire. Hardy grabbed her arm and yanked, dragging her from behind the sofa. He led her toward the laundry room. When they got to the door Hardy had used to enter the house, he saw three men coming from the woods, dressed in black tactical clothing and carrying MP5 rifles. He pointed his gun toward the men. "We're trapped."

Cruz saw them. "What now?" Bullets hit the wall opposite her. She stuck her gun out and fired three rounds at their assailants.

Hardy opened the door leading to the garage. It was clear. He gestured toward the men at the front door. "Keep them busy. I'm going to circle around from behind."

She nodded. Pressing her back against the wall, she drove out her gun and let loose a few rounds toward the front door.

Hardy exited the garage through the door that led to the front of the house. He crept forward and saw the men at the front door. There were three of them, each with silenced MP5 rifles. He saw one of them giving the other two hand signals before reaching for a stun grenade on his vest. They were preparing to rush Cruz and kill her. Hardy had to act fast. He took aim at the one in charge and shot him once in the back of the head at the base of the skull, instantly dropping him. He swung his pistol to the left and shot each of the other two men, aiming for the same spot. They fell to the concrete porch.

Hardy ran inside and rounded the corner of the living room. He skidded to a halt and found himself looking down the muzzle of Cruz's gun. Her finger was on the trigger and she would have killed him, if she had added another three pounds of pressure. She lowered her weapon.

He motioned for her to follow. "The way is clear. Let's go." They exited the house, leaping over the dead men and running toward Cruz's Charger. Approaching it, they saw all four tires had been slashed. A quick look at Ludlum's vehicle revealed the same thing.

Hardy jerked his head, "This way," before he and Cruz made a beeline for the trees to the side of Ludlum's house and went deeper into the woods. Turning to run back to where he had parked the Ford Ranger, Hardy saw the three men in black enter the house through the back door. He did not stick around to watch. He wanted Cruz and him to be gone before the men decided to search the woods.

They emerged from the forest and climbed into the Ranger. He started the engine and sped away, the truck tires throwing dirt and gravel when the vehicle transitioned from the loose stones to the concrete surface.

Chapter 20: Motel

Leaving Kent Island and crossing over the bridge, Hardy and Special Agent Cruz sat quietly. Hardy stared straight ahead, while Cruz looked out her window at the water. The sun was beginning to set behind her, so she had a clear view of the boats and other various watercrafts. People had begun celebrating the holiday weekend, frolicking on the Chesapeake Bay. The mood in the Ford Ranger was one of silence and unease. The gunfight had taken Cruz by surprise. She re-called her time with the Dalhart Police, specifically, the shootout with the Mexican drug trafficker. Like today, that gunfight had caught her off-guard, too. She felt the butterflies in her stomach. They had increased, since getting into the vehicle. She cocked her head to the right and glanced sideways at Hardy. *I'd be dead right now, if he hadn't knocked me down.* The Ford Ranger passed over dry land and Cruz went back to gazing out the window.

"Thank you...thank you for saving my life back there."

Hardy kept his eyes on the road. "You're welcome. I'm glad to see you up and around so soon after what happened this morning."

Cruz's mind went back to the incident and she half laughed. "That's got to be a record of some sort—*two* shootouts in *one* day."

Hardy grinned. His personal best was four.

"I suppose I should thank you for saving my partner as well. He would have died from that wound had you not helped him." Her eyes moved across every visible square inch of his body, scrutinizing him. "Who are you, Aaron Hardy?"

"Excuse me?"

"You're able to take out multiple armed men, sitting in the back seat of an SUV, practically naked. Then, you proceed to render medical aid to the wounded, call the police and escape." She squinted and barely shook her head, while gawking at him.

Hardy did not respond. He lifted the turn signal on the steering column and veered off Highway 50, near Yorktown. He had spotted a motel. He steered the Ranger into the parking lot of the motel and stopped in front of the hotel manager's office. "I'll be right back." He jumped out and jogged toward the office.

The man behind the desk of the dingy motel fit the stereotype. His black hair was greasy and matted to his head. He wore a pair of tattered jeans with a white, gray or black t-shirt. Hardy was unsure of what the original color had been. Hardy approached, but the man never looked up from the comic book he was reading. After nearly thirty seconds had passed, Hardy pushed the button on the tarnished bell on the counter.

"Hello," the man said, dragging out the word, his eyes glued to the magazine. "How can I help you?"

"I need a room. How much is it for one night?"

"Seventy-five and I'll need a credit card on file."

"I don't have a credit card, so how about I give you a Franklin and we call it good?

"You can give me a Franklin, but I'll still need a credit card." The man flipped a page.

Hardy put two, one hundred-dollar bills on the counter before repeatedly pushing the button on the bell.

The man lowered his reading material.

"Will two hundred dollars get you to forgo the credit card?"

"Listen, pal," the man leaned forward and pointed toward the credit card sign on the counter, "no credit card—no room key."

Since cash was no motivation, Hardy decided to appeal to the man's more slimy nature. "Come on, man, give me a break here. I've got my girlfriend out in the car..." Hardy gestured toward the Ranger. "...and she wanted to stop for a while, if you get my meaning." Hardy winked at the man and smiled. "I'm sure a guy like you has been in a situation like this before. Can you help me out? I only need the room for a couple of hours." Hardy added a fifty dollar-bill to the money on the counter.

The man stood and tilted his head around Hardy's shoulder. He saw the truck and the woman sitting in the passenger's seat. His eyes went to the money on the counter for a moment before he swiped the bills and stuffed them in his pocket. He plucked a room key from one of several hooks. "No smoking, you clean up any messes you make and you're gone before the sun goes down." He gave Hardy the room key, returned to his perch and raised the comic book.

Hardy left the office, got in the truck and drove around to the back of the motel.

Cruz had watched Hardy, while he was in the office. "What took so long? Did you know that guy?"

Hardy thought about telling her the ruse he had used to get the room key, but decided against it. He shook his head. "He just wanted to haggle over the price." Hardy backed the truck into a parking space directly in front of the window to their room. He and Cruz got out and Hardy tossed the room key to her before grabbing his duffle bag from the bed of the truck.

Inside the room, Hardy took a few steps forward and threw the duffle bag on the end of the bed. He slid the zipper to the right and took out the tablet. He walked to the desk in front of the window that faced the parking lot, plugged the tablet into the wall outlet and pressed the power button. As the machine went through the startup process, he took a few steps to his left and closed the motel door before returning to the window. He scanned the area and closed the blinds.

Cruz glanced at the room's décor. Not usually known for sarcasm, she could not control herself. "Wow, you sure know how to treat a lady." She strolled to the bed and sat. As soon as her butt hit the mattress, she sprung to her feet and went to the corner of the room, opting to sit in a hardwood chair next to a floor lamp on the other side of the door. *I think I'll take my chances with this.*

Hardy sat in the other wooden chair and began typing on the tablet. He established a connection to the free Wi-Fi the motel provided and was surfing the Internet.

"So, you never answered my question." She rested her arms on the chair and crossed her legs.

"What question was that?"

Cruz did not respond, but continued to stare at him. She knew he knew what she wanted to know and she was not going to play games.

Hardy had to tell her about himself, but he did not know *how much* he should divulge. She was an agent of the FBI and he, as he recently had been informed, had been carrying out unsanctioned military operations, involving the death and abduction of many, many people. This was another moment-of-truth, like the one at Ludlum's house when she picked up her pistol. He was uncertain about trusting her then, and he had his doubts, now. Everything he had learned about her, pointed toward a professional who faithfully carried out her duties, regardless of the circumstances. He had grown fond of her, however, and he thought she might have had feelings for him. He closed the tablet and picked up his chair, rotating it to face her.

"I'm sure you're aware of my military background...just as I'm aware of *your* background, Special Agent Raychel Elisa DelaCruz, corporal in the military, sergeant for the Dalhart P.D., Miss Texas."

Her eyebrows shot upward before she relaxed. After what she had witnessed, she should not be surprised that he knew so much about her.

Hardy leaned forward, rested his arms on his thighs and clasped his hands together. "What you are not aware of is what I've been doing for the last three years." He paused to collect his thoughts. "Up until two hours ago, I had thought I was the squad leader of a covert unit, working for the United States Marine Corps. We conducted clandestine missions around the globe designed to disrupt the actions of foreign governments, rogue nations and terrorist cells hostile to the United States. I was responsible for three teams of four men each." Hardy stopped and looked at the floor. A flood of memories came rushing back to him.

Cruz uncrossed her legs and leaned forward in her chair. She had heard his voice crack. "Were those men with you at the tavern?"

Hanging his head, Hardy nodded. "I lost all of them." He massaged his forehead with his fingertips.

Cruz was silent. She remembered what she had felt when she lost a good friend a few years ago. She could not imagine what Hardy was going through.

Hardy leaned back. "Before Colonel Ludlum shot himself, he told me that I, and my entire team, worked for *him*. As far as the U.S. government was concerned, we had been discharged from active duty."

108

Cruz held up her hand. "Wait a minute. That doesn't make any sense. Colonel Franklin Ludlum *is* a member of the United States Marine Corps."

"I know he *was* in the Marine Corps. After what he told me...I'm not so sure." Hardy crossed his arms in front of his chest. "He said our operations were given to us by a private corporation." Hardy thought for a moment, trying to remember the name. "He said the name of the company was called...The Tucker Group. We were all employed by this group, not the Marine Corps."

Cruz's body stiffened. "Did you say *The Tucker Group?*"

Hardy nodded. He had heard the change in her voice. "What is it?"

She stood and paced between the chair and the bed, one hand on her hip and the other hand pressed against her forehead.

Hardy sensed she knew something. "What's going on, Cruz?"

She stopped pacing. "I'm thirsty. Are you?"

Hardy frowned. "W-What?"

Cruz left the room and came back a few minutes later with two cans of Coca Cola. She had seen a pop machine on their way from the motel manager's office. She handed one can to Hardy before opening and taking a long drink from hers. She put the can on the desk and told him what she knew about The Tucker Group.

Before she had finished, Hardy was filling in the blanks on his own. The corporation was the key to figuring out who killed his team members and how he had been tricked into working for them. He opened his tablet and navigated to the home page of The Tucker Group before finding the page with the names and faces of the CEO and board of directors.

Standing behind him, she looked over his shoulder, rubbing the back of her head and grimacing. Her head was aching.

Hardy heard her grunt and looked back. "Are you okay?"

"Yeah, my head started hurting again after you pushed me into that bookshelf."

Hardy glanced away before focusing on the screen.

She noticed the change in his demeanor. "Don't worry about it. I would've done the same thing in your situation." She motioned toward the tablet. "What are you doing?"

"I need to speak with someone in charge over there at The Tucker Group." Hardy clicked on the picture of one of the board of directors.

"Good luck. I've made several calls to them and no one of importance has returned my calls."

Hardy opened his cell phone and dialed the number to the company. "Sometimes, it's not *what* you say, but *how you say it* that makes all the difference." Even though it was after five o'clock, Hardy was certain someone would be staffing the phones—he was right.

A bright and cheery voice came from the other end of the phone. "The Tucker Group, this is Angela. How may I be of service?"

Hardy was the epitome professionalism. "Hello, Angela. How are you?"

"I'm doing very well. And, you, sir?"

"I'm good. Thank you for asking...I need to speak with Mr. Robert Tucker, please."

Cruz stared at him, slack-jawed. If she had not been looking at him, she would have thought he was dressed in a three-piece suit and sitting behind a mahogany desk. She shook her head. *Why am I surprised anymore?*

"I'm sorry, but Mr. Tucker has left for the day. May I take a message?"

"No, I'm afraid I need to contact him, personally. I tried his other numbers, but he doesn't seem to be answering. Could you tell me where he is? It's very important that I reach him."

"I'm sorry, but Mr. Tucker left explicit orders that he is not to be disturbed. I'd be more than happy to take a message for you and make sure he gets it first thing Monday morning."

Hardy studied the screen on the tablet. He changed his businesslike persona to one of haughty executive. "Mr. Tucker is going to want to be disturbed for me, Angela. My name is Edward J. Hawthorne, the *second*. Perhaps, you've heard of me. I'm the Chairman of the Board of Directors for The Tucker Group—*your employer*, Angela." Hardy sensed he had the young woman's attention. "Now, I am only going to ask you this question one time, miss. *Where* can I get in touch with Mr. Tucker?"

The young secretary was caught in the middle. Her boss had left instructions that he did not want to be disturbed, but now she was talking to her boss's boss—or so she thought—and he wanted to know Mr. Tucker's whereabouts.

Having stated his authority, Hardy softened his tone with the secretary, giving her a way out of her predicament. "Listen, Angela, I know you are just trying to follow the orders of your boss. I respect that. I really do. That is why I am *not* going to tell Mr. Tucker that *you* were the one, who gave me the information. It will be our secret." He heard Angela let out a sigh. His one-person act was a spin on the 'good cop, bad cop' routine.

"Okay, Mr. Hawthorne. Mr. Tucker is away with his family for the weekend. They're staying at a cabin up North on the lake."

Hardy wrote the information on a nearby notepad, thanked Angela for her help and disconnected the call. Turning to his left, he saw the look on Cruz's face. "What?"

She was shaking her head. "Where did you learn to do that?"

Hardy raised his eyebrows, waiting for her to connect the dots.

She realized it was a dumb question to ask. Of course, a man with his experience would have many talents. "Never mind...so, we know where he is. What are we going to do?"

Chapter 21: My Operation

Hardy stood at the end of the bed, wearing a pair of boxer shorts and socks. He fished around inside the duffle bag and withdrew a pair of black six-inch A.T.A.C. Storm Boots, TacLite Pro Pants and a long sleeve shirt. He threw the items, made by 5.11 Tactical, on the bed. He saw Special Agent Cruz in his peripheral vision. She was standing near the head of the bed with her hands on her hips, her weight shifted to one foot. "This is *my* operation and I'm doing it *alone.*" He pulled up the pants and grabbed the shirt. They had been arguing ever since Hardy disconnected the call to The Tucker Group. Cruz had been pleading her case for getting the FBI involved. At the very least, she wanted to accompany him.

"I'm an FBI agent for crying out loud. Don't you think it would be wise to have someone in my position there, asking the right kind of questions?" Her eyes glimpsed his chest and she bit her lower lip. Hardy's five-foot eleven-inch frame was ripped with muscle. *He must have less than five percent body fat.* She lowered her gaze. His stomach was flat and showed the ribbed lines of his abdominal muscles—the proverbial 'six-pack.'

"Cruz, I plan to ask Tucker only one question." Hardy buttoned the shirt. "Once I have my answer, I plan to put a bullet in his brain." He put on his boots, tightened the laces and retrieved the VTAC LBE Tactical Molle Vest from the duffle bag.

She leaned forward and closed her fingers around the vest, preventing him from taking it. "What you're talking about is tantamount to murder."

"That's why *you*, as an FBI agent, have no business being anywhere near that cabin." Hardy covered her hand with his hand and regarded her, his mind snapping a mental picture. *If I'd met you another time, another place... We might have been good together.* He slipped his fingers between the vest and her hand and loosened her grip. She did not fight him. He slid the vest closer to him and attached equipment to it before shoving it into the duffle bag.

Cruz watched him check the MP5 rifle and insert a fresh magazine, which had a coupler attached to it. The other end of the coupler held a second magazine, allowing for quicker magazine changes when the rifle was empty. After his gear was stowed, the last thing he did was unplug the tablet from the wall outlet, stuff it into the duffle bag and zip the bag shut.

As an FBI agent, she knew she could not be involved in an assault like this without a warrant; however, she did not like the idea of Hardy going after Tucker alone. A man like him would have several bodyguards, even on vacation. While Hardy may not have been outgunned, he would be outmanned. She tried to reason with him from a

114

perspective he might understand. "As a squad leader, would you allow one of your teammates to go off on a mission like this *alone*?"

Having picked up the duffle bag, Hardy let it fall to the bed. She was right. His men acted as a team. No one went into battle alone. There was always another man backing him up. There was one important element missing from Cruz's logic, however, and he was quick to point it out to her. "That's just it. I have no team. They're all dead. Tucker ordered them to be killed." Hardy picked up the duffle bag and slung it over his shoulder. "Now, where can I drop you?"

With her hands folded in front of her chest, she appeared to be praying he would listen to her. "You have no idea what Tucker's role may have been in all of this, or if he was even involved." She was grasping at straws at this point. Her argument was weak. All of the evidence pointed toward Tucker.

"That's what I plan to find out." Hardy motioned with his chin. "Where do you live? I'll take you home."

Cruz's argument was not swaying him. She was witnessing a stubborn side to his personality and she was not going to succeed in talking him out of this, especially something of this magnitude. She brought her still folded hands to her mouth. After a few moments, she let her hands fall to her sides, relenting with a word of caution. "If you go through with this, there's no way I'll be able to protect you. Your name will be added to the FBI's most wanted list and every agent in the country will be looking for you." She walked toward the door. Drawing even with him, she stopped. "That includes *me*." Cruz opened her mouth to add something, but stopped herself, opting to walk away.

Hardy pondered the possibility that one day she may be the agent who finds him and tries to bring him to justice. The thought did not set well with him. She may have been a talented agent when it came to investigating crimes, but she would be no match for his combat skills. He watched her leave him. His chest rose and fell before letting out a sigh. *Another time, another place...*

Chapter 22: Potomac River

The silence in the Ford Ranger hung like a heavy fog over water. The constant hum of the tires rolling over the pavement added to the tension. Although Special Agent Cruz's house was only a short distance from the motel, the drive seemed like a cross-country trek. Her house was on Cripplegate Rd., a stone's throw away from the Potomac River. Hardy stopped the Ranger in the driveway, a short distance from the garage.

She got out and closed the door. She leaned over and looked at him through the open window. "Take care of yourself, Hardy." She paused before adding, "Don't take this the wrong way, but I hope we never meet again." After one last look, she managed an awkward smile before walking toward the front door.

Watching her, Hardy knew what she meant. If they ever met again, they would be on opposite sides of the law. He waited until she had entered the house before shifting the truck into reverse and backing away, his gaze never leaving the front door.

Chapter 23: Oval Office

6:46 p.m.

Director Jameson tossed his cell phone on the desk and leaned back in his chair, interlocking his fingers behind his head. He had not been able to reach Special Agent Cruz for the past three hours. It was unlike her not to take his call, even if it was after hours. After Senator Hastings had called to inform Jameson of the meeting between Hastings and Cruz, Jameson had called her. After several failed attempts, he finally contacted Martin O'Neal, who brought the Director up to speed on everything that had transpired. The last time anyone had heard from Cruz, she was on her way to meet with Senator Hastings.

Jameson had wanted to speak with Cruz personally before going to the President, but Jameson felt he needed to get the President involved sooner rather than later. He called President Conklin on the President's private number. When the President answered, he sounded distracted. Jameson could hear a sporting event in the background.

"I apologize for calling so late, Mr. President, but I have to talk to you about a matter that has come to my attention."

"Can it wait until tomorrow?"

"I don't think so, sir."

The President knew his Director would never have bothered him so late, unless it was important. "Let's meet in the Oval Office in fifteen minutes."

"Thank you, Mr. President."

When Director Jameson entered the Oval Office, the President was sitting on the couch with his legs crossed, holding a coffee cup. He had recently turned fifty-five and was in great shape for a man of his age. His hair was gray, but showed no signs of balding. He wore a white dress shirt, sleeves rolled up to the elbow, top button undone, and a pair of black slacks and black casual loafers. When he saw the door open, he put the cup on the coffee table and motioned for Jameson to join him.

Armed with the information he had received from Martin O'Neal, Jameson told the President everything that had happened in the last twenty-two hours, starting with the explosion at the tavern. When he had finished, he sat back on the couch and waited for the President. After several moments of staring at the documents on the coffee table in front of him, the President took a deep breath and spoke.

"Do you think these events are related?"

"The evidence would seem to suggest that, sir."

The President turned his attention away from the papers. "I didn't ask you what the evidence would suggest. I asked you what *you* think."

"I don't believe in coincidence, sir. These men showed up at the hospital within hours of the explosion. Only a handful of people knew there was a survivor. The media was still reporting that everyone in the tavern had been killed. That means someone high up tipped off someone else and that someone sent a team to intercept Hardy. So, to answer your question, sir, I think these events are related."

The President pursed his lips and slowly nodded. "And Hastings?"

Jameson thought for a moment before answering. It was no secret that he and Hastings had a strained relationship. They were cordial to each other out of respect for the President. Any accusations against the Senator could be construed as vengeful on Jameson's part; however, he had to be honest with his boss.

"I believe the evidence—" Jameson stopped himself. "I believe Senator Hastings is somehow involved, either directly or indirectly. I know he's a close friend of yours and he and I don't see eye to eye on most things, but I feel I need to be straight with you, sir."

President Conklin was well aware of how his director and the Senator felt about each other, and knew how difficult it must have been for Jameson to bring this matter to his attention. Chuck Hastings had been a close friend for many years, but the

President had great respect for his director, too, valuing the man's insight and opinion on serious matters.

The President stood and rested his hands on his hips, studying the papers on the table. "All right, but we're going to need a hell of a lot more than this," the President wagged a finger at the papers, "if we're going to go after a man of Hastings' power."

"I've already begun the process of getting search warrants for The Tucker Group and Senator Hastings." Jameson gathered the papers and put them in the manila folder.

The President cautioned the FBI Director. "None of this reaches Hastings until we are one hundred and ten percent sure he's guilty. He's smart, really smart."

"I understand, sir." Jameson stood. "But if Hastings *is* involved, he'll know something is up shortly after we raid The Tucker Group."

"Then we'll have to be prepared to move fast, Phillip."

Jameson nodded and left the Oval Office.

Chapter 24: Peephole

7:13 p.m.

Special Agent Cruz peered through the peephole in the front door, watching the truck back away. When it was out of sight, she turned around and leaned against the door. She closed her eyes and let her head fall backward against the wood panel. She tried to reconcile her feelings for Hardy and her duties as a government agent. It had been a long time since she had felt this way for any man. If he continued on his current path, he would be a fugitive from justice, if he weren't killed first. She entertained the idea of going after him and trying to talk him out of it one more time. Her mind on Hardy, she sighed when the house phone rang. She did not want to talk to anyone right now. Pushing her body away from the door, she shuffled into the kitchen. The phone rang again. "Yeah, yeah, I'm coming." She picked up the receiver. "Hello?"

"Cruz, its Jameson. Why haven't you been answering your cell? I've been calling you for hours. Is everything all right?"

She checked her pockets for her mobile, but came up empty. She must have lost it somewhere at Ludlum's house. She relayed the events to Jameson, and he told her about his meeting with the President.

Chapter 25: The Cabin

Robert Tucker had rented a simple, yet gorgeous, rustic cabin, surrounded by woods and nestled in the Appalachian Mountains, overlooking a beautiful lake. It was a steep 'A' frame chalet, built into the side of the hill. Stone columns ran across the back of the cabin, supporting the deck outside the master bedroom on the second level. Wooden stairs led from the deck to the ground. From there, a dirt path wound its way to the water's edge.

The main level was a large, open space. The kitchen area was against the wall opposite the huge bay window facing the water. Halfway between the bay window and the kitchen area, against the wall, was a stone fireplace, complete with built-in cavities for firewood, kindling and tools. Finishing off the look was a black bearskin rug on the floor. The entire cabin was finished in knotty pine, except for the floor, which was made of a dark-stained oak.

Bare-chested and dressed in a pair of sweat pants, Tucker sat in an Adirondack-style chair on the deck outside the master bedroom. He was in his mid-forties and had a very athletic physique. His dark hair and goatee gave him the look of a younger man. He took a couple of puffs on his cigar and gazed at the lake. The sun had almost set on the other side. The surface of the lake glimmered, as the last few rays from the sun spilled across it. Tucker tipped his glass back and finished off his drink. A sultry voice called to him from the master bedroom.

"Come back inside, Robert," said the woman. "I'm lonely."

Tucker smiled and rose from the chair. *I know what she's lonely for. This is going to be an exhausting weekend.* As Tucker walked inside the cabin and closed the sliding glass door, he had no idea he was being watched.

Chapter 26: Caged Rat

Down by the lakeshore, hidden among the trees, Hardy decided to wait another twenty minutes after Tucker had closed the sliding glass door. He had been at the cabin for some time and had walked around the entire property. Tucker had two guards posted in front of the cabin and two more in the back. He had not seen anyone else moving around inside, except for Tucker and a woman.

When the sun went down, all available light went with it. A half-moon overhead allowed Hardy to see a few feet ahead of him. He turned on his PVS7 Night Vision Goggles, made by ATN Corporation, and the area in front of him was cast in a green hue. He crept up the path, until he got to the edge of the tree line. He was able to see the entire back yard. He squatted and waited for the guard to his right to start his return trip to the side of the cabin. When he did so, Hardy moved along the tree line and took a position near where the guard would stop when he came back. A few minutes later, the guard came toward Hardy, unaware of Hardy's presence. The guard did a final sweep of the area and turned to walk away. Hardy sneaked forward a few steps and struck the base of the guard's skull with the butt of his MP5 rifle. The guard's body went limp. Hardy caught him and guided his fall to the ground before dragging him into the woods. He secured the man's hands and feet and stuffed a piece of cloth into his mouth before covering him with tree branches.

Coming back to the edge of the yard, Hardy waited and watched. The guard on the opposite side of the cabin came around the corner. After a few seconds, he turned around and disappeared from sight. Hardy ran in a low squat across the deck attached to the main level of the cabin, stopping at the far corner. Facing the cabin, he cocked his head to see around the corner of the cabin. The guard was making his way back. Hardy wrapped an arm around the man's neck and choked him, until he went limp in Hardy's arms. Dragging the unconscious guard out of sight, he laid him near the cabin. He bound the man's hands and feet with zip ties and stuffed his mouth full of Hardy's Washington Redskins t-shirt, which he had shredded. Now that the guards were not a factor, he could move to the upper level.

At the top of the stairs, Hardy watched the sliding glass door through which Tucker had disappeared. The way seemed clear. Hardy ascended the last few steps, pressed his body against the building and sidestepped to the edge of the sliding glass door. The room was casting a soft glow from a low wattage light bulb. He removed his NVG's and stowed them. He did not want to risk a look inside. There was enough moonlight that if anyone was looking in his direction, he would have been spotted. He waited a few moments more. Hearing two somewhat muffled moans coming from the room, he saw his chance to gain access to the room, while the occupants were otherwise engaged.

Hardy pushed the handle on the door and it moved. Tucker had not locked it. *Why would he? He thinks he's alone on the mountain.* Hardy readied his MP5 and slipped into the room.

The woman in the bed with Tucker let out a low squeal and pulled the covers around her naked body. Tucker sat against the headboard, taken by surprise.

"What the hell is this? Who are you?" Not getting a reply, Tucker threw back the covers to get out of the bed.

Hardy leapt forward and leveled the rifle at Tucker. "Stay where you are."

Tucker froze in place, one leg in the bed and the other hanging over the edge.

Hardy's eyes dropped and he saw more than he wanted to see. He motioned toward the man. "Please feel free to use the blanket." He picked up the woman's lacy negligee with the sound suppressor attached to his MP5 and tossed it toward her. The twenty-year-old, if that, scrambled for the robe.

"Your secretary said you were away with family for the weekend." Hardy looked at the woman, donning the negligee. "Something tells me this isn't your wife. And, I certainly hope she isn't your daughter." He looked at the woman. "You should leave now, miss."

The woman turned toward Tucker with a look of disgust on her face. "You're married and you have a kid?" She got to her knees, wound up her right hand

and delivered a slap to Tucker's face that even Hardy felt. "You're a sick bastard." She slinked out of the bed and left the room. Tucker was rubbing his cheek, looking at the door the woman had exited, when Hardy pressed the trigger of his rifle and sent a couple rounds into the headboard near Tucker's right ear. The man flinched and covered his head.

"Do I have your attention now, Mr. Tucker?"

Tucker asked a question of his own. "What's this all about?"

Hardy shook his head. "That's not how this is going to work. I will ask the questions and you will give me the answers. Is that clear?"

Tucker's eyes shifted to the open door leading to the deck.

"Your men have been neutralized. It's just you and me."

Tucker was a caged rat. A man of his power was not accustomed to being in such a compromising position. Hardy could see Tucker's mind working overtime, trying to come up with a way out of this situation. "Did you bomb that tavern last night and kill my men?"

Now, the wheels in Tucker's mind were really spinning. His eyes got wide and his mouth opened. "Hardy," he said. "Sergeant Aaron Hardy. So, that's what this is all about? Why would I do that? You work for me. Why would I want to kill you or my men?"

"Your men? We work for the United States Marine Corps, not The Tucker Group. Why would you say that we work for *you*?"

Tucker did not respond. His mind had begun to spin a lie. Hardy was under the impression he was serving his country. Tucker stammered, as he chose his words. "Well...I know your commanding officer...Colonel Ludlum. It was only a figure of speech, I guess. I meant nothing by it."

"Ludlum is dead."

Tucker was silent.

"He shot himself...*after* he told me about your operation. It's over, Tucker."

Tucker glared at the man dressed in black.

Hardy fired two more rounds. The bullets penetrated the headboard next to Tucker's left ear.

He nearly bounded out of the bed before cursing at Hardy. "Ludlum always was a weak link. I should have gotten rid of him a long time ago. But you, Hardy, you're the real deal. No one else could have figured out what was going on." Tucker stroked his chin. "I have a job for you. I want you take over for Ludlum. I'll find you more men. What do you say? I'll double what I was paying Ludlum."

Hardy wanted to empty his MP5 into the man's chest, reload and repeat. He relaxed his trigger finger. "Why? Why did you have all those good men killed?"

"What about my offer?"

Hardy shook his head. "Forget it, Tucker. The FBI is involved. It's only a matter of time before you fry for what you've done." There was more cursing from Tucker. "Why did you kill my men?"

Tucker shrugged. "Loose ends, I guess. They were loose ends. Those men, *and you*, were just pawns on a chess board, puppets whose strings were being pulled by—"

Hardy shot back, "Those were American soldiers, serving their country."

"Don't give me that. You jarheads are all the same. You'll murder anyone who stands in opposition to you and then wrap yourself up in the American flag. Besides, I didn't give the order to have them killed. If it were up to me, they'd still be alive and working for me." He held up his hand and rubbed his thumb and forefinger together. "You boys made me a...lot...of...money."

"Who was it, then? Who ordered them to be killed? Was it Hastings?"

Tucker nodded. "He got soft. He was afraid everything we had done would be exposed and he'd go down in flames."

"You make me sick." Hardy raised his rifle and centered Tucker's chest in the weapon's rear peep sight. The time had come. His right forefinger applied steady pressure to the trigger before stopping in mid stroke. Hardy wanted justice for his men. They deserved it. But, was this the way to administer that justice? Was this the way to honor his men? Hardy questioned his motives. *Am I thinking of them or me?* Was he trying to alleviate his guilt for the things he had done the past three years? He thought about what Special Agent Cruz

131

had said to him. If he shot Tucker, Hardy would forever be a wanted man. Interrupting his thoughts, Tucker shouted at him.

"Well, get it over with you rotten son of a—"

Chapter 27: Muzzle Flash

Hardy's peripheral vision caught sight of the muzzle of a pistol above the top step of the staircase leading to the main level. One of Tucker's men had gone undetected and was coming up the steps. Hardy spun away from the weapon before he saw the muzzle flash. Hitting the floor at the foot of the bed, he felt a burning sensation in his left shoulder. He twisted his body and crawled to the corner of the bed. The guard's head appeared above the floor. Hardy stuck his rifle between the bottom of the bedframe and the floor. His right forefinger, curled around the rifle's trigger, twitched three times. Three bullet holes opened on the guard's head and neck, felling him. The body slid down a step and came to a halt.

Hardy jumped to his feet and swung the rifle toward Tucker, but he was gone. The only other way out was through the sliding glass door. Hardy ran outside and raced down the steps leading to the dirt path, swapping out the magazines of his MP5. Landing on the third step from the bottom, he leapt and was on the run as soon as his boots hit the dirt. He reached for his NVG's, but his hand came up empty. He was sure he stowed them before entering the cabin. He must have lost them when he dropped to the floor. He activated the Surefire flashlight attached to his rifle. He would have to find Tucker the old-fashioned way.

The burning sensation in Hardy's shoulder intensified. He swiped his right hand across the area. Rubbing his fingers together, he felt a sticky wetness—blood. He could not feel an entry wound, so the bullet must have cut his skin.

Hardy moved down the path, swinging the rifle from left to right and back again. When he reached the bottom, he lit up the shoreline with the flashlight. Tucker was nowhere to be found. There was no way he had made it this far. Hardy wheeled around and went back the way he had come. Tucker might have gone around to the front of the cabin. Hardy advanced a few feet. Feeling a presence behind him, he stopped. Before he could address the threat with the rifle, a heavy object struck him in the back of the head. Stars danced in his vision, but they were not the ones from the night sky. His legs buckled and he collapsed, falling to his knees before landing face first on a bed of fallen tree needles. The scent of pine filled his nostrils. He never lost consciousness, but a full minute passed before he regained his senses and got to his knees. He heard a voice behind him.

"That's far enough." It was Tucker.

Hardy cranked his head around to see the man pointing Hardy's MP5 at his head. He was at a disadvantage, disarmed and in an execution-style position.

"Stay right where you are. This will be over soon."

With his back to his adversary, Hardy's torso was rotated slightly to the left. Tucker could not see Hardy's right hand. Hardy eased the hand closer to his body and the knife he had on his vest. He could see Tucker aligning the sights of the rifle with Hardy's face. Hardy wrapped his fingers around the handle of the knife, flexing the muscles in his right arm. Before he could act, bright lights shone on the two of them. The men appeared to be two actors in a play.

"FBI—Drop the weapon! Drop the weapon! Drop it now!" shouted the members of the FBI SWAT team, positioned in front of Hardy, ten meters up the path. In the light beams, Hardy saw Tucker's eyes. He was not going to drop the rifle. The FBI's rules of engagement were most likely 'fire only if fired upon.' Hardy could not let Tucker start the shooting, especially while he was staring down the muzzle of the MP5.

Hardy ripped the knife from his vest, pivoted to the right and threw the knife at Tucker. As soon as the tip of the blade entered the man's right pectoral muscle, he fired the rifle, sending rounds into the ground where Hardy had been kneeling.

With Tucker fulfilling his part of the rules of engagement, the SWAT team carried out their part, returning fire and perforating the man's body with nine-millimeter bullets. He took three steps backward and fell on his back. The rifle in his hands sounded once more. After that, the only noise heard was the pounding of combat boots on the hardened earth. With their rifles trained on Tucker, the

SWAT team moved forward, bypassing Hardy. They had orders not to touch him. One operative kicked the rifle away from Tucker, while a second removed the pistol from the waistband of Tucker's sweat pants. A third SWAT team member rolled the body over and handcuffed him. Even though the man was probably dead, the action was necessary to ensure the safety of the team.

Sitting in the brush and leaning against a tree, Hardy watched the action. His peripheral vision caught sight of a fourth member of the team. This one had a slender frame and moved differently. Before the person had knelt in front of him, Hardy sensed the person was a woman, sensed it was Cruz.

Special Agent Cruz carried a rifle and had the same clothes on from earlier, exchanging her blazer for a bulletproof vest with the letters FBI on it. The beam of her flashlight lit up the blood on his shirt. "Hardy, are you hurt?" Slinging the rifle behind her, she examined the wound.

Hardy glanced at his shoulder. "I'm all right. The bullet only sliced me." Bringing his attention back to her, he added, "What are you doing here, Cruz? I thought you said you never wanted to see me again."

Cruz called out to the nearest SWAT member and motioned for him. "No, I said I *hoped* we never *met* again." After taking the SWAT member's medical pack, she flashed her eyes toward Hardy and grinned. "I never said I didn't *want* to see you again." She dressed the wound, and applied a bandage, while telling him what took place after he had taken her home.

Director Jameson had secured search warrants for both The Tucker Group and Senator Hastings' office. After the SWAT team had raided The Tucker Group and gathered enough evidence against Hastings, the second SWAT team moved in and arrested Hastings at his home.

"Were you there to take him down?"

Cruz shook her head. "I couldn't be in two places at once. I had to be *here* to pull your butt out of the fire." She smiled and winked at him.

Hardy laughed. It was good to know she had a sense of humor. He had not seen that side of her. He was glad she was there. She had saved his life.

Cruz stood and held out her hand. "Come on, let's get going."

He took her hand and pushed himself away from the ground. Getting to his feet, he felt a rush of blood to his head and his legs wobbled. He staggered and took a giant step toward Cruz. She clutched his waist to stabilize him. Hardy wrapped his right arm around her shoulder.

"Easy now," she said.

"I'm okay. I just need a minute."

For a few moments, they stood there, not saying anything. Hardy was trying to regain his balance, enjoying the touch of Cruz's body. Secretly, he wanted it to last a little longer.

"Listen, Hardy," Cruz tilted her head back, her right hand on his chest, "I know this isn't exactly how you wanted this to go down, but we got them.

Hastings is going to jail and The Tucker Group will be dismantled. I promise you that everyone involved in the deaths of your team members will be brought to justice. You have my word."

In that moment, Hardy knew he wanted to see more of this woman. Moving up the path, he stopped and looked at her. "What time is it, Cruz?"

She checked her watch. "It's almost Midnight— 11:43 to be exact." Thinking that was an odd question to ask at a time like this, she said, "Why? You got a hot date or something?"

He shrugged. "I don't know...maybe." They picked up their pace again. "Since it's still my birthday for the next...*seventeen minutes*...would you like to have a drink with me?"

Her head down, arm in arm with him, Cruz smiled. "I'd love to. The first round's on me." They took a few more steps and she looked at him. "Happy Birthday, Hardy."

Chapter 28: St. Matthew's Cathedral

July 8th, 11:49 a.m.

It was a beautiful and sunny day. The temperature was seventy-five degrees. A light breeze blew, while fluffy, white clouds hung low in the sky. The day would have been perfect, if not for the somber occasion taking place in downtown Washington D.C. inside St. Matthew's Cathedral.

Constructed in a Roman style with Byzantine accents and built with red brick and sandstone trim, St. Matthew's Cathedral was the location for the memorial service, remembering those who had died in the blast at the tavern the previous week. It was decided that since they had perished together, they would be remembered together. Large pictures of each victim were placed on stands on the altar. Hundreds of potted plants and flowers surrounded the pictures. Among the pictures were those of the twelve members of Hardy's team. Hardy had learned the President had made sure that every one of them had been re-instated as members of the military. They had their service records changed to reflect their service up to the point where they were killed, and were given a full military funeral. Hardy sat on the end, a few rows back from the front, listening as the priest prayed a final blessing.

"O Loving Father, we pray that you would welcome your departed children into the realms of everlasting life. We ask that their tears be wiped away and their sufferings cease to exist. May the joy and splendor that is Heaven, be theirs for all of eternity."

"Finally, we ask you to look after the family and loved ones they have left behind. Comfort them when they grieve. Rejoice with them when they remember the good times shared. And, above all, never let the fire of the love within them burn out. In Jesus' name we pray."

And, all the people said, "Amen."

Special Agent Cruz, sitting next to Hardy, made the sign of the cross and said, "Amen."

Hardy saw her out of the corner of his eye. He had never been a man who really believed in God. It was not that he did not think there was a God, but rather he did not know for sure. In his line of work, he dealt with facts, not beliefs; however, he liked and respected Cruz, so he respected her beliefs. They had spent quite a bit of time together over the past week. They went out for drinks a couple of times. They went for short walks during her lunch breaks. And, last night, they had dinner at a nice restaurant. Hardy was grateful she had come into his life, especially during this difficult time. He was still having the nightmares about his team members, but the nightmares were less intense and getting further apart. He credited the time he had spent with Cruz for helping him find some closure. Despite the difficulties ahead of him, she had given him hope that brighter days would follow.

Chapter 29: We Must Act Now

July 9th, 7:57 a.m.

"Please show him in, Courtney." President James Conklin hung up the phone and continued his conversation with his White House Chief of Staff, Peter Whittaker.

Peter Whittaker was a short, lean man in his late forties. His black hair was parted on the left side. A thin mustache lay beneath his long, narrow nose. His eyes were small and close together. When he spoke, he had a very distinct Ivy League accent, having grown up in Massachusetts. His words were always carefully chosen. The President had tapped Whittaker to be his chief of staff, because of his attention to detail. Nothing made it to the President without Whittaker's knowledge. The President respected and trusted Whittaker and allowed him a great deal of latitude in all things related to the Presidency.

"Are you absolutely sure about this, Mr. President." Whittaker sat in a chair across from the President's desk in the Oval Office, his legs crossed. "We know nothing about him."

"The events of this past week have made it perfectly clear to me that we need a man with his talents." The President spun his chair a quarter-turn and stared into the distance. "This war on terror has been no war at all. The terrorists attack and we go on the defensive. In the military, if you're not advancing, then you're retreating. We must go on the offensive. We must act swiftly and we must act *now!*" The President pounded his fist on the desk.

The door to Oval Office opened. A young woman appeared and held the door open. A moment later, Aaron Hardy walked into the Oval Office, wearing a gray suit, white shirt and a red tie. A handkerchief in his left breast pocket matched the color of his tie, which was held in place by a gold clip. A collar bar under the knot of the tie drew the points of his shirt collar closer together. Striding across the room, his black shoes were without blemish.

The President stood and met Hardy halfway. The two men shook hands in front of the couch, standing on the rug, emblazoned with the seal of the President of the United States. Whittaker stood behind the President.

"It's a pleasure to you meet you, Aaron. May I call you Aaron?"

"Of course, Mr. President," replied Hardy. "The pleasure is mine, sir."

The President extended his arm toward Whittaker. "This is my Chief of Staff, Peter Whittaker. I've asked him to join us for this meeting."

Whittaker stepped forward and shook Hardy's hand. "It's good to meet you, Mr. Hardy."

"It's nice to meet you, Mr. Whittaker."

"Please, sit down." The President motioned Hardy toward the couch, while Whittaker sat on the opposite end of the couch. Across from Hardy, the President sat in a wooden straight back chair with leather trim, and crossed his legs.

The commander in chief clasped his hands together and rested them on his lap. "First of all, let me say how truly sorry I am for your loss. I want you to know I personally read the file of every member of your team. Those were fine American patriots. I wish I could have attended the memorial service, but I didn't want my presence to disrupt the service and take away from the grieving family members."

Hardy nodded his head. "I understand, sir. Thank you for everything you did to clear their service records."

The President waved his hand. "It was the least I could do."

Hardy was waiting for the President to get to the reason for the meeting. As busy as the President was, a face-to-face meeting to extend condolences was a little odd. Ever since Hardy had gotten the call from his secretary, Courtney, arranging the meeting, Hardy questioned what was going to take place. He did not have to wait long to find out.

"I'm sure you're wondering why I've asked to meet with you. So, I'm going to get right to the point. The war on terror isn't going exactly as I had planned. During the first two years of my presidency, I have been bogged down in bureaucratic bullsh—" the President stopped. "Pardon me—bureaucratic red tape."

Hardy smiled. *That's getting to the point, all right.*

"Members of Congress are afraid of offending...well...*everyone* these days, but especially the Muslim population. It's precisely because of this political correctness that I haven't been able to gain any traction in this war. I campaigned on a tough-on-crime/national security platform and I plan to keep the promise I made to those who elected me." The President uncrossed his legs and leaned forward in his chair.

Without realizing it, Hardy leaned forward and mirrored the President's posture.

The President pointed at Hardy. "That is where you come in, Aaron. I've read your service record and I've seen what you're capable of, both abroad and on American soil. Your actions last week, helping bring Senator Hastings and The Tucker Group to justice were icing on the cake, if you will." The President paused. "I need a man like you. This *country* needs a man like you. A man who's not afraid to take action and do whatever is necessary to get the job done...to take the fight to the terrorists." The President leaned back in his chair. "So, what do you say? I'm offering you a job, putting your special skills and talents to work, keeping the American people safe from terrorists around the world."

Hardy's eyes widened. He felt his lower jaw hanging open slightly. He quickly shut it and glanced at Whittaker. In one week, Hardy had gone from

Special Forces operator, to unsanctioned patriot, to being offered a job by the President of the United States. Before he could say anything, the President leaned forward and continued.

"This would have to be kept top-secret." He held up his index finger. "You would have one boss," he pointed his thumb at his chest, "who would report directly to me. At your disposal, you would have all the resources necessary to get the job done..."

Hardy listened to the details of the job. After the President had finished, he fielded questions from Hardy before standing, his body language indicating the meeting was done. "I'm sure you'd like some time to think it over, so take the weekend and contact Courtney on Monday. She'll put you through to me." The President held out his hand.

Standing, Hardy did not take the hand. He stared at the Presidential Seal on the rug, his mind replaying everything the President had said. Hardy had been reconciling the things he had done over the past three years, while believing he was doing those things in the service of his country. Was this his chance at redemption, his chance to honor his men? Or, would it be a constant reminder of his deeds? He wanted to put the past behind him and start fresh. He thought of Special Agent Cruz. The time they spent together had been fantastic. He wanted a relationship with her. How would this job offer affect that relationship? While he was mulling over the President's words, the final blessing the priest gave at the memorial service resounded in his mind—'Above all, never let the fire of the love within them burn out.'

Hardy raised his head. "With all due respect, sir, I don't need the weekend to think it over."

The President's hand dropped a bit. He had learned that whenever anyone started a sentence with 'with all due respect' bad news usually followed.

Hardy grasped the President's hand and said, "I accept. When do I start?"

AMERICAN INFLUENCE
Aaron Hardy Series
Book #2

Chapter 1: Cemetery

Kneeling, her butt resting on the heels of her boots, Natasha Volkov kissed her fingers and placed them on the new headstone in front of the freshly disturbed earth. "Mnogo lyubvi, papen'ka — *Much love, Papa*," she said before standing. Natasha's mind wandered to a time from her youth when her father would put her on his lap and tell stories. Mostly, the stories were from Russian folklore, but the ones young Natasha enjoyed were those about Russian history. She had been captivated by her father's voice, telling heroic tales of czars and emperors, leading their troops into battle, defeating the enemy and saving Mother Russia from the invading hordes. Natasha smiled. To this day, she had no idea if the stories had been true, but it made no difference. The story was not important. It only served as the backdrop to spend time with her father, her Papa.

Natasha tilted her head back and let the sun's rays shine on her face. The warmth felt good. Even though the calendar showed that spring had come to Moscow, the warmer temperatures were slow to follow. It had been a brutal winter with record cold

149

temperatures and snowfall. An overnight snowstorm had dropped a few more inches. Piles of snow still dotted the landscape, reminders of where the wind had made huge drifts over the winter. She could not remember there being a colder winter in her lifetime. She lifted the collar of her short-length fur coat around her neck and shoved her hands into the pockets.

A few minutes later, her hand vibrated. She retrieved a cell phone. Her heart beat faster. She slid her right thumb across the phone's screen and turned her head swiftly to the right to throw her long blonde hair over her shoulder. "Volkov...da — *Yes.*" She listened for a few seconds. "YA na moyem puti — *I'm on my way.*" Stowing the phone, Natasha gave her father's headstone one more look, her eyes settling on the last line: 'Predannyy Muzh i Lyubyashchiy Otets — *Devoted Husband and Loving Father.*' She did not want to leave her papa, but she had work to do.

Natasha spun around on the heels of her boots and trudged down the slope toward her waiting vehicle, her pace slow and methodic. The slope leveled off. Her mind shifted from her father to her job, and her strides grew longer and her pace quickened. With each step, the pull-tabs on her boots tapped against the metal zipper. She opened the door of her dark gray UAZ Patriot, a four-door, four-wheel drive, sport utility vehicle. Pulling up her skirt slightly, she climbed inside the SUV. Once inside, Natasha stared straight ahead. She took a deep breath and let it out. She forced herself to focus on her destination, her assignment. Having left the engine of the SUV running, she put the transmission into 'drive' and sped away.

Chapter 2: Assault

The wheels of the Patriot rolled to a stop. Through the windshield, Natasha spied a house in the distance. The structure was a simple and neglected one-story residence. Smoke rose from the chimney on the far left side. A small car was parked in the driveway. The vehicle's condition matched that of the house. Getting out of her vehicle, she went to the rear and swung open the door to the luggage compartment, revealing a cache of weapons and tactical gear. She removed her coat and threw it inside before picking up a bulletproof vest. Standing, she noticed Sergei at the corner of the Patriot.

Sergei Gagarin was a member of the Spetsnaz (Special Forces) of the Federal Security Service of the Russian Federation (FSB). He was a ruggedly handsome man, although his features were hidden by the tactical gear he wore. He was three inches over six-feet tall and weighed two-hundred and twenty-five pounds. His shoulders were broad and his body was well sculpted. From behind his goggles, Sergei stared at her. His deep blue eyes met her blue eyes. He adjusted the strap attached to his SR-3M Vikhr rifle.

Natasha and Sergei had been dating for the last two years. Their relationship had been great from the beginning; however, since the death of her father, they had begun arguing more. Usually, the arguments started over small matters before escalating to full-blown fights.

Last week, Natasha had told Sergei she had wanted to take some time to be alone. She needed to sort things out. The death of her father had been difficult, and she was slipping deeper and deeper into an anger-induced way of life. To make matters worse, her job was demanding more and more of her time.

Natasha was an FSB Agent, specializing in counter-terrorism, defending Russia from terrorist attacks. Over the past several months, there had been numerous assaults across the country. Citizens were terrified, never knowing when, or where, the next attack would occur. Natasha had been working overtime tracking down a serial bomber, who had exploded bombs at many locations, in and around Moscow, in the last three months. Sergei had called to inform her that a tip had come in, placing the bomber at this house. His team was in position, waiting for the order to storm the house.

"YA dumayu, chto vy dolzhny sidet' eto odin iz — *I think you should sit this one out.*" Bracing for the backlash, Sergei's muscles contracted.

Natasha glared at him. He was trying to protect her. As far as she was concerned, they were not dating anymore and her personal welfare was no longer his concern. Pointing her finger at him, she opened her mouth to speak, but stopped. Afraid of what she may say, she kept her thoughts to herself. She finished attaching the straps on her protective vest. "Bez shansov — *No chance.*" Her voice left no doubt she was angry. She picked up her SR-3M Vikhr, pulled back on the bolt and saw a round in the chamber. Releasing the bolt, she removed the magazine and made sure it was full.

Sergei did not have time to get into an argument with her that would most likely turn into a shouting match. He had a mission to complete and the other members of his team were relying on him to have his head in the game. He ogled Natasha from head to toe. "Vy deystvitel'no dumayete, chto vy odety dlya etogo — *Do you really think you're dressed for this?*" He made no effort to hide the sarcasm in his voice.

With more force than necessary, Natasha slammed the magazine into the rifle and examined her clothing. She was wearing a black bulletproof vest over a tight red knit sweater dress. The hem of the dress fell three inches above her knee. Black knee boots with chunky three-inch heels completed the outfit. She knew her clothing was not appropriate for an assault, but she had taken part in other operations and her heels and dress had been much higher.

Seeing the look on her face, Sergei made an appeal to her sensibility. "Pust' moi lyudi pnut' v dveryakh. Kogda vse yasno, mesto vse tvoye — *Let my men kick in the doors. When everything is clear, the place is all yours.*"

Natasha relented. The last thing she wanted to do was put his men at risk. She nodded her head and held out her hand, flexing her fingers. "Dayte mne naushnika — *Give me an earpiece.*" She put her rifle inside the SUV, before removing her vest and tossing it alongside the rifle.

Sergei handed her an earpiece and started jogging toward the house, two team members at his side. He gave commands over the radio. Over his shoulder, he heard Natasha call out to him.

"Byt' ostorozhen — *Be careful.*"

Sergei smiled. *Maybe not all is lost between us.*

Standing near the left-rear corner of the SUV, Natasha drew back her hair and tucked the tiny communication device into her ear. She heard Sergei's commands, while watching him and his team approach the front door. She folded her arms across her chest and rubbed the backs of her upper arms. The heels of her boots rubbed against each other, while she shifted her weight back and forth. She saw Sergei give hand signals to the men near him. The teams were preparing to breach both doors to the house, simultaneously. Natasha felt a chill run down her back. She lowered her head and realized she was standing in the cold, wearing only a dress and boots. Leaning to the right, her left foot came off the ground and the fingertips of her right hand touched the collar of her coat. Before she could close her fingers, a loud blast pierced her eardrums and the ensuing shockwave slammed into her chest like a sledgehammer.

Already off-balance, Natasha was thrown backwards several feet. She landed on her back in a spread-eagle position. Her ears ringing, she laid on the ground, staring at the sky. Particles of debris floated down around her. A hot ember, the size of a quarter, fell on her left thigh and burned a hole through her nylons. She felt nothing. It took more than a minute, but the ringing in her ears subsided. She sat up. The house was reduced to rubble. Sections of it were on fire. Black smoke rose into the air. Her senses returning, she felt searing pain in her leg. She swiped away the hot ember. There was a large hole in her nylons. The skin—usually milky white in color—was bright red. She gathered a handful of snow and held it on her thigh. She closed her eyes and sighed. A few seconds later, she opened them to the sight of the house in shambles. A teardrop ran down her cheek and her voice cracked when she whispered, "Sergei."

Minutes later, her legs began shaking and the muscles in her butt contracted. The coldness of the damp snow had seeped through her dress and nylons. Like an ocean wave, crashing against the shore, the cold ran up her body, until she was shivering from head to toe. Convulsing, she let her body fall backward. Lying on the snowy ground, she saw images of Sergei and her father flash across her mind. Fatigue set in and her eyelids drooped before closing. *I'm so tired.*

Chapter 3: Oval Office

July 8th, 8:43 a.m.; the Oval Office (the White House)

Aaron Hardy sat on the end of the couch in the Oval Office. The President of the United States, James Conklin, sat across from him in a wooden, straight back chair with leather trim. The men were discussing the details of the job the President had offered Hardy, which he accepted.

Hardy was wearing a gray suit, white shirt and a red tie. A handkerchief in his left breast pocket matched the color of his tie, which was held in place by a gold clip. A collar bar under the knot of the tie drew the points of his shirt collar closer together. The suit fit his five-feet, eleven-inch, one hundred and eighty-five-pound frame, perfectly. One week ago, he celebrated his thirtieth birthday and was in the best physical shape of his life.

Hardy had enlisted in the U.S. Marine Corps when he was eighteen years old. He spent the first four years of his career serving overseas, primarily in Iraq, before becoming a member of the Second Marine Special Operations Battalion, headquartered at Camp Lejeune, North Carolina. For the next five years, he was involved in direct-action, special reconnaissance and counter-terrorism missions, until Colonel Franklin Ludlum asked him to take command of a team and conduct top-secret missions all over the world.

One week ago, at the start of the Fourth of July holiday weekend, Hardy's teammates had been killed in an explosion at a tavern in Washington D.C. Hardy was the only survivor. During the next twenty-four hours, he tracked down those who were responsible for killing his men. With the help of Special Agent Raychel DelaCruz of the Federal Bureau of Investigation, he was able to bring the perpetrators to justice.

The President arranged a meeting with Hardy after discovering what he had done. During the meeting, the President offered Hardy a top-secret job, working directly for him. Hardy's main objective was to go on the offensive against the terrorists. Since the position did not officially exist, he would operate under special rules of engagement—his own. He would do whatever was necessary, and use whatever resources he had, to stop the terrorists before they could carry out further attacks. The President's exact words were 'to take the fight to the terrorists.'

"As I said earlier, you would have all the resources you need to get the job done." The President checked his wristwatch. "I'm sick and tired of the terrorists tying our hands and forcing us to play defense. When I campaigned for this job, I told the American people I would be tough on terror. Since taking office, I've been wrapped up in political battles that have virtually sidelined my efforts to make real progress in this war." The President shifted in his chair. "And, make no mistake, this *is* a war."

James Conklin was a man dedicated to serving the American people. He had served two terms as Governor of Massachusetts after he had returned home from serving his country. Conklin was a marine with the First Battalion 8th Marines and stationed in Beirut, Lebanon in 1983. He was among the 128 who were wounded when a suicide bomber detonated a truck bomb near the building serving as the barracks. Two-hundred forty-one American service members were killed. Conklin's hero status had helped him in his campaign for the governorship. He won in a landslide victory.

Now, at age fifty-five, he was two years into his first term. The man was in great shape for his age. His hair was gray, but showed no signs of balding. He wore a black suit with a white dress shirt. His tie was deep blue and he had a handkerchief in his left breast pocket that matched the color of his tie. Lastly, he wore a pair of black casual loafers. "Are there any—" the President started to say, but stopped when someone knocked on the door. The door to the Oval Office opened and the President's Director of the Federal Bureau of Investigation, Phillip Jameson, entered.

The President stood and glimpsed his watch. "Thanks for coming, Phil. I know you've got a lot on your plate."

"It's not a problem, sir." Jameson's long strides made short order of the distance between the door and the couch. He extended his hand toward the President, who shook it before introducing Jameson to Hardy.

"Aaron, this is my Director of the FBI, Phillip Jameson." The President faced Jameson. "Director Jameson, I want you to meet Aaron Hardy, your newest special agent. Aaron has accepted the position you and I discussed earlier, and is eager to start as soon as possible." After Jameson and Hardy had shaken hands, the President checked his watch. "Now, if you'll excuse me, gentlemen, I have a press conference in fifteen minutes." He shook Hardy's hand. "It was a pleasure meeting you, Aaron. I'm glad to have you on our team." He tipped his head toward Jameson. "You're in good hands."

"Thank you, Mr. President."

The President acknowledged Jameson. "I trust you'll fill him in on the specifics of the position as well as the details of his first mission."

"Of course I will, sir."

"Splendid," said the President, who patted Jameson on the back before heading toward the door, straightening his tie.

Jameson faced Hardy, who was already sizing up his new boss. Hardy knew Jameson had played an active role in the Fourth of July events in which Hardy was involved. He studied Jameson, taking in his demeanor and physical characteristics.

The fifty-year-old FBI Director was physically fit, regularly lifting weights and jogging. He was five-feet, eleven inches tall and weighed one hundred and ninety pounds. He was bald and wore rounded, rectangular eyeglasses with thick black frames. His work attire was always the same—black suit, white shirt, red tie. He changed the shade and print of the tie, but it was always red. His shoes were black and always polished—no smudges. His clothing was a projection of what you could expect from him. He was a man who brought to bear rock-steady leadership and decision-making skills and always backed his agents. He was also quick to get to the point.

"Let's get started." Jameson tossed a manila file folder onto the coffee table before sitting in the chair the President had vacated. "Before we go over your first mission, we need to discuss the details of your employment."

Sitting, Hardy nodded his head and leaned forward.

"Officially, your position does not exist as the President outlined it." Jameson reclined and crossed his legs. "You'll be working for the FBI and have an office in Washington D.C. Your title will reflect your cover story. You'll be acting as a consultant, advising corporations, foreign nationals, other nations...you name it...on matters pertaining to terrorism." Jameson spread his hands apart. "Keep it broad and vague when you have to discuss your credentials." He wagged his finger. "That reminds me. Here's your badge." He handed Hardy a leather bi-fold with an FBI badge and documentation with his photo and official title.

Hardy opened the leather bi-fold and read his title: Special Agent Consultant to the Director. *That's a mouthful.*

"Now, about your first mission," Jameson pointed toward the manila folder, "The details are in that file. Let's go over what you need to do."

Chapter 4: Mission

Thousands of feet above the Atlantic Ocean

Hardy sat back in his seat aboard a Gulfstream V jet, flying high above the Atlantic Ocean. He was the only passenger on the flight. The FBI used the jet to transport agents around the world. The aircraft had taken off from Washington D.C. at 1 p.m.; its destination was Moscow, Russia. After the plane had leveled off and reached its cruising speed, Hardy unbuckled his seatbelt and picked up his new phone.

He stared at the satellite phone. Even though it appeared to be exactly like any other smartphone on the market, it was a state-of-the-art piece of technology, capable of getting a communication signal where normal smartphones could not. Plus, it contained a Global Positioning System tracker that was accurate within one square block. He was not staring at the sat phone in awe of its technological advances, however. Before the Gulfstream V had taken off, Hardy made a call to Special Agent Raychel DelaCruz of the FBI. The conversation had not gone well.

Special Agent DelaCruz, her colleagues shortened her name to Cruz, had been the lead agent investigating the explosion at the tavern that killed everyone, except Hardy. His first encounter with her was at the hospital after the explosion. He had been captivated by her from the moment he opened his eyes and saw her standing over his hospital bed. Twenty-nine years old, she was both beautiful and professional. She was tall, standing five-feet, eight inches. She had dark brown hair that fell below her shoulders. Her hair was paired with an equally beautiful set of dark brown eyes. She had a long face with high cheekbones and a flawless complexion.

During the past week, Hardy and Cruz had been seeing each other, taking walks during her lunch hour and going out for drinks. Two days ago, they went out for dinner for the first time. They had a great time and made plans to go out again tonight, which made the call to her more difficult.

Hardy had told her he was going out of town, which had prompted her to ask the usual questions— where are you going?, why are you going?, how long will you be gone? Since the President had made it clear his new job was top-secret, Hardy had to tiptoe around the inquiry, unable to get into specifics. Even though she sounded like she was okay, he had sensed she was not happy with his vague responses.

Hardy closed his eyes and rested his head on the seat. He did not want to ruin what he had with her. In his line of work, it was difficult to have a serious relationship with a woman. He would be gone for long periods and he could not discuss where he had been. Since Cruz had spent long hours at her job, he had hoped she would be better able to understand his unconventional schedule. Still, no woman wanted to be separated from her man for long stretches.

He put the sat phone in his pocket and reached for the manila file folder on an adjacent seat. *I'll take her somewhere nice when I get back.* Shifting his thoughts to the mission, he opened the file and studied its contents.

Director Jameson had spent the rest of the morning briefing Hardy on the mission. It was simple in nature. He was to locate Anton Rudin, a Russian bomb maker, and kill him. Rudin was a bomb maker for hire. He made sophisticated and powerful explosive devices and sold them to anyone, or any organization, for the right price. He may not have been a terrorist, but he supplied them. The theory behind the mission was stop the bomb maker from making bombs, and the terrorists have one less resource at their disposal.

For the past five months, Russia had been experiencing a wave of domestic terrorist attacks, including several bombings in, and around, the city of Moscow. The Russian authorities suspected Rudin had supplied the bombs, but had not been able to find him. In a spirit of cooperation, Russia had contacted the White House and agreed to share the information they had on Rudin in the hopes of stopping further terrorist attacks. It was a real 'olive branch' of a gesture, since the two nations were not on the best of speaking terms.

Hardy peeled back a sheet of paper, skimmed the page beneath it and let go of the paper. The dossier of Natasha Volkov, the Russian FSB agent he was scheduled to meet in Moscow, was lengthy.

Volkov was twenty-seven years old. She had been working for the FSB for the last four years, serving in various positions. Her most recent appointment, which began shortly after the terrorist attacks had started, specialized in counter-terrorism. She was fluent in three languages, one of which was English. She graduated from Moscow State University before completing her training at the FSB Academy, where she was recognized for numerous talents, including marksmanship and criminal investigation. Hardy rubbed his eyes with his thumb and forefinger. Even though he had not met her, he could see she was an accomplished woman, at least on paper. Reading the file, he began the task of committing to memory everything the dossier contained.

Three hours later, Hardy tossed the file onto the seat. He retrieved his sat phone and checked the time before reclining in his seat. He was tired and his eyes burned. The flight to Moscow was going to take nine hours, and there was an eight-hour time difference between Washington, D.C. and the Russian capitol. He would be landing at 6 a.m., local time. He closed his eyes and relaxed. He needed to get some sleep before his 8 a.m. meeting with the FSB agent.

Chapter 5: Moscow

After the jet touched down at Moscow Domodedovo International Airport, Hardy de-boarded the aircraft, cleared the customs process and made his way to the front doors of the airport. He was to rendezvous with an American asset, who would take him to the meeting with Agent Volkov.

Outside the airport, Hardy scanned the area and spotted a man matching the description he was given. The man was tall and in his late thirties, leaning against a Volkswagen Polo Sedan, reading a newspaper. He wore a light gray suit, white shirt with a black tie and black dress shoes. On his head was a fedora-style hat, tilted backwards. Black sunglasses covered his eyes. Hardy strode toward the man. "Did the Tigers win yesterday?"

The man lowered the newspaper. "Not only did they win, but they shut out the Yankees, three to nothing."

"Myself, I'm a Lions fan."

The contact information having been verified, the man folded the newspaper and threw it into the car. He held out his hand. "I'm Tom MacPherson."

MacPherson was an American asset stationed in Moscow. He worked out of the embassy. MacPherson's American handler had contacted him and given him explicit instructions. He was to pick up Hardy at the airport, assist him during his time in the city and drop him at the airport when Hardy was finished with the mission. MacPherson was not to inquire about the nature of Hardy's visit.

The two men shook hands. "Aaron Hardy."

"Hop in." MacPherson took Hardy's suitcase and put it in the trunk of the car. He sat in the driver's seat, started the engine and navigated the sedan into traffic.

Hardy did not waste any time. "Were you able to get what I asked for?"

MacPherson tipped his head backward. "It's in the back." He was given a list of items he was to acquire for his passenger.

Hardy twisted in his seat, retrieved a duffle bag and plopped it onto his lap.

"You'll find everything you asked for is in there."

Hardy unzipped the bag and inspected the contents. "It looks good." He closed the bag and pushed it to the floor. "How far are we from the hotel?"

MacPherson scratched his chin. "About an hour, I'd say."

Hardy looked at the time on the dashboard of the car—it read 6:13. The café, where the meeting was taking place—Apartment 44—was only a few minutes away from his hotel, the Marriott. "Good. That'll give me time to get cleaned up."

For the next hour, the two men made small talk, until MacPherson brought the sedan to a stop in front of the Marriott. He popped the trunk and jumped out. Handing over Hardy's suitcase, along with a room key, MacPherson motioned toward the hotel. "You're already checked in, so you can go straight to your room.

"Thanks." Hardy accepted the items. "I'll meet you in the lobby in twenty minutes."

MacPherson nodded before getting back into the sedan and driving away.

Chapter 6: Marriott

Inside his room, Hardy started the shower and stripped, laying his clothes on the bed. He waited until the steam began to rise over the top of the shower curtain before he climbed into the stall. The hot water hit him like tiny pellets, but it felt good. He had been stuck on a plane for nine hours. After another hour in a small car, this was like a therapeutic massage. Standing with his back to the showerhead, he let the water loosen his tight muscles. He took a few extra minutes to enjoy the moist heat, before lathering and rinsing his body and hair. He rotated the shower handle to the right. Stepping out of the shower, he picked up the towel he had left on the toilet seat and wiped the remaining beads of water from his body. He tossed the towel onto the floor and left the bathroom.

Naked and standing by the bed, Hardy put on a pair of boxer shorts and blue jeans before adding a light brown t-shirt, white socks and brown hiking boot-type tennis shoes. Unzipping the duffle bag MacPherson had given him, he retrieved a Glock 19 handgun, holster, magazine pouch and two magazines. He tucked the small holster inside his waistband before attaching the clip over his belt to secure the rig. He picked up the Glock 19, retracted the slide to verify that the pistol was loaded and slid it into the holster. He put the magazine pouch on the other side of his belt and stuffed two fifteen-round magazines into it before draping his t-shirt over the gun and the magazine pouch. Slinging the duffle bag over his shoulder, he exited the hotel room.

Entering the lobby, Hardy spied MacPherson, sitting in a chair and thumbing through a magazine. Noticing Hardy, MacPherson tossed the magazine onto the table next to him and rose to his feet. The two men left and got into the sedan. Hardy put the duffle bag in the back seat.

MacPherson eased the sedan into traffic.

Hardy twirled a finger in the air. "I want to make a slow trip around the café before we park the car. Go slow, but don't make it conspicuous."

MacPherson acknowledged him.

Less than ten minutes later, the sedan turned right down a narrow side street. MacPherson pointed. "The café is up ahead on the right."

Hardy's eyes scanned the street and buildings for anything, or anyone, that seemed out of place. He did not have reason to suspect anything was going to go wrong. Being acutely aware of his surroundings was something that came natural to him; furthermore, this skill automatically kicked in whenever he was in unfamiliar territory. The street was mostly deserted. A few people mingled on the sidewalk, talking as they walked. Cars were parallel-parked on the right.

After passing the entrance to the café, MacPherson gestured. "This street dead ends up ahead. I'll have to turn around if you want to make a second pass."

"No, park up there, the last one," Hardy said, referring to the row of parallel parking spots on the right. He did not want to risk another drive past the café, in case there was someone watching.

MacPherson parked the sedan and shut off the engine. "How do you want to play this?" He removed his handgun from its holster. Pinching the slide near the muzzle between his thumb and forefinger, he pulled back the slide only enough to see a round in the chamber.

Hardy shook his head and held out his hand. "Let me see your phone."

MacPherson flicked his eyes toward the outstretched hand. "Why?"

"I'm going in alone. I want you to text me if you see anything on the street."

MacPherson relinquished his mobile.

Hardy punched in the number to his sat phone and returned the man's phone to him. After verifying his gun was loaded, he gave the street one more check before getting out of the sedan. He maintained a brisk pace toward the café, his eyes taking in every detail around him. Approaching the café, he swung open the door and stepped inside.

Chapter 7: Café

Apartment 44 was a small café. There were several round-shaped, wooden tables in the center. Matching wooden chairs with circular seats complemented the tables. Straight ahead was a dark mahogany bar. Bottles of alcohol lined a shelf behind it. A full-width mirror behind the shelf gave the illusion there were twice as many bottles. A few patrons sat at the tables. The bartender nodded at Hardy. He nodded back before choosing a table off to the side next to a large brick wall. On one side of the table were two chairs. The other side had booth seating.

Hardy sat on the booth side, his back to the wall. He placed his sat phone on the table and removed a folded newspaper from his back pocket. He placed the newspaper on the table, making sure the section heading was visible and hanging off the edge of the table. His sat phone read 7:48. He glanced around the café, noting where the exits were located.

A few minutes later, a young woman in her twenties showed up at his table, placed a menu in front of him and said something in Russian. He presumed she wanted to take his order. He tapped his finger on the rim of an empty water glass and smiled. The woman had a blank stare on her face for a split-second before she smiled back and nodded her head. She left, returned with a pitcher of water and filled the water glass. Hardy checked his sat phone again—7:55.

During the next five minutes, more patrons entered the café. Each time the door opened, Hardy observed the new arrivals. None matched the description of his contact, the FSB agent.

At eight o'clock, a woman in her mid-to-late twenties with long, blonde hair made an entrance. She stood inside the door and surveyed the people. She displayed a slender figure, five-feet, seven-inches tall, and was dressed in skin-tight blue jeans. A white short-sleeve camisole shell was tucked inside the jeans. When her eyes settled on Hardy, she paused. Dropping her cell phone into the right pocket of her black fitted knee-length blazer, she strutted toward him. Her long legs carried her across the hardwood floor with minimal steps, the hem of her blazer flaring. With each footfall, the two-inch chunky heels of her black pumps echoed in the confined space of the café. The patrons noticed her impressive entrance. They stopped their conversations and held their glasses in midair to glimpse the newcomer.

The woman stopped at Hardy's table. She put her right hand on the back of the nearest chair and eyed the newspaper. The section heading, 'sports,' was hanging off the edge of the table. "My money is on the Yankees this year."

Now that she was standing in front of him, Hardy saw her beauty. Her skin was white, almost like cream. Her blue eyes were set above a narrow nose and below impeccably manicured eyebrows. When she spoke, her full lips parted and revealed a set of white teeth, brilliant in color and perfectly aligned. Her photo in the dossier did not do her justice. "They'll never make it past Boston."

"Boston's bullpen is terrible."

Hardy stood and extended his hand. "I'm Aaron Hardy."

She shook his hand. "Natasha Volkov—it's a pleasure to meet you, Mr. Hardy." She slid the chair out from under the table and sat.

"Likewise, Ms. Volkov." He took his seat.

"Please call me Natasha. I find Ms. Volkov a bit too...*old*...for my tastes." She smiled and half-chuckled. "Perhaps if we meet again in forty years, you can call me, Ms. Volkov."

Hardy laughed as the young woman, who had brought him his water, spoke to Natasha. Natasha replied, and the woman left and came back with a pitcher of water and filled Natasha's water glass.

After the woman had left, Natasha directed her attention toward Hardy. *He's handsome.* She eyed his facial features. He had light brown hair, cut short. His jaw was square. His chin came to a slight point and had a tiny dimple in the center. She was drawn to his deep blue eyes. They made her feel as if he was peering into her inner being. His physique was muscular. His biceps stretched the sleeves of his brown t-shirt to the point where she was expecting the fabric to split at the seam.

She had always been intrigued by American men. They seemed to be freer and more relaxed than their Russian counterparts were, but every bit as tough. Inwardly, she laughed. Maybe she had seen too many American movies when she was younger. "My superiors tell me we're to work together."

Hardy detected a sarcastic tone in her voice, but dismissed it.

She opened the menu and pretended to be deciding on what to order. "So, let's work together. You can start by telling me what you know about Anton Rudin."

Hardy did not appreciate this woman's attitude; however, in this scenario, he was the visiting team and he wanted to get off to a good start. He opened the folded newspaper, took out a few documents and a map of a specific location in Russia. He placed everything in front of him. "A couple of weeks ago, the FBI uncovered and stopped a plot to blow up the Golden Gate Bridge during rush hour traffic. During the investigation, they captured the man who was going to set off the explosion. He had entered the United States from Russia, one week earlier."

Natasha closed the menu and set it aside.

Hardy took a drink of water. "Fast forwarding a little...during the interrogation, the FBI discovered the identity of the man who was to *make* the bomb that was going to be used on the bridge."

Natasha crossed her legs and leaned forward in her chair. "Anton Rudin?"

Hardy nodded. "The man in custody divulged the location of where he had met Rudin when he was in Russia." Hardy twisted the map and pointed to a location and the address of the house where the man had met Rudin. "My people believe this is the best place to begin our search for Rudin." Hardy slid the other documents across the table.

Natasha peered at the map and recognized the address. Without realizing what she was doing, she reached under the table and rubbed the top of her left thigh. She stared at the map in silence. Images of Sergei flashed across her mind. Even though it was not on the map, she envisioned the house, the explosion, the debris. The entire incident came rushing back to her.

Hardy thought she was inspecting the map, but when several awkward moments had passed, he knew something was wrong. "What's the matter?" She did not respond. Reaching out, he touched the map. "Natasha?" She flinched. "Are you okay?"

She blinked several times and took a drink of water. "I'm fine." Her eyes went back to the map. "No, there's nothing there. My people have already—" she paused before flatly stating, "There's nothing there."

"I'd still like to see the house. Maybe, something was overlooked. It can't hurt to have another pair of eyes—"

Natasha cut him off in mid-sentence. "Trust me." Her voice grew louder with each successive word. "There's *nothing* there."

Hardy had touched a nerve. He wanted to push her on the issue. The FBI had been certain there was a better than good chance Rudin used the house as a home base. After staring at her for several moments, he decided not to push it. He remained quiet, letting her read the rest of the documents.

Natasha held a sheet of paper in the air, while she read the next. She consumed everything Hardy and the Americans had on Anton Rudin. She frowned and her eyebrows curled downward. The Americans had no new information. She tightened her grip on the papers, crinkling them. Her government had insisted she work with Hardy in the spirit of cooperation to find Rudin. *Why?* It was obvious the Americans had nothing of value to offer. She put the papers in order and passed them back across the table.

Hardy wasted no time in quizzing her. "Now, it's your turn. What information do you have?" He took the papers and set them on the folded newspaper.

Natasha studied Hardy for several seconds. After taking a drink of water, she glanced over her shoulder. "Look, my government has ordered me to work with you. Why, I don't know. Your country has nothing new to offer in this matter; however," she tugged on the lapels of her jacket to straighten it, "in the spirit of cooperation, I will play nice." She smiled at Hardy, but did a poor job disguising her feelings. "I'm this close," she lifted her hand, her thumb and forefinger close together, "to finding Rudin. I'm waiting for a call from one of my contacts. He thinks he knows where Rudin is hiding." Natasha stood, the backs of her knees pushing the chair away from the table. "Where are you staying?"

"The Marriott," replied Hardy. *She's going to blow me off.*

"Good. Go back to your hotel and rest. When I find out more, I'll call you." She spun around, "I'll be in touch, Mr. Hardy," and marched toward the door.

Hardy watched her leave, his hand shaking from the death grip on the water glass. She had dismissed him with a virtual 'don't call me, I'll call you' attitude. She had not given him any information. This meeting had been a disaster. *So much for cooperation.* Still fuming, he considered his options; go after her and insist on being involved in the conversation with her contact, follow her or visit the site on the map himself. He was contemplating a fourth option when he noticed something odd on the other side of the café.

Chapter 8: Surprised

Natasha left the café. She had no plans to contact Hardy when she found Rudin. She had worked hard, tracking the man to that dilapidated house, only to have him slip though her fingers. Sergei's death would not be in vain. No, when she found Rudin, she was going to be the one who brought him to justice. No pretty boy American was going to take from her the satisfaction owed. After Rudin was in custody, she would call Hardy and give him an excuse for why she had not called him sooner. *It was a matter of urgency and I needed to move fast. That should placate him.*

Reaching the sidewalk, she heard her phone ring. It was her contact. She swiped a finger across the screen before tucking the phone under her hair. "Tell me you found him." Focusing on the voice on the other end of the phone, she listened.

Striding up the sidewalk of the narrow, deserted street, she was paying too much attention to the caller and did not see the slow-moving black van to the right, until it was too late.

The van accelerated and came alongside Natasha before swerving left and coming to a halt, the tires screeching. The side doors were open. Two men jumped out and rushed her. She dropped her phone, threw back the right lapel of her open-front blazer. Before she could get to her weapon, the first man latched on to her right arm and twisted it behind her back. The second man took her pistol from her holster. The first man, who still held her arm behind her back, grabbed a handful of hair, took two steps toward the van and threw Natasha through the open doors.

She threw out her left hand to break her fall, her palm skidding across the rough fibers of the van's carpeted floor. She landed on her stomach, her knees hitting the metal trim of the van's running boards. The surge of adrenaline kept any pain from reaching her brain. She rolled onto her left side and brought her right foot up, ready to drive the heel of her shoe into the first target presented. She lined up her foot with the center of the man's chest, the one who had thrown her into the van. She never got the chance to deliver her strike, however.

As the men approached the van, Natasha heard several loud bangs. The men's shirts split open in several different spots. The second man staggered backward and hit the open door of the van before sliding to the pavement. The first man dropped to his knees, his upper body landing inside the van. Staring at Natasha, he appeared to have been shot. She was not going to be denied her revenge, however. She thrust her leg toward the man, the heel of her shoe landing squarely on the man's nose. After a loud crack, streams of blood stained the carpet. His head rocked backward and he disappeared from sight. Before she could get to her feet, she noticed movement to the right.

Chapter 9: Newspaper

Hardy followed a man from the café. The man had sat in the corner, pretending to read a newspaper. Hardy had noticed the man never flipped a single page of the newspaper. Occasionally, he would peer over the paper, looking at Natasha. After she had gone, the man chucked the newspaper, tossed a few Rubles on the table and left.

On the street, Hardy saw the scene unfold. The van came to a quick stop, blocking Natasha's forward movement. Two men jumped out, rushing toward her. Watching them throw her through the side doors, Hardy knew what was coming next and he had to act. Drawing his Glock 19, he took a step to the right to get a clear shot at the two men near the van. He pressed the pistol's trigger several times, shooting the man to the left four times, hitting him in the torso. The last shot penetrated his ear, sending him crumpling to the concrete. Transitioning to the second man, Hardy shot him multiple times, until he fell through the van's open doors. The man from the café telegraphed a move for a holstered weapon. Hardy had been waiting to see what the man would do. He had to make sure the newcomer was not coming to Natasha's aid. When Hardy saw the pistol on the man's hip, he had seen enough. He put his pistol's front sight on the man's nose and pulled back on the trigger. Mr. Newspaper collapsed into a heap, never getting the chance to draw the pistol.

Hardy sprinted toward the van. Keeping a safe distance from the open doors, he swung his pistol around and pointed it inside. Natasha was on the floor, a man squatting behind her and pressing the muzzle of a gun against her right temple. His other arm had her in a headlock. She was off-balance, unable to fight back.

The man said something to Hardy in Russian and drove the muzzle deeper into her skin. Natasha's eyes squinted and she groaned. Her windpipe was being crushed. Hardy leveled the Glock at the man's right eye. "I'm sorry, but I don't speak Russian."

Again, the man spoke to Hardy in his native language.

Not taking his eyes off his adversary, Hardy spoke to Natasha. "Natasha, this ugly oaf doesn't know what I'm saying, so this is what's going to happen." Hardy waited again to see if his comment got any reaction from the man. It did not. "When I count to three, you're going to tilt your head to *your* left as far as you can. Understand?"

Struggling against her captor's grasp, Natasha held her hands in front of her, her eyes wide. She managed to shake her head, no.

"Trust me, Natasha. You're not the only one who graduated at the top of the class in marksmanship. On three, tilt your head to your left." Hardy gripped his Glock a little tighter. "One."

Natasha's adrenaline coursed through her body. Her heart pounded in her chest and she could feel her pulse throbbing in her temples.

"Two."

Natasha had met Hardy less than thirty minutes ago. He was expecting her to place her life in his hands. She was not a religious person, but she said a quick prayer and lowered her hands, hearing Hardy say the next number.

"Three!"

Natasha put all of the adrenaline surging through her veins to good use. She yanked her head to the left as hard as she could. The muscles on the right side of her neck burned. She thought if she did not die from a gunshot wound to the head, she would break her neck.

Hardy had noticed the gun being held to Natasha's head was a Sig Sauer, a double-action/single-action pistol. The hammer was forward and in double-action mode. The man's trigger finger would have to travel further and exert more energy to discharge the gun. Hardy took advantage of those factors.

He applied steady pressure to the trigger of his Glock. Natasha had jerked her head far enough to give him a clear shot. He only needed one. The gun in his hands roared. The muzzle rose and fell.

The muzzle of Hardy's pistol settled and he saw the man's body go limp. The grasp around Natasha's neck loosened and the arm slid off her shoulder. The arm holding the Sig Sauer dropped to the floor of the van. The man's body slowly leaned back and came to rest against the unopened door of the van.

Natasha rolled to her left, clutching her neck and coughing. In between coughs, she shouted at Hardy, using her native tongue.

An interpreter was not necessary. He had learned a few Russian words, starting with the curse words she was spewing. She was not was angry. Adrenaline and fear were driving her emotions.

Hardy started searching the dead men, while Natasha regained her senses. The first man had a badge. He was a member of law enforcement. Hardy felt a lump form in his throat. He had killed a cop. He held the badge, so Natasha could see it.

Climbing out of the van, she retrieved her handgun from the ground and holstered it. She snatched the badge from Hardy's hand and examined it. "What the hell?" she said. Her voice was deeper and hoarse. She held the shield she carried on a daily basis. *They're FSB.*

Hardy checked the other bodies. Each one had the same badge.

Natasha rubbed her throat. "I don't understand this."

Hearing the gunshots, MacPherson came running from the parked sedan, surprising Natasha, who spun and reached for her gun.

Hardy stopped her. "It's all right. He's with me." He pointed at the dead men. "Are these friends of yours?"

Moving from one to the next, she examined each of their faces. "I've never seen them before, but that doesn't mean anything. The FSB is a large agency with many, many agents in its employ."

"What happened," asked MacPherson, holstering his gun?

Hardy gestured at the corpses. "They tried to kidnap Natash...Agent Volkov." Without formality, Hardy introduced them to each other. "Agent Volkov...MacPherson...MacPherson...Agent Volkov."

MacPherson said, "Pleasure."

Not making eye contact, she replied, "Pleasure."

Natasha reached into her pocket. "I've got to call this in." Not finding her phone, she jerked her head left and right. The cell was lying on the ground where the man had grabbed her arm. She picked up the device and brushed off the dirt.

"Wait a minute." Hardy held up his hand. "Are you sure you want to do that?"

"I have to. I'm an FSB agent. I have to report this." She tapped the screen, dialing the number for her supervisor.

"Exactly. These are *your people*. Why would they want to abduct you? That makes no sense."

She stopped dialing and looked at him.

"You don't know who you can trust. You don't know who ordered this."

In the distance, wailing sirens grew louder. MacPherson joined the conversation. "In a few minutes, this area is going to be crawling with police. Whatever you plan on doing, you need to do it, *now.*"

Hardy saw patrons from the café, peeking out the window. Some were making their way outside to see the commotion. "He's right. We need to leave."

Natasha held out her arms. "And, go where? We don't know what's going on here. I need to find out who these people are and what they wanted from me." She coughed before massaging her throat.

"You're not going to find answers if you're arrested by the police. Instead, you'll be answering *their* questions."

Natasha stared at the dead bodies. He was right. Without more information, the police would assume she and Hardy were guilty of killing four FSB agents. She slid her phone into her blazer pocket. "All right, let's go." She hurried up the sidewalk. "My vehicle is right around the corner."

Hardy waved off MacPherson. "Get out of here. I'll find my way home, somehow. Thanks for your help."

MacPherson nodded. "Take care, Hardy."

Hardy ran to catch up with Natasha at the corner of the main cross street. Her SUV was a few parking spaces away. After they got into the vehicle, she brought the engine to life, peeled away from the curb and accelerated as fast as she could without drawing attention.

Chapter 10: Roadside

Once they were a safe distance away from the scene behind them, Natasha stopped the Patriot on the side of a deserted road. She slammed the gear selector into 'park' and leaned back, running her fingers through her hair before interlocking them behind her head. She mulled over the incident outside the café. *Could my own people be responsible? They were definitely FSB agents. Their badges seemed real enough.* Letting her arms fall, her hands smacked against her thighs. She let out a long breath and her bangs shot upward.

Hardy knew what she was feeling—betrayal. Recently, he had faced a similar situation. He gave her a few minutes before pressing her. "What are we going to do, Natasha?" He would have loved to take charge, but he was in uncharted waters. The mission had taken a left turn.

She rolled her eyes toward him. Her head followed. *That's a good question.* She had been attacked by her fellow agents and was essentially on the run from the police. Staring at Hardy, her thoughts lingered over whether she could trust him.

"Who knew about your meeting with me?"

Natasha thought for a moment. "I was ordered to work with you by my boss, the director of the FSB." She paused. "There were several other agents who knew about it." She stared out the window. The sun was rising and the day was getting warmer. "Anyone could have known about it. It wasn't exactly a secret."

"So, you can't trust anybody in your agency. Everyone's a suspect. It looks like it's up to us to find out what's going on." Moments of silence passed, while they pondered their options. "Again, what are we going to do? What's our next move, Natasha?" He was in a foreign country and did not have any sources to contact, a position with which he was unfamiliar. Like it or not, he was reliant on his new 'partner.'

Hardy's words, 'you can't trust anybody in your agency,' echoed in her mind. Calling the police would likely result in her arrest and a possible murder charge. No, contact with her agency was off the table. Someone there wanted her out of the way. She was confident this attack was related to her search for Rudin. She had focused most of her resources on capturing him. In fact, during the last three months, every other case on her list had been sidelined. To find out who was behind this attack, she would have to catch Rudin and squeeze him for information. Natasha glimpsed Hardy out of the corner of her eye. Reluctantly, she would have to confide in him. Unfortunately, the next phase in their working relationship was about to begin on a sour note, the revelation of a lie.

Natasha studied her fingernails. She picked at one and flicked her fingers.

"Natasha?"

She waited until the silence became more unbearable than the truth. Whipping her head away from him, she came clean. "I was on the phone with my contact," she spoke as if reading from a script, "when those men attacked me. He told me where I could find Rudin." Staring at the floor, she felt his eyes, penetrating to her core.

"You weren't going to tell me about it, were you?"

She rubbed the palm of her left hand, the hand that had saved her face from skidding across the floor of the van.

"You were going to give me a courtesy call...*after* you had already picked him up." Hardy's pulse beat faster and the muscles in his jaw tightened. "If this is what *you people* consider cooperation, then I don't want any part of it. It's no wonder diplomatic relations between our two countries have soured. You people—"

Natasha whipped her head toward him. Fire burned in her eyes. "And, what is *your* angle in all of this? I'm sure you and your country aren't solely interested in helping us find a bomb maker devastating my people *out of the kindness of your heart*. What's the *real* reason you're here, Hardy? Can you tell me...without using the word 'cooperation' in the sentence?"

"I'm here to end Rudin's life. He's a bomb maker, who sells to the highest bidder. I take him out and he can't make any more bombs. It's that simple. There's no angle other than I want to see him dead."

"Oh, if it were only that simple. But it seldom is, though. You Americans look out for your own interests. You intervene in the affairs of other nations to accumulate wealth and power, influencing those nations to do your bidding. You're a selfish and self-centered people. You think you are the greatest nation to grace the face of the earth." Natasha looked up and raised her hands—"God's gift to the human race." She shook her head. "You people are so arrogant." She started to turn away, but stopped and jabbed a finger in his Hardy's direction. "Believe me when I tell you...your American Influence does not hold the power you *think* it does with my country."

Hardy and Natasha sat in silence for several minutes. She gripped the steering wheel hard enough to turn her knuckles white. Resting on his legs, Hardy's fists were clenched. Afraid of what they may say if the conversation continued, the agents remained quiet.

Natasha had lost much in a short time. She had not recovered from her father's death when Sergei was killed less than a month later. Her nerves were raw. Lately, she had lashed out at anyone who crossed her, even over trivial matters. She glimpsed Hardy out of the corner of her eye. If their working arrangement had any chance of succeeding, she was going to have to temper her feelings. *Maybe, he has no ulterior motive in this. We need to start over...if that's possible.*

Natasha released her grip on the steering wheel and flexed her fingers. She twisted in her seat to face him, making a mental note to soften the tone of her voice. "I know this may seem odd, coming at a time like this, but I never got a chance to thank you for saving my life back there. Thank you." She let her words hang in the air. "What made you come after me?"

Hardy gritted his teeth. Oddly, he had been asking himself the same question. Risking his life to save a woman, who repaid him with insults to his integrity—and his country—had not been part of the plan. If he had stayed seated in the café and not followed that man...he let his thoughts trail off before reprimanding himself. *You're not that kind of man.* He had done the right thing. Unclenching his fists and wiggling his fingers, Hardy made a conscious effort to relax his chest muscles.

He shot a look out the window. "There was a man in the café," Hardy's voice was matter-of-factly, "who pretended to be reading a newspaper. He left right after you did. I followed him and saw the whole thing." He faced her and struggled to add a touch of warmth to his tone. "You're welcome. I'm glad I was there."

Natasha noted his exaggerated attempt at a pleasantry; however, she felt an undertone of sincerity in his words. Like her, he was trying. *Yes, I think I might be able to trust him.* After those words entered her mind, she inwardly laughed. Hardy had killed four men to save her. If it were not for his actions, she would have been abducted, possibly dead by now. "Go after him."

Hardy's eyebrows furled downward. "What are you talking about?"

"You asked me, 'what are we going to do?' We know where Rudin is hiding. Let's go after him. That's why you're here, isn't it? That's why we're working together. And, I'm thinking he might have some answers about those FSB agents back there. What is it that you Americans say?" She paused a moment, thinking of the phrase. "It's a win-win." She cocked her head to the left and raised her eyebrows, hoping the idiom would lighten the mood.

Natasha's attempt at humor was lost on Hardy. His mind was elsewhere. Killing Rudin was the purpose of his mission. In order to accomplish that, he and Natasha needed to be on the same side. She had made an effort to make amends for her words—and actions. *A fresh start.* He nodded. "Where is he?"

A smile formed on Natasha's face. She took out her cell phone. "East of St. Petersburg, on the outskirts of town," she replied, touching her phone's screen. "My source told me he has armed men with him. So, we're going to need some help."

"Who are you calling?"

She hesitated and shot him a sideways glance. "Some friends of mine from the FSB..."

Hardy rolled his eyes.

"They can help."

"We've been over this. You don't know who's responsible for sending those men."

Natasha put the mobile to her ear. "Yes, but I know these men and they would do anything for me. I trust them with my life."

"I hope you're right, because it's not just *your* life on the line."

Natasha put her hand on his forearm. "I put my life in *your* hands in that van. Now, it's time to repay that faith."

Hardy glanced at her hand. Trust was a complicated issue. He was accustomed to being in control of missions and situations. He gave the orders and his men followed, trusting in *his* judgment.

Natasha patted his arm and smiled. A second later, the familiar, deep voice of a man she knew and respected sounded in her ear. "Victor, it's Natasha." She turned away from Hardy.

"Natasha," Victor's smile came through the line, "it's good to hear your voice. How are you?"

"I'm doing well, Victor, but I need your help."

"What is it?"

"How soon can you get your team ready for a trip to St. Petersburg?"

"Not long, why? What's going on?"

She took her phone away from her ear and tapped the screen several times. "I just sent you the address of the location. I need to find someone there and the people inside will not be receptive to a knock on the door. I'll explain when you get there."

"I'll send you a text when I know our ETA."

"Thanks, Victor." Natasha eyed Hardy. "Oh, I'll be coming to the event, *plus one*. Is there any chance you can bring a grab bag?"

"I'll see what I can do."

Natasha ended the call and stashed the phone. Not having shut off the Patriot's engine, she lowered the gearshift into 'drive' and re-entered the roadway. Not taking her eyes off the road, she addressed her passenger. "Settle in, we've got a long drive ahead of us. If the traffic isn't too bad, we can make it in less than nine hours."

Hardy checked his sat phone—8:37. Not looking forward to another nine hours in confined quarters, he reached between his legs and found the lever to move the seat back. Realizing it was already back as far as it could go, he groaned under his breath.

"Are you hungry?"

"I'm starving." He had eaten a bagel and cream cheese on the flight, but that was not nearly enough food.

"I know a place on the way. It's about an hour from here. We can get something there."

Chapter 11: Rudin

Anton Rudin sat on a stool, hunched over an old wooden farm table that had seen many family dinners throughout the decades. Children would have gathered at the table, eager to see what their mother had prepared. Never in their wildest dreams would past occupants of the house have imagined the table holding the items it now held.

Rudin pushed the bridge of his gold round eyeglasses further up his long, pointed ski-slope-shaped nose. Beads of sweat dotted his forehead. His black hair was cut short and parted on the side. He was a small man, barely five-and-a-half-feet tall, and had a thin build. Fortunately, his skills did not require him to use his brawn. No, he made his living with his mind.

Rudin finished wiring the remote detonator to the last of four bombs. His cell phone on the table vibrated. He leaned over and sighed. It was his current employer. The man had hired him to make the four bombs. The man had also hired him to make, place and detonate the bombs that had exploded in Moscow over the last six months. Rudin did not see himself as a terrorist. In his mind, he was a businessperson, a supplier. It was a simple issue of supply and demand. There was a need for what he made and he filled that need. The man he was about to talk to, however, had wanted Rudin to be more than a supplier.

Rudin despised the client, but the man paid very well for the bomb maker's services. Once these four devices were in place, Rudin would receive the final installment. The money would be enough to allow him to live comfortably for the rest of his life, which was going to be a long time, since he was only forty-five years old. He had made plans to use his newfound wealth to leave Russia. He hated the cold winters, and the older he got, the more his body protested. He had his eyes set on somewhere warm, somewhere tropical. A place with beautiful sunsets and miles and miles of coastline, speckled with pretty girls in skimpy bikinis. Rudin smiled, envisioning the scene.

Letting go of the pliers, he grabbed the mobile. "Da — *Yes.*"

"Gotovy li oni yeshche — *Are they ready yet?*" asked the man.

"YA tol'ko chto zakonchil — *I just finished,*" replied Rudin.

"Khorosho. Grafik byl peremeshchen vverkh. Vy dolzhny poluchit' ikh na meste v nastoyashcheye vremya. Moi lyudi vstretyat vas v tochke sblizheniya. K tomu vremeni, vy poluchayete k mestu, bezopasnost' budut udaleny, i u vas ne budet nikakikh poluchat' cherez vorota. — *Good. The timetable has been moved up. You need to get them in place, now. My men will meet you at the rendezvous point. By the time you get to the*

197

location, security will be removed and you'll have no trouble getting through the gate."

"Chto mozhno skazat' o zhenshchine iz FSB? Ona stanovitsya vse blizhe i blizhe — *What about the woman from the FSB? She is getting closer and closer.*"

"Ne bespokoytes' o ney. Ya dogovorilsya. Ona budet zabotit'sya — *Don't worry about her. I've made arrangements. She will be taken care of.*" The man paused and added, "Ne vint eto vverkh. Vy budete shchedro zaplatili, no tol'ko yesli vam eto udastsya. Otkaz ne budet dopuskat'sya — *Don't screw this up. You'll be paid generously, but only if you succeed. Failure will not be tolerated.*" As soon as the man had finished speaking, he hung up the phone, not giving Rudin a chance to respond.

Setting the cell on the table, Rudin began giving orders to the men. One of them, holding a spatula in his hand, tossed things into a plastic garbage bag, while another gathered large pieces of paper on a nearby table. Rudin screamed, "Ostav'te vse. My dolzhny idti! — *Leave everything. We have to go now!*"

Chapter 12: Popovich

General Popovich hung up the phone and leaned back in his chair. He swiped the tip of a wooden match across the matchbox. Sparks flew and a small flame grew. He brought the match to the cigar he was biting. After a few puffs, he shook the match and tossed it—and the matchbox—onto his desk. He put his feet up, his combat boots landing on the desk near a coffee cup. The surface of the black liquid inside vibrated. Thick smoke from the cigar hung in the air above his head.

General Popovich was fifty-seven years old. His gray hair had receded to the top of his head. A thick, gray mustache covered his upper lip. Above the lip was a large and bulbous nose, heavily pockmarked. His dark eyes were deeply set. Bushy eyebrows hung over them, almost coming together to form one brow. He was of average height, but he had gained much weight in the last ten years. His neck spilled over the collar of his uniform, while the buttons strained to keep the lapels together.

General Popovich was the head of the Premier's security team. Prior to accepting the job, he had been a high-ranking member of the KGB, Russia's intelligence agency, until its breakup in 1991. He continued to serve in the intelligence arena as an FSB agent, until his departure five years ago. Two years ago, the Premier had asked him to come out of retirement and lead the Premier's security team.

The General was a hardliner. He longed for the old days, when Russia was a superpower. His country had been feared and respected by other nations. Its citizens had been proud and could hold their heads high.

Russia had become weak, however. Western culture had invaded its borders, bringing with it decadence and decay. Young people wanted freedom, chanting in the streets, protesting against the government. Using technology, they took to the Internet to broadcast their message to others like them. What those fools did not understand was that freedom was not free. Freedom came at the cost of security. But, those immature idealists thought they could have both. Popovich needed to change their way of thinking before beautiful Mother Russia was lost forever.

General Popovich took the cigar from his mouth and tapped it on the lip of the ashtray. He returned the cigar to his mouth, clasped his thick, pudgy fingers together and put his hands behind his head. Plans had been set in motion that would bring about the change his country required. The Russian people were already living in a state of fear, teetering on the brink of surrender. Popovich's next move would show his fellow citizens that no one was safe from terror. The only thing that would save them was to give the government more power and more control. In this way, Russia would become great again.

Chapter 13: Farmhouse

5:16 p.m.; thirty-five minutes southeast of St. Petersburg, Russia

At one time, the old single-story farmhouse would have been attractive. Centered on several acres of rich farmland, the house would have sheltered families from the brutal Russian winters, while the land would have provided food. The dwelling was situated at the base of a sloping hill. There was a grove of trees at the top of the hill; oaks and pines, among others, standing guard for more than a century.

The structure was in a state of disrepair. The chimney was missing so many bricks that light passed through it. The wooden siding was rotted and many pieces had been blown away. Even the wraparound porch had not escaped the effects of the elements. The handrail was loose; large sections were missing. The floorboards were in place, but they were splintered and rough. Having long been abandoned, the farmhouse had stood its ground in silence, until three days ago when several men showed up.

On the other side of the hill, just past the stand of trees, a small SUV was parked near the edge of the tree line. Natasha gazed through the windshield of her Patriot. "The house is just over that hill." She checked the time on her cell phone. "Victor will be here soon." Exiting the SUV, she closed the door and climbed into the backseat. Once the door was shut, she drove her knees into the seat cushion and leaned into the luggage compartment.

With her back to him, Hardy saw her hauling items from the compartment and tossing them onto the seat; some fell onto the floor. He looked closer and noticed a bulletproof vest, a pair of black tactical pants and a pair of six-inch boots. He did not recognize the name on the items—everything was in Russian—but he could see they were of similar quality to the gear he used. Hardy flicked his eyes to the right; they opened wider.

Still on her knees and facing away from him, Natasha had removed her long blazer, kicked off her shoes and pushed her jeans to her knees. Only a couple of feet away from Hardy's face, a pair of white lace-trimmed bikini underwear separated him from her butt. She spun around, plopped onto the seat and wiggled out of the jeans. Out of the corner of her eye, she saw Hardy whip his head away from her.

Sitting on the seat, wearing only her underwear and a short sleeve camisole, she smiled and realized he must have gotten an eyeful. Her mind had been so focused on getting into her tactical clothing she had forgotten there was another person in the vehicle. She buttoned her pants and shirt. "It's all right. We're both adults. I don't have anything you haven't already seen."

"I'm sorry. I was just admiring your," Hardy shut his eyes and winced—*bad choice of words*—"looking at your tactical gear."

Pulling on her boots and slipping into the bulletproof vest, she grinned. "*Tactical gear*, huh? Is that what a butt's called in America? Is that slang?" She grabbed her SR-3M Vikhr rifle and placed it on the floor. "I'm dressed now."

Pivoting in the seat, his cheeks crimson, Hardy saw the playful grin on Natasha's face. "You know what I meant." The awkward situation had morphed into a moment of lightheartedness. It was good to see this woman had a sense of humor. He pointed at her with his chin. "I think I'm a bit underdressed for the occasion."

Wearing full tactical clothing from head to toe, including a bulletproof vest, Natasha removed the magazine from the weapon, checked to make sure it was full and re-inserted it. She pulled back on rifle's bolt and saw a round in the chamber. Hearing a vehicle behind her, she glanced over her shoulder. A black SUV had rolled up to the right of the Patriot. Opening the door, she got out and leaned back inside. "Not for much longer. Come on."

Hardy stepped out of the vehicle and stretched his arms before putting his hands on his lower back and bending side to side. He watched three large men exit the black SUV. Dressed similar to Natasha, each of the men greeted her with a broad smile, kissed her on each cheek and proceeded to talk to her in Russian. Even though Hardy could not understand what they were saying, he could tell from the facial expressions that Natasha meant a great deal to these men. Hardy waited patiently for them to finish their reunion. One of the men, the tallest and oldest of the three, stopped talking and noticed Hardy. The other two men followed suit. Natasha made the introductions.

"This is Aaron Hardy. He's assisting me in tracking down Rudin." She pointed to the man furthest away from her. "Aaron, meet Nikolai Pushkin and Ivan Strovsky. They don't speak any English." Both men were similar in appearance; short blonde hair, square jaw, six-feet, two inches tall and weighing at least two hundred and twenty pounds. The only discerning feature between them was Nikolai's cleft chin. Both men nodded their heads and shook Hardy's hand.

"And, this big ox is Victor." She put her hand on the man's shoulder, which was almost higher than the top of her head. Victor Yedemsky smiled at Natasha before stepping forward and extending his hand toward Hardy.

Victor was easily six-feet, five inches in height and weighed thirty pounds more than either Nikolai or Ivan. Victor had dark hair, cut short, but not in a military-style crew cut. His green eyes were set far apart, beneath his sparse eyebrows. A well-manicured mustache rested below a wide nose with flaring nostrils. Even though he was in his mid-forties, his skin was weathered and displayed light pockmarks, especially the cheeks.

All members of the Russian Spetsnaz knew the name, Victor Yedemsky. He was a living legend in the Spetsnaz community. During his twenty years of service, he had seen action in many of the terrorist attacks that had taken place in his country, including the Moscow Theater Hostage Crisis in October 2002. In that incident, 40 terrorists took 916 guests hostage. The three-day standoff ended when security forces, which Victor was among, stormed the theater and stopped the terrorists from triggering bombs that would have brought down the building.

Victor had also been assigned to combat the worst act of terrorism in Russian history, the September 2004 hostage crisis at a school in Beslan, North Ossentia. One thousand, one hundred, twenty-eight people were taken hostage; 333 of them were killed, including 186 children. That had been a difficult day for Victor. Months later, he was still mentally recovering from Beslan. To this day, images from that attack haunt him in his sleep.

"It's nice to meet you, Mr. Hardy." Victor had a strong Russian accent.

Hardy shook Victor's hand, feeling the strength of the man's grip. "The pleasure is mine."

"Come," said Victor. "I have something for you." Everyone moved to the back of the black SUV. Victor opened the back door, dragged a duffle bag closer and unzipped it. "I think they'll fit." Inside the bag was the exact same black tactical clothing all of them were wearing, including a bulletproof vest, helmet and goggles. "Finally, this is for you, too." He picked up the same type of rifle that Natasha had been holding earlier and handed it to Hardy. "If you need a crash course in operating it, Nikolai or Ivan can help with that."

"Thanks, but I've handled one before." Hardy dropped the magazine, slid the bolt back and forth a few times, re-inserted the magazine and operated the bolt to chamber a round.

Victor was impressed. Not many people outside of Russia were familiar with a Vikhr. "Very good," he said, before pointing toward the hill and giving his men instructions. The two men checked their weapons and took off toward the hill, each in a different direction. When they had gone, he turned back to Natasha. "I heard you were involved in a shooting in Moscow that killed four FSB agents. Is that true?"

Natasha glanced at Hardy, who was in the process of emptying the duffle bag. He stopped and the two of them exchanged glances.

Victor's eyes shifted from Natasha to Hardy before coming back to Natasha. He saw the body language. "It's true, isn't it?"

"Yes," said Natasha, who described the incident at the café.

Victor put his hand on her shoulder. After she had recanted the story, he faced Hardy, who was buttoning the black shirt. He put his meaty hands on Hardy, one on each shoulder.

Hardy's muscles contracted and he clenched his fists, a kneejerk reaction.

Victor drew Hardy closer and kissed him, once on each cheek. "Thank you, Mr. Hardy, for saving Natasha's life. I am in your debt, sir."

Hardy relaxed. He thought he was going to have to fight this mountain of a man. He smiled. "We can start by dropping the 'sir' and 'mister.' Call me, Hardy."

Victor smiled and slapped Hardy on the back.

Hardy showed no emotion, but Victor's slap reminded Hardy of his high school days, specifically, being hit with a wet towel in the locker room. *That's going to leave a mark.*

Hardy put on the rest of the tactical clothing. The shirt and pants were a good fit, but the boots were too big. He opted to wear his own boots. He gazed at Victor and Natasha. They had walked several feet away and were talking in Russian. The discussion grew more intense. Natasha was animated, moving her hands and arms, while Victor remained calm. Her behavior was similar to when she was upset with Hardy back in Moscow. There was one major difference, though. At this moment, she was twice as upset. Hardy finished attaching the straps on his bulletproof vest before joining them.

Re-positioning the vest to get more comfortable, he stood next to the Russians. "Is everything okay?"

"What do you think?" Natasha tilted her head toward Victor. "Do we go in now or should we wait until dark?"

Hardy could tell from her tone she was in favor of raiding the house before dark. Victor's facial expression displayed a different opinion. Hardy felt as if he was caught between two friends, being asked to choose one over the other.

Tactically, it was better to go in under the cover of darkness. If they went now, there was a chance they could be spotted before they made it to the house; however, there was no telling how long the target would be inside. If they waited too long, they could lose their window of opportunity.

Victor raised a huge paw. "All I'm saying is that we need to stay focused. We don't want another incident like..." his voice trailed off, when he realized the implications of his words.

Natasha's eyes narrowed and she glared at Victor. "Go ahead and finish—like the one that got Sergei killed. You think it's *my fault* he's dead, don't you?"

"I didn't say that." Victor was smoothing over his words. "I know he would have—"

Natasha interrupted him. "No, you didn't *say it*, but it was on your mind. You think Sergei might still be alive, if I hadn't been there, distracting him from his job."

"Natasha—"

"Go to hell, Victor." She stormed off toward the trees.

Hardy faced the big man. "What was *that* all about?"

Victor jerked his head toward Natasha, as if to say 'ask her.'

Chapter 14: Guilt

Hardy caught up with Natasha at the tree line. He took hold of her elbow. She spun around, her long hair flying over her shoulder. She glanced at Hardy's hand—still clamped onto her arm—and locked eyes with him.

Hardy's upper body leaned backward. *If looks could kill.* He had been on the receiving end of her fury before and was not looking forward to another round. Still holding her elbow, his other hand shot up. "I just want to talk. What happened back there?"

She yanked her arm away. "It's none of your business." She took a few steps and looked over her shoulder. "You wouldn't understand, anyway."

Hardy skirted around her and blocked her way, but did not make physical contact—he was not entirely convinced she would *not* hit him. "Listen, it may not be any of my business, but I can see that whatever happened is affecting you. And, since we are working together, I should know what is going on—not only for my safety, but for the safety of this team as well."

Natasha started to speak, but stopped.

Hardy saw the muscles in her face relax, while she mulled over his words. He coaxed her. "What happened?"

Natasha crossed her arms in front of her chest. She was not in a mood to talk. Victor had brought back memories she had spent months trying to reconcile. *How dare he?* Cupping her elbow in her left hand, she covered her mouth with her free hand.

Hardy squared his body and clutched her shoulders. "Talk to me, Natasha. What's going on?"

She raised her eyes toward him. She did not intend to tell him anything; however, maybe it would be good to open up to someone, having not spoken with anyone about Sergei's death. She rolled her eyes and let her arms fall to her sides. Natasha relented, "All right, fine," before launching into her story.

Hearing about the explosion that killed Sergei and his teammates, Hardy had flashbacks of the blast that had taken the lives of *his* teammates. The incident was still in the forefront of his mind and had caused him to have the same nightmare almost every night for the past week.

In the nightmare, Hardy saw the faces of his teammates gathered around the table at the tavern. Everyone was laughing, drinking and having a good time. Their faces became distorted and they desperately tried to tell him something. He could not hear anything they were saying. Their mouths were moving, but no sounds could be heard. At that moment, he felt something hit him in the back. The force threw him to the pavement. After that, everything went black.

"That's not all." She turned away from Hardy and folded her arms across her chest. She saw Victor leaning against the SUV and she recalled her harsh words to him. "My father died three weeks before that explosion. Actually, he was killed...killed in an explosion at a bus stop. He wasn't waiting for a bus. He was just walking by..." She closed her eyes and dropped her head to her chest. Seconds later, she whirled around and thrust her finger toward the top of the hill. "And, that son-of-a..." she stopped talking when her voice cracked. First, pausing to get control of her emotions, she finished the sentence, her voice deeper. "He's responsible."

Hardy was at a loss for words. Not only had she lost her boyfriend to Rudin, but her father as well, less than a month apart from each other. He understood why she had been quick-tempered with him and Victor. "Natasha, there was nothing you could have done to save your father, or Sergei."

"I could have at least been there with Sergei. I could have—and should have—gone in with him. I was the reason he was there."

Hardy shook his head, no. "What would that have accomplished? You would have been killed, too."

"At least I would have been there with them. It was my job. I should have been the first one through the door. Instead, they're dead and I'm..." her voice trailed off.

Hearing her last words, Hardy understood the source of her anger—*guilt*. "You're what—still alive? Isn't that what you were going to say?"

Natasha glimpsed Victor, regret filling her heart. If not for him, she might have died in the aftermath of that explosion.

Victor and his team had been en route to the house. By the time he had arrived, the house was in pieces and Natasha was lying on the cold ground, shivering and her body convulsing. Victor had picked her up and taken her to the SUV. Once there, he wrapped her in blankets and kept her warm, while a member of his team drove them to the hospital. The doctors had said if she had spent any more time exposed to the elements, she might have died.

"Natasha, I understand what you're going through." Hardy put his hands on his hips. "You're feeling guilty that you're still alive and those men are dead."

Leveling her eyes on him, her face flush, she snapped, "How do *you* know what I'm going through?"

He held his hand to his chest and shot back at her, his voice on the verge of yelling. "I know, because I lost my team...in an explosion. They all died. Twelve of the best men I've ever known. They're gone," he pointed toward the ground, "and I'm still here." He lowered his voice. "So, yes, I know what you're going through."

Natasha took a half step backward.

"I've felt the guilt you're feeling, now." He held his arms out to his sides. "Every day, I ask myself the same question—what could I have done differently to save them?"

Natasha waited, hoping for insight.

"I still haven't found an answer where I could have changed the outcome of that day." He ran his fingers through his hair and scratched his head.

"Does it get any better?" Her voice was an octave above a whisper. "Does the guilt go away?"

Hardy watched the leaves flutter in the breeze. "I don't think it will ever go away...*completely.*" He paused. "Honestly, I'm not sure I would want it to."

Natasha cocked her head. "What do you mean?"

Hardy dropped his head, his eyes settling on a broken tree branch on the ground. "I carry those men with me every day. Sometimes, I think they carry me when I'm down and need a boost." He kicked the tree branch and looked at her. "My point is you need to find a way to channel your feelings toward something good. Make their lives—your father and Sergei—matter. Let them live on through what you do."

Natasha's eyes bore a hole through Hardy's brain. She saw, no, she felt his pain. He had taken an emotional beating, but he was still on his feet, fighting. He was tough—she thought of the four, dead FSB agents in Moscow—however, he had a softer side, too. She speculated it was a side not many people had seen.

Hardy thought about the funeral service for his men and the priest's words that day. His words had made Hardy think, differently. He debated sharing those words with her. "I don't know if you believe in God or not, but at the funeral service for my teammates, the priest said to the people, 'Never let

213

the fire of the love within them burn out.' For some reason," he shook his head back and forth, slowly, "those words have stuck in my brain and heart. Every day I wake up and every mission I will go on, my men will be with me."

Natasha listened to this American as if she was ten-years-old, sitting at the feet of her father and hanging on his every word. Maybe she was dreaming, but even Hardy's voice, his inflections and pitch almost matched those of her father.

Hardy's eyes met her eyes. "I can't explain it. I do what I do, not only for myself and for my country, but also for them. I know they would have wanted me to go forward and make a difference in this world. If they could have, they *would've* been doing the same thing." Hardy stuffed his hands into the front pockets of his pants.

Several moments of silence passed. A light breeze blew a lock of hair in front of Natasha's face; she brushed it away. "Thanks, Hardy." She touched his shoulder and let her hand slide down his upper arm. "I'm sorry about your team."

He regarded her and nodded. "Thank you."

"Thank you for sharing that with me. I know it must have been hard for you, but I appreciate it." Natasha cranked her head around and spied Victor before turning back to Hardy. She had unfinished business with Victor, but she did not want to abandon Hardy.

He rolled his eyes and head toward Victor. "Go, I'm fine." He saw a faint smile flash across her face before she slipped past him.

Natasha strolled to where Victor was leaning against the SUV, her fingers tucked into the front pockets of her pants. "Look, I'm—"

Victor raised his hand, stopping her. "There's no need to apologize."

"Yes, there is. Friends don't treat each other the way I treated you."

"But, friends forgive each other." Not letting her respond, Victor changed the subject. "Now, let's talk about this raid."

Natasha nodded her head. "Thank you, Victor." She took a couple steps forward and hugged him, his long arms and wide body enveloping her torso.

A few minutes later, Hardy ambled toward them.

Victor gestured toward him. "So, Hardy, now that you've had some time to think it over, when should we raid the house?"

Hardy glanced at Natasha. "My preference is for waiting until dark." Out of the corner of his eye, he saw her body bristle. "However, we may not get a better opportunity than right now."

Victor saw his men coming from the hill. "Maybe, my men can help with this."

Nikolai and Ivan gave a report of the layout of the property as well as any movement in and around the house. Natasha translated for Hardy.

"In that case, I say we go now." Hardy pointed. "We come over the hill from the west and use the setting sun to our advantage. Since it will be at our backs and just above the trees, we should have some cover. Victor, you, Nikolai and Ivan will break off at the bottom of the hill and take a position at the back

215

of the house. Natasha and I will go to the front door. We simultaneously breach both doors, sweep the house and get our man."

Victor contemplated the plan. "All right, I like it." Victor explained the details to Nikolai and Ivan, who nodded their agreement.

All of them began prepping their gear. Victor distributed earpieces to everyone and gave Hardy a small camera attached to a flexible cable. Hardy would use it to scan for bombs or tripwires before breaching the door. After a final check of their gear, they climbed the hill.

Chapter 15: Raid

Squatting on the ridge, Hardy and the others observed the house below. He pointed. "We'll break up at that oak tree and get into position. I'll give two clicks on the radio when we're ready to breach. Five seconds later, we go in hard and fast."

"Got it," said Victor before translating for Nikolai and Ivan.

Natasha adjusted her weapon. "Remember, we need Rudin *alive*."

Hardy looked at her. She nodded. Getting the 'thumbs up' from Victor, Hardy stood. "Go!"

The two teams ran down the hill, single-file and in a low crouch to minimize their visual imprint on the landscape. Hardy was leading, followed by Natasha, Victor, Nikolai and Ivan. At the oak tree, Hardy and Natasha went right, while Victor's team moved to the back door. As Hardy and Natasha rounded the corner of the house, he saw Victor in the process of slipping the flexible camera under the door.

Hardy and Natasha moved alongside the house, staying below the windows. They came around to the front and ascended the stairs, making sure not to step on the broken floorboards of the porch.

Hardy had the flexible camera in his hand by the time he knelt at the door. Sliding the device under the door, he moved it around and watched the screen in front of him. He saw no one inside. There were no signs the door had been rigged to trigger an explosive device. He withdrew the camera wand and stowed it.

Using hand signals, Hardy told Natasha what he had seen and what they were going to do. She nodded, got to her feet and prepared to open the door. She twisted the knob. The door was unlocked.

Hardy gave two clicks over his radio before counting down from five with his hand. When he got to zero, Natasha pushed the door open. Hardy raised his rifle, dashed inside and moved right. Natasha followed and went left. The living room was dark. Mold and mildew filled their nostrils. The beam from their rifles lit up the area in front of them. There was an old coffee table in front of a couch and a reclining chair. They moved around them, sweeping their rifles back and forth. They cleared the living room and moved to the dining room area, where they met Victor's team. Hardy flashed hand signals before he and Natasha went to the right, while Victor's team went the opposite way.

With Hardy in the lead, he and Natasha moved down a narrow hallway, clearing each room. Coming to the last door, he saw it was closed. Hardy was getting ready to kick in the door when he saw the light pattern under the door, break up. Natasha had seen it too. His earpiece crackled.

"All clear," said Victor in Russian and English.

Hardy looked at Natasha, who nodded. He drove his boot into the door and it flew inward. She entered and cleared the left half, while he did the same with the right half.

Chapter 16: Bedroom

The room appeared to be the master bedroom. It was empty. After a quick check under the bed, Natasha moved toward a partially open closet door. With Hardy's rifle pointed at the door, she swung it open and took a step backward. Hardy and Natasha heard a scuffling sound before a scrawny cat came out of the closet, darted between them and out of the bedroom. Natasha relaxed her posture and let her rifle hang from its sling, giving Victor's team the 'all clear.'

Hardy and Natasha met Victor's team in the kitchen. Nikolai and Ivan were opening and closing cabinet doors and rummaging through everything on the floor, while Victor stood at the kitchen table.

"He was here, all right." Victor was scanning the items on the table. "These are components used to make bombs." He held up a cell phone. "He's using a cell phone as the detonator."

Hardy stood on the other side of the table, while Natasha walked to the kitchen counter and stood with her back to Victor.

Hardy was the first to say what everyone must have been thinking. He picked up an empty container of vanilla frosting. "Since when is frosting used to make bombs." There were at least fifty cans scattered around the kitchen. Most were empty, except for a dozen unopened ones.

Victor shrugged his shoulders, continuing to examine the other items.

Hardy stared at the kitchen table. There were items everywhere, including globs of white frosting, except for a rectangular space in front of him. The space was clean.

Natasha leaned against the sink, holding a piece of blue cardstock. "I think I know where Rudin is going." She gave the cardstock to Victor.

Hardy glimpsed them. "What is it?"

Victor skimmed the document. "It's an invitation to a birthday party for the Russian Premier. The party is tonight at nine."

Hardy snapped his fingers. "Of course," he said, his eyes shifting to the table. He stretched out his hands and measured the length and width of the clean spot. "They're going to put the bomb inside a cake. That's why they needed all this frosting." Hardy twisted his upper body. He saw boxes on the floor behind him. "Only thing is...there's no cake. They covered the device with a cardboard box and frosted it."

Natasha observed the boxes and the frosting containers. "Won't it be a dead giveaway when the first person chomps down on a piece of cardboard?"

Hardy shook his head. "The cake was never intended to be *eaten*, so it doesn't have to be real. That means Rudin plans to detonate the bomb before anyone has a chance to cut it, most likely when it's placed in front of the Premier."

221

Her eyes wide, Natasha pivoted her head back and forth from Hardy to Victor. "We have to warn them."

Hardy held up his hands. "How? You and I are wanted for killing those FSB agents. They won't believe *anything* you have to say. And, I'm a *foreigner*."

Victor planted his hands on his hips. "This is a big party. The Premier turns fifty this year. Heads-of-state, foreign dignitaries and high-ranking officials will be there."

Natasha joined the men at the table. "All the more reason to warn them."

"Once again," Hardy held out his hands, "How?"

Victor wagged a finger at no one in particular. "I know the man in charge of the Premier's security, General Popovich. I'll call him...tell him I have reason to believe there will be an assassination attempt on the Premier. He'll listen to me." Victor stepped away.

Natasha picked up the invitation. "In the meantime, we need to find a way into this party."

"For fear of sounding like a broken record...how do we do that? You are *definitely* not on *that* guest list."

Flicking the invitation between her fingers, Natasha's mind went back to her adolescent years.

Hardy saw her smiling. "What is it?"

"The party is being held at the Summer Palace."

Hardy bobbed his head. *Okay, sounds like a swanky place.* "So, what?"

222

"Most everyone is familiar with the Winter Palace in St. Petersburg. It's a large and gorgeous structure, built to portray the might of Imperial Russia. It was the home of the Russian Monarchs, until 1917. In late October of that year, Vladimir Lenin and the Bolsheviks stormed the palace and took control. The soldiers stationed there put up little resistance. After—"

Hardy leaned forward and rested his folded forearms on the table. "What does this history lesson have to do with the birthday party, Natasha?"

"People are *not* familiar with the Summer Palace. It was a favorite retreat for the ruling class during the summer months. As I was saying," she cocked her head at him, "before you interrupted me...After the Bolshevik Revolution in 1917, the Summer Palace was abandoned and neglected."

"For my thirteenth birthday, my father took me there. He said the government had made plans to restore and modernize it. They were going to turn it into a venue for fancy gatherings, royal weddings...*birthday parties for the elite*. It was no longer going to be open to the public." She waved a hand as if she was shooing away a bug. "Anyway, that afternoon, my father and I explored every square inch of that place, including the basement." Natasha smiled, remembering running through the rooms and down the hallways. Having not been cared for in many decades, the palace was in shambles. At the time, she had imagined its former glory, members of royalty, wearing beautiful garments, gliding across the marble floors, dancing and conversing.

Hardy got in her line of sight. "You were saying..."

Her mind came back to the present and she locked eyes with him. "The basement is where we found a secret passageway."

Hardy's eyebrows went up and he stood straight. Whenever the term 'secret passageway' was used, his curiosity was piqued. The allure of finding something hidden intrigued him; however, more importantly, a passageway meant something simpler—a way inside.

Natasha smiled. "I see I have your attention now."

With two fingers, he curled an ear toward her. "I'm all ears."

"My father and I followed that passageway, until we came out on the other side of the hill, far away from the palace. It was common to build secret passageways. In case of attack, the occupants had a way to escape. I think we can use that passageway to get *into* the palace and attend the party."

Victor returned to the table.

His head hanging down, Hardy slowly shook it back and forth, drawing out his words. "I...don't...know, Natasha. It's been a long time, since you were there. How do you know where the entrance is located?"

"The first thing I saw when we came out was a large boulder. There were no other rocks in the area. That one must have been put there to mark the location, in case anyone needed to sneak," she cleared her throat and leaned heavily on the next word, "*inside.*"

"What if it's been moved? What if the opening has been sealed shut? The passageway could have collapsed in the last ten years. What if we find the entrance and get to the palace, only to discover the opening on *that* side has been sealed? Those are some big 'what ifs.'"

Natasha noticed Victor. "How'd it go?"

The muscles in Victor's jaw were taut. "Not good," he said, through clenched teeth. "I told him everything we've discovered and that I had good reason to suspect there would be an attempt on the Premier's life and..."

A bad feeling swept over Natasha. "What happened?"

He stared at the table. "Once he found out I was with you," Victor motioned toward Natasha, "he told me you were wanted in the deaths of four FSB agents and I was to bring you in, immediately. If I didn't, then I was going to be charged with insubordination for disobeying a direct order. I would also suffer the same fate that awaits you." He raised his eyebrows. "Whatever that is, I'm not sure."

"Oh, Victor, I'm so sorry I got you involved in this." Natasha put her hand on his shoulder. "I should have never called you."

"No," replied Victor, his voice getting louder. "You are a soldier, defending your country. It is General Popovich who should be sorry." Victor shook his head, disgusted that his friend had

225

become what he is today. "He was a good soldier, too, in his day. I think he has become a part of the political machine, caring more about how he is viewed by his peers, than carrying out his duty."

"Victor, Hardy and I can take it from here." Natasha glanced at Hardy; he nodded his head. "You and your team have done enough. Just give us a head start..."

"You are *not* going anywhere without us." Victor's eyebrows pointed toward the bridge of his nose. "I say 'to hell with Popovich.' I'm a patriot and I will continue to serve my country and my Premier." Victor gestured toward the invitation in Natasha's hand. "What's the plan?"

Hardy informed Victor of Natasha's plan. Victor had reservations, too, voicing the same concerns Hardy had voiced.

She chucked the invitation and Hardy caught it before it slid off the table. "Well, if either of you have a better one, I'd love to hear it." Her head pivoted back and forth from Victor to Hardy. "Anything?"

After more than a minute, Hardy and Victor realized her plan was the best they had and gestured their compliance to each other.

Hardy scanned the invitation. "I don't know how Russians celebrate birthday parties, but in America, a 50th birthday party for our President would be a formal affair." Hardy pinched his shirt between his thumb and forefinger and tugged. "We're not dressed for the occasion."

"I think I can take care of that." Once again, Victor had his cell phone out, making a call. He looked Hardy over from head to toe and said, in Russian, "I have a brother who lives nearby. He, too, is a *short* man." Victor, Nikolai and Ivan laughed, while Natasha smiled.

Hardy's eyes went back and forth from Natasha to Victor. "What did he say?"

Natasha pursed her lips and stifled her laughter. "He said his brother, who lives nearby, has a black suit that would fit you."

Hardy knew that was not exactly what Victor had said. Upset, but not with Victor, he was mad at himself for not learning more Russian than a few curse words. It was good; however, that Victor and his men were busting Hardy's chops. That meant they were starting to accept him. And, that was good for morale. He laughed with them.

Chapter 17: Jameson

Once the plan to infiltrate the Summer Palace was finalized, Hardy stepped away and placed a call to Director Jameson; he answered on the first ring.

"Hardy, you're late checking in. How's it going? Have you found Rudin?"

Hardy brought Jameson up to speed on the progress of the mission, including the assassination plot on the Premier's life. The director was not pleased with the last part.

"That wasn't your objective. Let the Russians clean up their own messes. You have a job to do and that job is finding and killing Rudin." Jameson was a man who followed the rulebook to the letter. He and Hardy had made a plan to catch and kill Rudin and get out of the country. Thwarting an assassination attempt was not part of that plan. The way Jameson saw it the additional time spent in country only served to make it easier for something to go wrong.

"I understand the mission, sir. In order to complete it, I need to *find* Rudin, and that involves getting to the Premier. I see our goals and those of our Russian counterparts as being the same. I—"

"Damn it, Hardy," said Jameson, his voice boomed through the phone's speaker. "Is this how it's going to be? I gave you an order. I expect you to carry out that order. I don't expect you to change things as you see fit."

"With all due respect, sir, circumstances in the field change and agents need to pivot when required—"

"Don't lecture me on being a field agent, Hardy. I know events can change. I was in the field, too. Unlike you, however, I didn't change the parameters of the mission. I changed my course-of-action to complete the mission."

Hardy gripped the sat phone tighter. He knew Jameson had a lot of experience, but Hardy was no rookie. He understood the importance of following orders. He also knew that, sometimes, a plan did not work as it had been laid out. A soldier, or field agent, had to make quick decisions based on the changing landscape of the battlefield.

"Are you still there?"

"Yes, sir," replied Hardy.

"Tread carefully, Hardy. Your actions will have a direct impact on your job status. This may end up being your first and *last* mission."

"Yes, sir...I'll contact you again, when I have more information." He disconnected the call. The director had been clear. Hardy may come back to the States no longer in the employ of his country. He pinched the bridge of his nose between his thumb and forefinger and closed his eyes. With his mind on the conversation with Jameson, he did not hear Natasha.

"Is everything okay?"

Not wanting to discuss the call, Hardy nodded and changed the subject. "Are we ready to go?"

Natasha noticed the diversion, but did not push him for details. "First, we have to make a stop at Victor's brother's house. From there, we need to get some supplies before leaving for the Summer Palace. But, yeah, we're good to go."

Chapter 18: Palace

Facing a hill, Natasha stood by the only large boulder in the area. She looked in the direction of the Summer Palace. Tall trees surrounded her and the other members of the team. A few of the setting sun's rays found their way over the hill and through the trees, giving her enough light to identify the landscape. She took fifteen measured steps, stopped and told everyone to fan out and check for the door leading to the secret passageway.

Hardy, Victor, Nikolai, Ivan and Natasha began poking metal rods into the earth, trying to locate the hidden door. After moving up the hill for several meters, they found nothing. They fanned out a little further and repeated the process, going down the hill and ending where they had started.

Hardy stared at Natasha. "Are you sure this is the spot?"

"I'm positive." She pointed at the boulder. "That's the same rock I saw as a teenager." Standing in place, she acted out what had taken place more than a decade earlier. "As soon as I came out of the passageway," she pointed, "I looked straight ahead and saw that rock. It was about fifteen steps away."

"How do you know it was *fifteen* steps?" questioned Hardy.

"I was curious. It's my nature. I started there and paced off the distance," she swung her arm toward the hill, "to the entrance. It took me fifteen steps to get there."

Hardy gave Natasha an onceover, beginning at her feet and ending at her head. "You said it was your thirteenth birthday?"

She nodded her head.

Hardy trotted back to the boulder and stood where she had been standing. He took fifteen half steps and stopped. "Let's start searching from here."

They formed a line and poked their metal rods into the earth, while climbing the hill. They had not taken three steps, when Nikolai's metal rod hit something solid. He poked the rod into the ground in several places. Each time, he was met with resistance, and everyone heard a 'clunking' sound.

They cleared away the dirt and debris, revealing a large iron door. It was four-feet wide, six-feet high and parallel to the slope of the hill. Nikolai and Ivan took hold of the door's latch and tugged. Grunting, they applied more force, while Hardy and Victor each grabbed a corner. The four men were able to loosen the rusted hinges and swing open the door. The earth shook beneath their feet when they let go and the heavy iron slab landed on the ground. Cool, musty air rushed out of the opening to greet them. Natasha tapped the button on the back of her flashlight and directed the beam inside.

The opening was only four-feet high for the first few meters. After that, the passageway rose to more than six-feet in height. The width appeared to be wide enough for two people to walk side-by-side.

"What made you think it was closer to the boulder?" Natasha leaned over and examined the darkness.

Hardy squatted and followed her flashlight's beam. "I figured you're taller now than when you were thirteen-years-old. Your fifteen steps, just now, took you further away from the boulder. In short, we started searching too close to the hill."

Victor held two backpacks.

Hardy stood and strapped on one of the backpacks before adding a tactical helmet and goggles. A small sledgehammer and pickaxe hung near his leg. He turned on the flashlight attached to the helmet and faced Natasha. She was wearing the same gear. They resembled miners more than they did members of a tactical team ready to crash a high-profile birthday party. "Are you ready?" She gave him the 'thumbs-up' sign. "Ordinarily, I'd say 'ladies first,' but in this case..."

Victor put one hand on each of them. "Good luck." When Natasha acknowledged him, he added, "Be careful."

She nodded her head before following Hardy into the blackness.

233

Chapter 19: Passageway

The passageway had a gradual incline. The air was moist and smelled horrible. It had been musty at the opening, but now it was rank, getting worse the deeper Hardy and Natasha went. Water dripped from the ceiling in places and mold was growing on the walls, ceiling and footpath, which were made of stone.

After twenty minutes, Hardy came to a spot where there was a large expanse of pooled water. He was unsure of the water's depth. He stepped slowly, one footfall at a time, not wanting to drop into a deep hole, possibly a sinkhole that had opened at some point in the last decade. He and Natasha were probably the only ones who had been down here in almost fifteen years.

A few minutes later, they had passed the water and continued forward. There were a few more water pools, but they were smaller and it was obvious they were not concealing a hole.

Hardy stopped when he came to a 'Y' in the passageway. One leg veered off to the left, while the other leg went straight. He shined his handheld flashlight down each leg. "Which way?"

Squinting, Natasha moved her head back and forth, trying to recall the way she and her father had come. At the time, they had been going in the opposite direction. She did not remember the passageway being anything but straight. If she and Hardy chose wrongly, they would lose precious time, having to backtrack.

In the beam of his helmet-mounted flashlight, Hardy saw her indecisiveness. He trusted her instincts. Her memory had gotten them get this far when he had doubted the plan from the beginning. "Natasha?"

"Yeah," she said, studying each route.

"Look at me."

She whipped her head around, her helmet-mounted light shining on his forehead.

"Don't think right now. What's your gut telling you?"

She glanced at the left leg before pointing to the right one. "It's this way."

"All right, let's go."

The corridor seemed to go on forever. They had walked another twenty minutes and still not come to the end.

Natasha was thinking she had made the wrong choice. "Maybe, we should turn around and go back."

Hardy moved forward, never hesitating. He and Natasha had come too far not to see this through.

Less than five minutes later, he stopped when the pathway unceremoniously ended. Hardy shined his flashlight all around the wall in front of him as well as the surrounding area—nothing but stone.

Natasha examined the wall. "Did we miss something or is this a dead end?"

"Well, we've come this far." Hardy removed the pickaxe before setting the backpack on the stone floor. "It would be a shame not to at least knock on the door. Stand back."

He checked the clearances on either side of him. He swung the pickaxe, aiming for the same spot with each swing. Chips of stone flew back at him, striking his face and goggles. He jerked away each time a piece hit him. His pickaxe connected several more times with the wall before he stopped and took a closer look at where he had been aiming. He had made a tiny hole. "Kill your light." He turned off his flashlight. No light was coming from the hole. He put his hand up to the hole and felt a slight breeze. "We broke through. I think there's a chamber on the other side."

Natasha slid her backpack from her shoulders. "I don't believe it." She grabbed her sledgehammer.

"Believe it. You've got good instincts. You need to trust them." He exchanged the pickaxe for the sledgehammer. Taking turns striking the wall, Hardy and Natasha opened a section of the wall big enough for Hardy to squeeze through.

Natasha held up her hand and he stopped. She stuck her head through the opening, the light on her helmet illuminating the cavity. After a quick scan, she snaked her way between the jagged bricks. Hardy tossed in their packs, while she shined her flashlight around the area and confirmed that this was the basement of the Summer Palace. She looked back at the opening she and Hardy had made. At some point, the entrance she and her father had gone through had been covered to keep people from accessing the passageway. She was still staring at it when Hardy contorted his body and made his way inside.

Wiping the sweat from his forehead with his sleeve, he depressed the switch on his flashlight and followed its beam. "Which way do we go from here?"

Natasha got her bearings and pointed. "The staircase should be over there."

Hardy headed in that direction, stopping at the bottom of a stone spiral staircase. With Natasha on his heels, he ascended the stairs, careful not to make too much noise. At the top, a heavy wooden door impeded their progress. Slowly, he twisted the doorknob; it was not locked. He let the doorknob go back to its resting position and motioned for Natasha to go back down the steps.

Once they were standing near the backpacks, she unbuttoned her shirt. "On the other side of that door is a hallway that leads to the kitchen area. We'll need to change here. I doubt if anybody will come down here, but we should stow our gear out of sight."

Hardy nodded, while he took off his goggles and unfastened the strap on his helmet. He stripped out of his tactical clothing and boots, revealing another layer of clothing. He was dressed in a black suit with a white ruffled shirt and a red bowtie. After removing a pair of black dress shoes from his backpack and putting them on, he straightened his suit and bowtie before retrieving a pistol holstered at the small of his back. A quick check of its status later, he tossed the backpack, helmet and goggles through the opening in the wall.

"Hardy, can you give me a hand with this?"

He directed his flashlight toward Natasha's feet. The beam bounced off the floor, casting a glow on her. She was standing with her back to him, holding a fake diamond necklace in her hand. Hardy took it, wrapped it around her slender neck and joined the two ends of the crab-claw clasp.

She spun around. "How do I look?"

Hardy tapped a forefinger to the top of his head. "Is that part of the ensemble?"

Natasha's eyes went upward. "Oops." She was wearing her helmet. Removing the tactical gear, her hair fell. She twisted her head and shoulders several times before running her fingers through the long locks, adding fullness. "Now, how do I look?" Wiggling her fingers, she slid her hand into a black glove that came to rest above her elbow.

Natasha's long, blonde hair, which normally came to the middle of her back, was now black and stopped at her shoulders. Victor's sister-in-law had helped Natasha cut and dye it, in case anyone at the party knew what she looked like. She was wearing a royal blue sleeveless satin dress, the hem coming to her knees. Black nylons and royal blue high-heeled pumps completed her outfit.

Not getting a reply, she glanced at her 'date.' "Do I look that bad?" She tugged on the second glove.

Seeing her dark hair in this light, Hardy had a brief image of Special Agent Cruz flash across his mind. For a split-second, he felt homesick. He had never seen Cruz in any other clothing besides her business attire, slacks and a blazer. He imagined she would look every bit as stunning as Natasha was, now. He blinked his eyes a few times to re-focus his mind on the mission. A thin grin formed on his lips. "You look dressed...*to kill*."

Natasha returned his smile, while attaching a pair of fake clip-on diamond earrings that dangled more than an inch below her earlobe. "Thanks...You look pretty good, too."

Claiming a small semi-automatic pistol from her backpack and verifying the gun was loaded, she lifted the hem of her dress well above her thigh. A holster, near the innermost part of her left leg, was tucked inside the lace band of her thigh-high stocking. A garter belt helped support the weight of the pistol. She slid the weapon inside the holster and let the dress fall to her knees. Natasha gave Hardy her pack, which he chucked through the opening, while she adjusted her dress and finished primping.

Hardy moved toward the staircase. "Let's go." Natasha followed, her heels clicking on the stone floor.

Chapter 20: Kitchen

Exiting the basement, Natasha led Hardy through the narrow hallway and toward the kitchen. Halfway there, a large man in a brown suit appeared ahead of her. Natasha caught a brief glimpse of a small communication device in his ear. *Security.* Fortunately, he was more concerned with the food on the serving trays than he was with doing his job.

Natasha whirled around, grabbed the lapels on Hardy's suit coat and pushed him against the wall. "Put your arms around me and kiss me." She pressed her lips to his mouth and passionately kissed him.

Hardy tensed. *What is she doing?* Grabbing her shoulders, he pushed.

She dipped her head toward the guard, her eyes burrowing a hole into Hardy's brain, while she barked at him under her breath. "*Kiss* me."

Hardy glanced left and saw the man; he had spotted them. He wrapped his left arm around Natasha's waist and jerked her closer. Their bodies slammed together. He cupped the back of her head and leaned into her.

Hardy and Natasha's lips mashed together. She felt a warm sensation flood her body. Her attention drifted away from the situation. She tasted his lips and felt his strong arms around her. Tugging on the lapels of his suit coat, she kissed him back. Lost in the moment, she nearly forgot about the ruse.

The guard had dropped the food he was holding and was moving toward them. He approached and said, "Chto ty zeds' delayesh'? — *What are you doing here?* Eto zapretnaya zona — *This is a restricted area.*"

The guard's voice brought Natasha's focus back to reality. She spun her head toward the guard, pretending he had startled her. She hunched her shoulders. Covering her mouth, she giggled like a teenage girl.

"Nikto nedopuskayetsya za predely kukhni — *No one is allowed beyond the kitchen,*" said the guard.

Natasha took Hardy's hand. When they were even with the guard, she smiled seductively and said, "My sozhaleyem — *We're sorry.* My prosto khoteli nayti mesto gde my mogli by...pobyt'v odinochestve — *We just wanted to find a place where we could...be alone.*"

The guard inspected Hardy, who slapped a goofy grin on his face and shrugged. Still giggling, Natasha dragged Hardy away from the guard.

Once they had moved through the kitchen, they entered the reception area, adjacent to the Great Room of the Summer Palace. Hardy looked over his shoulder to make sure the guard was not following. "That was nice back there."

Natasha licked her lips. The taste of his kiss was still there. She smiled. *Yes, it was.*

"That was some quick thinking. You got us out of a tight spot."

Her smile faded and she felt a dull ache in her chest. "Thanks," she mumbled.

Approaching the archway leading to the Great Room, Hardy held out his arm. "Shall we?"

She glanced at his arm before faking a smile and driving her feelings deeper inside. The mission was all that mattered. She curled her gloved arm under his elbow. Arm in arm with him, she walked into the Great Room, her eyes shifting left and right in search of Rudin.

Chapter 21: Great Room

The Great Room was packed. People were dressed in the finest attire. The men wore black tuxedos with tails and bowties over ruffled shirts. The women displayed everything from conservative evening gowns with low-heeled shoes to risqué mini dresses paired with exotic heels. Really wanting to draw attention, some women had worn high-heeled boots that rose to their thighs. Champagne glasses in hand, people talked along the outside edges of the room, while others slow-danced in the middle.

At the far end of the room, a large stone fireplace captured people's attention the minute they entered the Great Room. The opening was easily ten feet wide and six feet high. A six-inch thick dark wooden mantle stretched across the opening, extending two feet past each side. Large portraits of the ruling class sat on the mantle. The wall around the fireplace was made of stone. The remaining three walls of the room were made of teak paneling and stained a dark color. The floor was white marble, streaks of black crisscrossed throughout it. Four black marble pillars, rising to the ceiling, seemed to serve as unofficial boundary points for those dancing. The ceiling was high above the floor. Large wooden beams, set at specified intervals, crossed the entire width of the room. Beautiful crystal chandeliers were strategically placed to provide a well-balanced amount of light. Dressed in white suits and white gloves, waiters traversed among the guests, offering drinks and hors d'oeuvre's and taking empty champagne glasses. The scene seemed to be taken from the pages of a fairy tale.

Hardy lifted two glasses of champagne from the tray of a passing waiter before giving one to Natasha.

"Thank you." She took a sip.

Hardy scanned the room. "The cake will be easy to spot; Rudin, not so much. We need to move around and get a look at this whole place."

Natasha twisted her left wrist. She had worn a simple, yet elegant, fake diamond watch from the collection of Victor's sister-in-law. "It's almost 8:45—let's split up. We'll meet back here in ten minutes."

"You keep an eye out for Rudin and I'll try to locate the cake."

She nodded her head and slinked off to the right.

Hardy made his way to the left, casually slipping around and in between groups of people. They were talking in many languages in addition to Russian. He smiled and nodded to them in passing. Standing with two others, a young girl in her late teens smiled at him when he approached them. It was clear from her smile she had not brought a date to the event. She grabbed his forearm, and he almost spilled the glass of champagne in his hand.

"Oops." The girl put her hand to her mouth. "I'm so sorry."

Hardy smiled. "No harm done."

"You're American, aren't you?"

"Yes." He looked beyond the girl, searching for the cake.

"It's so good to meet someone else who speaks English." She put her hand on her chest. "I'm Michelle," she pointed to the girls to her right, "and this is Ivanka and Sasha." They smiled at Hardy and gave him a short wave. "They speak very little English."

He flashed another smile, "Aaron," before glancing around again.

"My father works at the embassy here. He's the ambassador. So, naturally he was invited," said Michelle, trying to impress the handsome stranger.

"It was nice meeting you, but I can't stay. I'm looking for someone." Hardy started to walk away, but stopped. "Some birthday party, huh? Where's the cake? You can't have a birthday party without cake. Am I right?"

"Oh, there's cake," said Michelle. "They wheeled it in about half an hour ago." She spun around on the three-inch heels of her boots and pointed toward a small room to the left of the fireplace. "They took it in there. It had vanilla frosting, but I hope it's chocolate cake. Chocolate is my favorite." She grinned at Hardy. "Why don't you stick around and we can share a piece."

Hardy studied Michelle. She was a young girl acting like a grown woman. She was pretty, but immature. He noticed her plump cheeks and saw two small pimples she had covered with makeup. *She's probably not even eighteen yet.* He whipped his head left and right before coming back to her. *She shouldn't be here. If Rudin detonates that bomb...* "You said your father was the ambassador. Is he here tonight?"

"No, he couldn't make it. He gave me his tickets and said I could come."

Good. Hardy squinted at the young girl. "Listen, Michelle, I need to find someone first, but why don't you and your friends head outside." Hardy gestured toward the front doors. "I'll meet you there in a little while." He smiled before adding, "I'll bring cake."

"All right, it's a date." She translated for her friends, while they left and headed toward the front doors.

Hardy walked closer toward the fireplace and glanced at the room where Michelle had said the cake had been taken; he saw it. No one was near it. He thought about checking for explosives, but that would draw too much attention. He made a right turn and continued past the fireplace. The Premier and his top generals were talking. Several of his security guards were nearby, their heads pivoting back and forth, looking for threats. One of them locked eyes with Hardy. If he averted his gaze too quickly, he would draw suspicion. If he stared too long, the guard might assume Hardy was a threat. He maintained eye contact with the guard for two seconds then turned away. Smiling and nodding at people, he headed back to meet Natasha.

Chapter 22: Dancing

Natasha was waiting for Hardy. She saw him coming and met him at the edge of the dance floor. "Any luck?"

He motioned with his head. "The cake's in the room near the fireplace. And, you?"

She shook her head, no. "What do we do?"

Hardy put his hand on the small of her back. "What everyone else is doing...*dance*." He escorted her to the edge of the crowd. Taking her right hand and putting his right arm around her waist, he led Natasha around the floor, both of them swaying to the gentle music. "We can't make a move on the cake, until we find Rudin. He's got the detonator and he might trigger the bomb if he sees anyone messing with it." In perfect harmony, Hardy and Natasha glided over the marble floor as if they had been dance partners for years. "I think Rudin is waiting for the cake to be brought out to the Premier. We've got until then to locate him." Hardy looked into Natasha's eyes and grinned. "For now, let's try to blend in."

Natasha stared back. He had a firm hold of her. She felt his bulging bicep pressing into her side. The dark stubble on his face would have felt course on her cheek. They moved back and forth, keeping in time to the music. Her eyes fell on the long black gloves around his neck and the silky dress she was wearing. She could not remember the last time she had dressed like this and danced with a man. Hardy was a good dancer. *He's a great dancer.* Light on his feet, he made her feel as if she was floating above the floor. Over his shoulder, she caught a glimpse of one of the waiters and the moment was shattered.

"Slow down." She bobbed her head left and right, searching for the man. He was walking toward the kitchen with a serving tray in his hand. She never took her eyes off him. When the waiter went toward the kitchen, she got a quick look at the side of his face and saw his gold, round eyeglasses. He matched the picture from Rudin's file, perfectly.

Hardy spun her. "What is it?"

"It's Rudin. He's heading for the kitchen." She let go of Hardy and moved past him. A hand latched onto her upper arm, and she was twirled around. "What are you doing? He's getting away."

Hardy was staring at the room near the fireplace. "We've got another problem. They're bringing in the cake."

A man in front of the fireplace clanged a fork against a champagne glass. Everyone stopped dancing and moved closer to the fireplace. The people were standing shoulder to shoulder.

Natasha rotated her head back and forth from the kitchen to the two waiters, pushing the cart with the cake on it. "We can't be in two places at once."

"We'll have to split up." He still had a hold of her arm. He moved around her toward and guided her toward the guests, who were crowding closer to

248

the fireplace. "You get the cake out of here and I'll go after Rudin."

"No, Rudin is mine," she shot back. "I'm taking him down."

"There's no time to argue, Natasha." He gave her a push. "I don't speak Russian, so it's up to you to convince them there's a bomb in that cake and get it the hell out of here. I'll deal with Rudin."

She regarded the partygoers, jammed together, jockeying for a better position. "I'll never make it through that crowd."

"Just start pushing," he trotted backwards, "I'll clear the way," before he spun around and sprinted for the kitchen. Stopping at the entrance to the Great Room and drawing his pistol, he fired several rounds into the ceiling before disappearing from sight.

Everyone on the dance floor scattered, giving Natasha a clear path to the cake.

Hardy ran through the kitchen, his pistol in hand. The waiters and kitchen staff ducked under the counter and jumped onto the counters. Coming to the hallway, where he and Natasha had kissed, he stole a quick look. *There's no way for him to escape that way.* He gained speed and crashed into the only other door in sight. The door flew open and he glanced over his shoulder. Two security guards were following him, shouting at those in their path.

Chapter 23: Van

Hardy spotted Rudin; he was hurrying toward a delivery van, a cell phone in his hand. *He's going to detonate the bomb.* Before the door had closed, Hardy saw the guards were closing the distance. He searched the area and spotted a rectangular trashcan. He dragged the trashcan over to the door and wedged the top part under the doorknob. Lifting his leg, he drove his foot down onto the bottom of the can. Seconds later, the guards slammed into the door, but the trashcan did not move. *That should hold them.*

Hardy focused his attention on Rudin, whose fingers were tapping on the cell phone's screen. Hardy raised his pistol and put the front sight on the cell phone. He took a breath, let out some of the air and held the rest. He slowly pressed the trigger, until the pistol recoiled. He missed the cell phone. The bullet skipped off the delivery van. Sparks shot off the van's side panel.

The report of the gunshot surprised Rudin. The phone slipped out of his hands. Squatting, he drew a weapon of his own and fired at Hardy.

Hardy dove behind a metal dumpster; bullets ricocheted off its side. Instead of peeking out from the same side of the dumpster, Hardy moved to the other side and peered around the edge. He saw

Rudin snatch the phone and climb into the van. From Hardy's angle, he could see all of the van's tires, except for the right-front tire. He steadied his pistol against the solid steel wall to his left and fired three shots, while the van sped away. Each bullet struck a tire, releasing the air it contained with a 'boom.'

The van swerved left and right, accelerating toward the main gate. Rudin had both hands on the wheel, trying to keep the vehicle moving straight. He glanced at the passenger's seat, and the cell phone on it. All Rudin had to do was push the 'send' button to complete his mission; however, self-preservation was at the forefront of his mind. The van veered left and Rudin yanked the steering wheel hard to the right. The two tires on the right side lifted off the ground. The hulking vehicle hung in the air for a few seconds before slamming back down.

Rudin navigated his approach to the main gate. Two security guards were holding up their hands, wanting him to stop. When it became evident the van was not going to stop, they drew their pistols and began firing at the van's windshield. At the last second, they dove out of the vehicle's path, one to the left and one to the right.

Rudin raised his right hand in front of his face as if his hand was going to stop the bullets coming through the windshield. He pushed his foot—and the accelerator—to the floor. The van lunged forward and rammed into the vertical bars of the gate. The speed and weight of the vehicle was too much. The doors swung open, the right one coming off its hinges and landing on the front lawn, several meters away.

Hand over hand, Rudin cranked the steering wheel to the right. The van lurched in the same direction. Its speed and top-heavy weight were too much to overcome. The van heaved to the left, appearing to be suspended. Rudin wrenched the steering wheel back to the left. For a split-second, it seemed as if the van was going to right itself; however, it keeled over, the box banging against the pavement. The vehicle slid forward several lengths, the metal box scraping across the concrete, creating a trail of sparks. Rudin opened his eyes and the first thing he saw was the cell phone.

Chasing the van, Hardy came up from behind the security guards. They saw the pistol in his hands and shouted at him, pointing their pistols at his head. He dropped his weapon and raised his hands into the air. One guard broke away and approached the van, while the other moved toward Hardy. The guard was issuing commands, while taking turns pointing the muzzle of his weapon at Hardy's chest and the driveway. Hardy had taken many men captive during his time in the military and he knew what the guard wanted.

Hardy dropped to his knees, before going prone on the hard surface of the driveway. He waited to feel the cold steel of the handcuffs around his wrists. *I wonder if they use zip ties, too.* A loud explosion came from over his shoulder. His hand shot to protect his head. Cranking his head toward the blast, he saw smoke rising from the palace. Two boots appeared in his line of sight followed by a hand. Hardy tilted his head back. "Victor?"

Chapter 24: Smoke

Victor and his team had been positioned in the woods, outside the main gate. They had seen the whole act play out before their eyes. Victor used his status in the Spetsnaz to convince the security guards that Hardy was with him, while Nikolai and Ivan moved to the van. Before they were able to secure him, Rudin had detonated the bomb.

Hardy grabbed Victor's hand and the big man hoisted him to his feet.

"Are you okay?"

Hardy nodded.

"Where's Natasha?"

Hardy gaped at the palace. The gray smoke had gotten thicker. He bolted toward the front door. Coming to the steps, he took them three at a time. Glimpsing Michelle and her friends, he saw the look of abject terror on their faces. Other than that, they were fine. Racing past them, he shouted and flung his arm at them. "Get out of here." If there was a secondary explosion, he wanted them far away.

Making it to the Great Room, all he saw was smoke. He plucked the handkerchief from his breast pocket and covered his nose and mouth. He pushed forward. People were stumbling, holding each other, while heading for the front door. Their blank faces were dirty, as they used their hands to shield their noses from the smoke. Men had their arms around women's waists, helping them exit the blast zone. Waiters were tending to the injured. Beneath the screams and cries for help, constant coughing could be heard.

With Victor a step behind, Hardy stopped at the fireplace. He took the handkerchief away from his face and shouted Natasha's name several times, coughing in between calls. He got on his knees and looked left and right of the fireplace. There was so much smoke that everything appeared black. His eyes started to burn.

Victor motioned. "I'll look over here."

"Wait," shouted Hardy. "I think I see her. Follow me." Hardy had caught a glimpse of royal blue fabric. He kept low and moved parallel to the fireplace, stepping over and around chunks of stone. Outside a small room, where the smoke was thickest, he saw one of the Premier's security guards lying face down on a woman with black hair. Of course, with so much blackness all around, she could have been a blonde for all Hardy knew. She was on her back. The guard on top had a large gash on the back of his blood-soaked head. Crimson streams ran down the side of his face, dripping onto the woman's dress. Drawing closer, Hardy saw the woman's face. *Natasha*. It appeared as if the guard had shielded her from the blast before being hit by one of the large pieces of stone on the floor around her. He felt for a pulse on the guard. He was dead. "Help me." Hardy pushed, while Victor wrenched on the guard's arm, until Natasha was free of the corpse.

Hardy leaned over and put his ear to her nose and mouth. While staring past her shoes, he listened for a breath.

Victor examined her body. "I don't see any wounds." He took her wrist in his hand. "I've got a pulse."

"She's not breathing." Hardy coughed. "We've got to move her away," he coughed again, "from here." He slipped his hands under her armpits. Staying in a crouch, he lifted her upper body and began walking backwards toward the center of the room. Natasha's head rested against his belly. Victor grabbed her knees and hoisted them.

The men carried Natasha away from the thickest of the smoke and placed her on the floor. Hardy put his hand under her neck and raised it to clear her oxygen pathway. He leaned over, opened her mouth and ran his forefinger all around the inside of her mouth, making sure there were no foreign objects. He pinched her nose with his right thumb and forefinger, took a deep breath and blew into her mouth. Out of the corner of his eye, he saw her chest rise. He turned his head to the side, sucked in more oxygen and blew into her mouth. He fought to suppress a cough. He repeated the procedure several times, stopping periodically to put his ear to her nose and mouth. She wasn't breathing.

Kneeling on the other side of Natasha, Victor held her wrist. "Her pulse is weak."

"Damn it," said Hardy, shoving Victor and swinging his leg over Natasha as if he was mounting a horse. Straddling her, he slipped his fingers inside the neckline of her dress and wrenched on it. The satin dress yielded to the force, splitting open to below her belly button and exposing her bra and underwear. He slid his fingers under her bra, between her breasts. Finding the area where her ribcage came together, above her stomach. He moved his fingers a couple inches higher, while raising his left fist above his head. Using the middle finger as an aiming point, he gathered all of his strength into his left arm and started to drive his fist toward her chest.

Before he could deliver a blow, Victor clamped onto Hardy's fist with both hands.

"What the hell are you doing? Let go of my arm." Hardy was enraged, his voice hoarse from inhaling smoke. Natasha was dying and he had to save her. He cocked his right arm and prepared to knock the giant into next Tuesday, if that was possible.

"Look." Victor gestured toward Natasha.

His arm poised to strike, Hardy eyed Natasha. She was rolling her head back and forth on the floor, coughing and gagging. Her head came away from the floor with every cough. She gasped for air. Her eyes opened and closed several times.

Victor slid across the floor and lifted her head and shoulders, cradling her in his arms. "You gave us quite a scare, you know that?" He pushed the hair out of her eyes and wiped dirt from her face.

She looked at him and managed a slight smile. She tried to speak, but was stopped by another bout of coughing, her body twisting.

After several minutes, Natasha was able to keep her eyes open and her coughing became more infrequent. Her eyes focused on Hardy, who was still straddling her. Breathing heavily, his chest rose and fell. Her eyes moved further down his frame. Below his groin, she spotted her underwear and the remnants of the dress. Her eyes meeting his, she pointed a finger at their adjoining nether regions. "I don't know how things are done in America." She let out a half laugh/half cough. "In this country, however, *one dance* doesn't get you to first base."

His hands fumbling with the torn fabric, Hardy covered her exposed skin as best he could. "Actually, that's not first base. First base is—" He waved his hand, "Never mind." He removed his jacket and handed it to Victor before rolling to his right and collapsing beside her.

Victor moved out from under her and placed her head on Hardy's jacket, which Victor had crumpled into a ball. He put his forefinger under her chin and tilted her head backward. "I'm going to help the others." He shifted his gaze to Hardy and pointed his finger at him. "You," he said, before pointing at Natasha, never taking his eyes off Hardy, "Stay with her."

"Understood," replied Hardy, not offended by the commanding tone in Victor's voice.

When Victor had gone, Natasha rolled her head toward Hardy. "Did you get Rudin?"

"He's in custody." A few moments passed, giving Hardy time to think. He felt guilty for sending her to take care of the bomb. She could have been killed. "Listen, I'm sorry. I should have been the one to go for the bomb."

She rolled her head back and forth. "No, you were right. Even though I speak Russian, I had a hell of a time getting someone to listen to me. If you had been there, they would have shot you on sight." She rolled her head to face him. "By the way, what were you thinking—discharging your weapon like that? I'm surprised the security guards didn't shoot you. That was crazy."

Hardy agreed. "Yes, but it was effective. And, for the record, the security guards *did* try to shoot me."

Natasha plopped her hand onto his forearm. "I'm glad you're all right." Coughing, she pulled her hand away and covered her mouth. "Thank you for your help. I'm not sure I could have gotten Rudin *and* saved the Premier's life."

Hardy re-called their heated conversation along the side of the road. He rotated his head toward her, a devilish grin on his face. "So, maybe Americans aren't so *selfish* and *self-centered* after all."

Without moving her head, Natasha shifted her eyes toward Hardy and saw his grin. The corners of her mouth slowly lifted to form a smile before a burst of laughter followed. She was still laughing when Michelle, the girl from the party, appeared and knelt next to Natasha. Her two friends were with her.

Hardy lifted his torso from the floor and leaned on his elbows. "Michelle, I told you to get away from this place. What the hell are you doing here?" His voice was hoarse, making his words sound even more scolding.

"I couldn't turn my back on these people. If it hadn't been for you," she glanced over her shoulder at her friends and came back to him, "we might have been lying where you are right now." She leaned forward and helped Natasha sit up. "Come on, let's get you out of here." She draped Natasha's right arm around her neck, while slipping her left arm around Natasha's waist. Michelle's friends helped from the other side. Together, the three of them helped her stand. Michelle pointed at Hardy, who was on his feet. "As soon as I saw you, I knew you were some kind of secret agent. My dad taught me how to recognize a spy when I saw one. Don't worry. Your secret's safe with me."

Hardy smiled at the girl. She had no idea what she was saying. Her innocence was both amusing and refreshing. One thing was for sure; she had a good heart, risking her own safety to help others. The world needed more people like her. He saw Natasha grinning at him. "Yeah, I'm a regular *secret agent man.*" Natasha snickered, while everyone shuffled out of the palace.

Chapter 25: Airport

July 11th, 11:43 a.m.; Domodedovo International Airport (Moscow, Russia)

Hardy stood at the base of the staircase leading to a small jet. The Russian Premier had arranged for the private aircraft to fly Hardy back to the United States. It was a small token of gratitude, acknowledging his part in saving the Premier's life. The Russian leader had also awarded him the Hero of the Russian Federation, the highest honor that could be bestowed on a Russian citizen or foreign national.

"The Premier wanted me to tell you how grateful he is for your help." Natasha handed Hardy a box. "He wanted to present this to you in person, during a formal ceremony; however, he respects your request to maintain a low profile."

Hardy opened the box. Inside was a gold star attached to a red, white and blue ribbon. The artifact was the official medal given to recipients of the Hero of the Russian Federation. He nodded his head and closed the box. "Please give the Premier my regards."

"He also wanted me to tell you that if you ever needed anything, and he was in a position to be of assistance, you should contact him."

Victor stood next to Natasha. "The same goes for us." He glanced over his shoulder at Nikolai and Ivan. "If you ever need our help, we will be there." Victor, Nikolai and Ivan shook Hardy's hand before each one gave him a kiss on each cheek. "Have a safe flight, my friend." Victor and his team walked away, leaving Hardy alone with Natasha.

She folded her arms over her chest and tipped her head toward the men. "Well, you've managed to endear yourself to some good people. He meant what he said, you know. I've seen it myself. No matter where you are in the world, he will be there for you."

Hardy stared past her shoulder at his new companions. "Judging from their devotion to you, I believe it."

Natasha glanced at the pavement, not looking at anything in particular. A gentle breeze blew strands of hair across her face. She pushed the locks behind her ear. "I found out this morning that Rudin gave officials the identity of the man who had orchestrated the bombings."

Hardy leaned closer, straining to hear her. A nearby jet engine roared when the aircraft accelerated down the runway.

Natasha raised her voice. "It was General Popovich. He was at the birthday party and left moments before the cake was wheeled out and placed in front of the Premier. Also, he was the one who sent those FSB agents to the café. Not sure what his motives were, but every officer in the country will be searching for him. He won't get far." She shifted her weight to her other shoe, a low-heeled, black pump. "As for Rudin," the noise from the plane died and her voice returned to a normal level, "he won't ever see the light of day again. I know you wanted him dead, Hardy, but he'll never make or sell another bomb."

"I suppose that's just as good." Hardy was unsure if his superiors would see it the same way.

More moments of silence passed between them. Jets took off and landed in the background. The wind blew stronger.

"Well, I guess I should be going." He pivoted to the left and put a hand on the staircase railing.

Natasha's stomach twisted. She stretched out a hand toward him, but quickly retracted it. Seeing him turn his back, an empty feeling washed over her. It was time to face the truth. He was leaving and she did not want that. *But, why? I hardly know him.* It had been three months since Sergei's death; however, it seemed like only yesterday that she and he were together. Being with Hardy these past couple of days had brought back the feelings of joy and happiness she had with her boyfriend. Hardy's kiss at the palace rushed into her mind. That kiss had meant something to her, but he did not seem to share the same feelings. Her heart told her to kiss him again—to either confirm or deny there was something between them. Her mind, however, was telling her not to put a strain on a good friendship. In the end, impulses won out over rational thinking.

Natasha curled her fingers around his arm and pulled gently, until he faced her. She placed her right hand over his left pectoral muscle and tilted her head backward. Her eyes going back and forth from his eyes to his lips, she leaned closer, only a few inches separated them. Staring into his eyes, she froze. Something in them said her kiss would not be received well. No, she sensed his mind was on something else. She pulled away and patted his chest twice. "It was good working with you, Hardy. Take care of yourself." She stepped back and dropped her gaze. "And, if you're ever anywhere even remotely close to Moscow," she looked up and forced a smile, "I would be deeply hurt if you didn't contact me." She stuck out her hand. "Have a safe trip."

Hardy was no fool. At the palace, he had felt the passion in Natasha's kiss. She had been reluctant to pull away from him then just as she was now. Though their relationship had started out cold, they had experienced combat together, and combat had a way of forging close bonds in a short time. He thought of her lying on the floor at the palace, not breathing. His heart ached and he would have done anything to save her life.

Hardy took a step forward, past the handshake, and put his hands on her waist; she put hers on his chest, arching her back slightly. "Natasha, I'm going home to a woman I met a week ago and I can't wait to see her and spend as much time as I can with her. My heart beats faster just thinking about it." Natasha lowered her gaze. Gently placing the pad of his forefinger under her chin, he lifted.

Natasha forced herself to make eye contact. She was rewarded with the same beautiful blue eyes that had captivated her when they first met at the café.

"I care a great deal for you. I really do...just not in that way." He paused. "The last thing I want is to hurt you. But, we've been through too much for me not to be honest with you."

Natasha stood still. Her heart thumped in her chest. His words brought pain and comfort. A relationship with him was not going to happen. In time, she would be okay. So much pain had consumed the past few months of her life. Right here, right now...all she wanted was to feel his hands on her waist, and the beating of his heart on her palm for a little longer. After more than a minute, but before the moment became awkward, she cupped the back of his neck, rose to her tiptoes and kissed him on the cheek. "Thank you...for being honest." She lowered her heels to the pavement and pointed a finger at him. "I will *still* be upset," she poked him in the chest, "if I find out you were in Moscow and didn't call me."

Hardy chuckled, gave Natasha a hug and kissed her cheek. "I promise I'll call if I'm ever in the area." He walked up the staircase. At the cabin door, he turned and waved before vanishing into the aircraft.

Ten minutes later, the jet taxied toward the runway, next in line to depart. As the plane made a left turn, Hardy peered out the window. He saw

Natasha standing in the same spot where they had said their 'good-byes.' The jet's engines grew in intensity and the aircraft lunged forward and gained speed. Hardy watched her, until she was too far behind the jet to be seen. He faced forward. He shut his eyes, took a deep breath and let the air slowly leave his lungs. He recalled the events that transpired, since their first encounter. A half grin spread across his face when their heated conversation came to mind. Once they had ironed out their differences, they had made a good team.

Hardy's chest felt tight; he rubbed it, thinking he had pulled a muscle. He stopped and cocked his head. He realized in his excitement to be heading home to see Special Agent Cruz, he had not processed the fact he was not leaving behind a team, but good friends. Reconciling the feelings, a greater sensation forced its way through the pain, a sense their paths would cross again.

He opened his eyes, retrieved his sat phone and began searching the Internet for restaurants in Washington D.C. He spent fifteen minutes reading reviews for different establishments. He smiled when he found the restaurant he wanted, the Bourbon Steak, one of the most luxurious restaurants in D.C. It was located inside the Four Seasons Hotel in Georgetown. It would be a perfect place to take Cruz for dinner.

Chapter 26: Washington

July 12^{\text{th}}, 7:55 a.m.; the White House

Dressed in the same clothes he had worn to the first meeting with the President—gray suit, white shirt, red tie—Aaron Hardy turned left at the end of the hallway. A secret service agent was escorting him to the Oval Office for an early morning meeting with the President. This was going to be Hardy's first formal contact with anyone, since his return from Russia.

After Hardy's plane had landed on American soil, Director Jameson had called to inform him of the meeting. The phone call had been short and to the point. Hardy had been unable to ascertain Jameson's mood. The man's personality was cold and his demeanor was rigid. Prior to that call, Hardy and the Director had only one face-to-face meeting, and a tense phone conversation from Russia.

Striding toward the Oval Office, Hardy passed several people—secret service agents, staffers and a few unfamiliar to him. All of them had taken special interest in him. One person cranked his head around, as he passed, continuing to stare. From the time he had stepped onto the grounds of the White House, everyone had acted in the same manner.

Their attitude teetered on the brink of admiration and... *'dead man walking.'*

Two secret service agents, standing on either side of the door to the Oval Office, sized up the newcomer, their eyes never leaving Hardy. Reaching the Oval Office, he heard the door to the Cabinet Room, which was down the hall, open. The President entered the hall with the Joint Chiefs of Staff; he was the first to see Hardy. He acknowledged him and continued his conversation with the Vice-Chairman. Rounding the corner of the hallway, the Joint Chiefs of Staff made eye contact with Hardy, nodded their heads and shook his hand. The last to do so was the Commandant of the Marine Corps, Wesley McIntosh, a four-star general.

General McIntosh was in his mid-sixties and bald, except for a patch of gray hair that surrounded the back of his head near his neck. The numerous medals on his uniform were proof of his professional prowess, having spent almost fifty years serving in the Marine Corps. He had seen action as a foot soldier in Vietnam and as a colonel in the first Gulf War before playing a major role in coordinating the invasion of Iraq in 2003. After the President had nominated him to be a Joint Chief, he was easily confirmed by the Senate. General McIntosh shook Hardy's hand the longest. "As a fellow Marine, I'm damn proud of you, son."

Hardy's eyebrows furled downward, while he shook McIntosh's hand. "Thank you...sir."

After McIntosh had left, Hardy saw the President beckoning him toward the Oval Office. Hardy sidestepped the commander in chief and entered the room. FBI Director Jameson and the President's Chief of Staff, Peter Whittaker, were sitting on the couch. Hardy gestured toward the closing door, more specifically, the scene that had unfolded. "Sir, if you don't mind me asking, what was that all about?"

The President put a hand on Hardy's back and extended his free arm. "Come, sit down and I'll tell you all about it." The President strolled to the other couch, directly across from Jameson and Whittaker. He sighed when his body sank into the soft cushions. "After spending an hour in one of those straight-back chairs, this feels pretty darned good."

Hardy shook hands with Whittaker and Jameson before sitting next to the President. He was still unsure of his future. In fact, the greeting he had received from the Joint Chiefs, especially General McIntosh, had only added to the confusion.

Whittaker started the meeting. He was a short, lean man, in his late forties. His black hair was parted on the left side; a thin mustache lay beneath his long, narrow nose. His eyes were small and close together. When he spoke, he had a very distinct Ivy League accent, having grown up in Massachusetts. His words were carefully chosen. The President had tapped Whittaker to be his Chief of Staff, because of his attention to detail. Nothing made it to the President without Whittaker's knowledge. The President respected and trusted Whittaker and allowed him a great deal of latitude in all things related to the Presidency. "Mr. President, I have scheduled a meeting with the Russian Premier for later this month. Considering how nice the weather has been, I thought the Rose Garden or the South Lawn would be appropriate. Of course, we will have this office made ready if the weather does not cooperate."

"Excellent," said the President, who appeared to be very pleased this morning. He shifted his weight to his right hip and crossed his left leg over his right, so he could face Hardy. "Aaron, you have managed to accomplish what no one has been able to do in a long time. Yesterday, the Russian Premier called me, directly. We spoke for a few minutes and talked about two things." The President held up his right forefinger. "One, he was willing to meet with me, regarding the war on terror; specifically, how our two countries might work together to stop future terrorist attacks." He held up two fingers. "Two, he had *high praise* for you."

Hardy raised his eyebrows. He knew the Premier was grateful, but he did not expect his name to come up during such an important phone call. He glimpsed the men sitting on the other couch. Whittaker was smiling, but Jameson was not.

"Your heroic actions, Aaron, have laid the groundwork for the United States and Russia to become allies in this war on terror. And, that meeting...later this month," the President pointed, "the one that Mr. Whittaker was referring to...the Premier requested that *you* be there."

The events of this morning fell into place like tumblers in a lock. The Joint Chiefs all knew about the upcoming meeting between the President and the Premier, and that Hardy had paved the way. He relaxed, feeling somewhat more confident his job was secure. Since he had gotten the call from Jameson, he had been obsessing over this meeting. Opening his eyes this morning, he was sure he was going to be fired.

The President stood—Whittaker, Jameson and Hardy joined him—and extended his hand. "You've done your country a great service, son. I can't tell you how pleased I am that you're working for me." Hardy clasped the President's hand. "Now, if you and Mr. Jameson will let yourselves out, Mr. Whittaker and I need to hammer out the details of the meeting with the Premier."

"Of course, Mr. President."

Jameson nodded, "Sir," before heading toward the door. Hardy followed.

The two men left the Oval Office and walked down the hallway. Neither one said a word. Hardy had to take longer strides to keep pace with Jameson. He sensed something was not right between him and his boss. The tension between them seemed to have gotten worse. As they approached the lobby, Hardy's intuition became fact.

Jameson planted both feet and stopped. Hardy had taken two additional steps before he could halt his momentum. "Everything may have worked out this time," said Jameson. "But, I guarantee that if you continue to go 'rogue' on these missions, you're going to wind up doing irreparable damage to yourself and to your country."

'Rogue?' I followed orders. I accomplished the mission. Hell, I even managed to get a Presidential 'attaboy.'

"I expect my agents to be disciplined and to follow orders when they are in the field. You got lucky, Hardy. If things had gone south and the Premier had been killed, who do you think would have made a perfect target for the Russians to blame?"

"As I said on the phone, sir, circumstances in the field can change and going to 'plan B' does not mean a soldier has gone 'rogue.'" Hardy held up his hand. "I know you have field experience, but with all due respect, how long has it been since you've been in the field, sir?"

Jameson's face and neck darkened. He glanced toward the lobby. He needed to keep his anger under control.

Thinking he had gone too far, Hardy regretted his words. A beat later, he stood taller. *No, I don't regret anything I said.* If he caved now, then Jameson would never respect him. He barreled ahead. "Terrorists don't play by the same rules we've been confined to for years. In order to do my job, I'm going to need to change the rules, too. And, that may mean changing how I carry out the mission, the orders I've been given."

The color of Jameson's face had made it to crimson.

"I assure you, sir, I have no other motive than to do what's best for my country."

"I don't question your motives, Hardy. Your *tactics* are what concern me." Jameson brushed past Hardy and strode toward the lobby.

Hardy watched the man storm off. He shook his head and spoke under his breath, mimicking Jameson. "My *tactics* led to the capture of my target and the saving of innocent life. My *tactics* got a meeting with the Premier of Russia. My *tactics—*" Hardy stopped himself. He was going down a juvenile path. He was above that behavior. *Maybe, I shouldn't have taken this job.* He ushered the thought out of his mind and meandered toward the lobby. He had a dinner date with Special Agent Cruz and wanted none of this to interfere with that. All he wanted was to go home and get some rest. His problems with Jameson could wait.

Chapter 27: Restaurant

Hardy slid the chair away from the table and waited for Special Agent Cruz to sit before he sat across from her. His plane had landed in Washington D.C. on Sunday around one in the afternoon. Exhausted from his travels, he had slept most of the day and had not seen her until a few minutes ago when she arrived at the restaurant. He was excited, almost giddy, to spend time with her. He had made reservations at a nice restaurant and wanted the evening to be perfect.

"This place is amazing." Cruz looked around the restaurant. She had worn a red short-sleeved dress. The hem stopped less than an inch above her knees. Tan-colored nylons and red high-heeled pumps accented the dress. Her long hair was up, tied loosely behind her head.

Hardy was dressed in a pair of khaki casual pants with a white polo shirt and brown loafers. He stared at her, while she admired the atmosphere. He was taking in the atmosphere, too, a different kind of atmosphere. She looked beautiful. In the time they had spent together, she had never dressed like this. As an FBI agent, she usually wore slacks and a blazer, her hair in a ponytail. Tonight, Hardy was seeing a different side to her and he loved it.

Cruz noticed him staring at her. She smiled and tilted her head slightly. "What is it?"

Hardy smiled back. "Nothing, I'm just happy we were able to make this happen." He lifted the bottle of wine he had made sure was waiting for them when they arrived. "Shall I?"

"Of course," she replied, picking up her glass and holding it for him. After he filled it, she thanked him and took a sip before setting the glass on the table. "So," the word was a sentence of its own. "How was your trip?"

Hardy filled his glass and placed it, and the bottle, on the table. He felt his stomach churn. He did not want to discuss where he had been. His whereabouts were a matter of national security and not up for discussion, not with her, not with anyone. "It was good." He changed the subject. "What about you? Is there anything new and exciting happening at the FBI these days?"

She noticed the diversion. It reminded her of the phone conversation they had had before his trip.

During her career, Cruz had developed a keen sense for when people were not being honest with her. This skill had served her well during her investigations; however, she also thought her expertise had contributed to her past failed relationships. She had speculated the men were intimidated by her and left. In reality, maybe her trust issues had driven them away.

Not wanting history repeating itself with Hardy, Cruz did not press for details. "Now, you know I can't talk about my work." She smiled flirtatiously and crossed her right leg over her left. "As they say, 'if I did that, I'd have to kill you.'"

Hardy laughed and reached for his wine flute. He retracted his hand when the waiter stopped at their table. Hardy let Cruz place her order before he asked for a medium-well steak with roasted potatoes and green beans.

"Very good, sir...I'll get those going for you right away." The waiter left.

Hardy and Cruz conversed for the next twenty minutes, talking, laughing and having a great time. Topics of conversation were anything and everything, except work. Both of them were relieved that the subject had not come up again. Hardy refilled their wine goblets. A few seconds later, the waiter returned and set plates of food in front of them. After asking if they needed anything else, he left.

"This looks delicious." Cruz placed both feet on the floor, unfolded a napkin and put it on her lap. She leaned over and breathed in the aroma. "It *smells* delicious, too." Looking at Hardy, she slid her hand across the table, palm up. "Will you say grace with me?"

Hardy glanced at her hand before wrinkling his nose. It wasn't that he did not think there was a God, but rather he did not know for sure. In his line of work, he dealt with facts, not beliefs.

Cruz smiled, knowing he was uncomfortable when it came to matters of faith and God. She glanced at her hand. "Just hold my hand."

Hardy took her hand. *This, I can do.*

Bowing her head, she prayed. "Bless us, O Lord, and these Thy gifts, which we are about to receive from Thy bounty, through Christ, Our Lord. Amen." She squeezed Hardy's hand and let go.

That wasn't so bad. He unfolded his napkin and placed it on his lap. Reaching for his fork, he felt his sat phone vibrating on his hip. Inwardly, Hardy groaned. Not many people had his new number. That meant there was a good chance the caller was Director Jameson.

Cruz heard the buzzing. After the third time, she gestured toward the source of the sound. "Aren't you going to get that?"

Hardy inspected the phone—*Jameson.* "Yes, I should probably take this. I'm sorry." He excused himself before answering the phone and walking away from the table.

Cruz had ordered spaghetti and meatballs with meat sauce. Twirling her fork in the mound of spaghetti on her plate, she watched Hardy. Her investigative nature crept to the forefront of her mind. Judging from his actions, the conversation was tense. At one point, he said something and looked back at her. She smiled at him. He forced a smile and turned away. Her mental synapses were firing. *Who's he talking to? He's definitely not happy.* She saw him end the call and make his way back to their table.

Cruz wiped her mouth with the napkin. "Is everything all right?"

Hardy was focused on the phone in his hand. "Not really." He paused, searching for the right words, but nothing seemed appropriate. "I'm really sorry. That was work on the phone. Something has come up and I need to leave."

"You must have an important job, getting called in after hours." She was unable to mask the disappointment in her voice.

Hardy heard it, too. He stood behind his chair. His eyes went from the plate of food to the bottle of wine to her red dress. He stared at her. She was gorgeous, the best thing to happen to him in a long time. And, he had to leave her. "Look, I'm really sorry—" he did not know what to say next.

It was Cruz's turn to force a smile. "It's all right." She took extra time to fold her napkin before setting it on the table. "I understand." *No, I don't.* Their relationship had started great, but his abrupt trip had left her with more questions than answers. Now, he was back and they were enjoying a wonderful meal and terrific conversation. One phone call later and he has to leave in the middle of dinner. She tried to make light of the situation, even managing an almost sincere smile. "I guess it's a good thing we drove separately."

"I'll make it up to you." He pushed his chair under the table, "I promise," and walked away.

Cruz watched Hardy leave. *I don't even get a kiss goodbye.* As if he had read her thoughts, she watched him spin around and return to her side before leaning over and kissing her cheek. Standing, he turned to leave and she grabbed his hand. "Be careful." *Why did I say that?* Even though she did not know what his job entailed, her gut told her it was dangerous. Hardy smiled and squeezed her hand, "I will," before leaving the restaurant.

DEADLY ASSIGNMENT
Aaron Hardy Series
Book #3

Chapter 1: Charity

Monday, September 16th, 4:37 p.m.; south of Dallas, Texas

Charity Sinclair sat in the backseat of a four-door black sedan, staring at her reflection in the rear-view mirror. Her shoulder-length dark hair, tinged red, was tousled; individual locks and strands stuck out on either side of her head. Her left eye was covered by a large lock; she pushed it away from her face, letting the hair slide between her fingers.

Charity was five-feet, six inches tall and weighed one hundred and fifteen pounds, but her slim figure gave her the appearance of a taller woman with longer legs. The lines of her bust, waist and hips flowed gracefully down her body, creating the outline of an hourglass. Her eyes were dark and large, set beneath dark eyebrows that followed the curvature of her round eyes. Eyeglasses with red plastic frames rested on her short, slender nose. Despite her attractive features, the one characteristic most people saw first was her smile. Her mouth was wide and paired with a full set of lips that Charity loved to color with red lipstick. A broad smile revealed large white teeth, her lips stopping short of showing her gum line. When she smiled, no one could resist the urge to return the gesture. It was her greatest physical quality. Men were enchanted by it. Women were jealous of it. Children were drawn to it.

Charity's eyes shifted to the man in the driver's seat. His chin rested on his chest and his head was cocked slightly to the right. One hand rested on his leg, palm up. The palm was bright red—the result of his efforts to stop the flow of blood from a bullet wound in his chest. She could not avert her eyes from the man. "What have I gotten myself into?" Several moments passed, but the body in the front seat still held her gaze. A nearby crow cawed and she blinked her eyes a couple of times before shutting them. Removing her eyeglasses, she set them on her lap and rubbed her eyes with the heels of her palms. *I've got to do something.* Sitting in the backseat of the sedan was not going to save her life.

Charity slid the bows of her eyeglasses past her ears, placed a hand on the back of the front seat and twisted her upper body. Peering through the back window, she saw no other cars in sight. She opened the back door on the driver's side and stepped out. Her fingers curled over the top of the doorframe and her right foot still inside the vehicle, she whipped her head left and right; her hair flew over one shoulder, and then the other. The road was deserted. Squinting, she gaped through a stand of trees on the other side of the road, her eyes straining to make out a few far away buildings and another road. With no other signs of civilization in the area, the storefronts were her best chance for help. She could not stay here much longer. If those men came, they would kill her for sure this time. They had found her once. They could find her again.

Charity slammed the door and ran across the road. Her thong shower sandals flopped against the heels of her feet. Roused from a late afternoon nap, she only had time to grab the sandals before she was rushed out of the house and pushed into the vehicle. A pair of light blue shorts and a white tank-top shirt accompanied the footwear.

Snaking between two large trees, she went deeper into the woods and disappeared from sight. Stepping over fallen limbs and zigzagging around low-hanging branches, sharp twigs scratched Charity's arms and legs. She felt the waistband of her shorts stretch to the rear, halting her forward progress. She reached around and grabbed her shorts before they were torn from her body. She stepped backwards and released the branch. Her eyes caught sight of the scratches on her arms. She sighed. "This is going to be fun."

For twenty minutes, Charity methodically made her way through the woods, until she emerged on the other side. Waving her hand in front of her face to clear away bothersome bugs, she got on her tiptoes to get a better view of the building she had seen from the road. The structure appeared to be a restaurant, but the sign was obscured. She lifted her right foot off the ground and slapped the back of her calf. A mosquito had enjoyed its last meal. Clearing the air in front of her once more, she entered the field, the only thing standing between her and the restaurant.

Tall blades of grass tickled her bare legs. Charity thought back to the moment that had started her current journey. She shook her head, wishing she had never opened her laptop computer that day. Being the inquisitive type, however, she was compelled to take a closer look at what had been displayed on her computer screen. If she had known then that her life would forever change, she would have closed the laptop and gone to the hotel pool. Without breaking her stride, she picked a red-colored wildflower and brought the blossom to her nose, breathing the aroma. She half laughed. *No, I wouldn't have. That's not me.*

Minutes later, Charity's sandals slapped the concrete parking lot behind the restaurant. In the open, she felt exposed and quickened her pace, her sandals making a 'flop-flop-flop' sound. She tossed the flower aside and ran to the front door.

Chapter 2: Jameson

"Slow down, Charity, and tell me what happened."
FBI Director Phillip Jameson leaned forward in his
chair. Charity was scared and talking fast, taking
deep breaths of air in mid-sentence. Even though he
had heard enough, he let her continue. Her voice
told him she was getting tired. That would calm her
nerves.

"Where are you, Charity?" He picked up a pen
and slid a pad of paper across his desk. He
scribbled. "Listen to me and do exactly what I tell
you." He paused, waiting for an acknowledgment.
"Stay where you are. Do not leave the restaurant.
Don't even go to the bathroom. Stay where you can
be seen at all times. Do you understand me? Good.
I'm sending an agent to pick you up. You will be out
of there and safe within the hour. Remember to stay
visible, Charity. You're going to be all right." Once
Jameson had confirmed she knew what to do, he set
the phone's handset back in the cradle. Removing
his eyeglasses, he tossed them onto the desk. With
his elbows on the desk, he closed his eyes and
rubbed his forehead with his fingers. His eight-hour
workday had just gotten longer.

Jameson had always worked hard. When he was ten, working as a newspaper carrier, he made a decision to give more to his employer than he received. That work ethic carried over to every job he worked, including his current position. He never expected more than his paycheck at the end of the week. As a result, his superiors had taken special notice and promoted him as soon as the opportunity had arisen. Two years ago, when James Conklin became the President of the United States, he had a short list of names, actually one name, for the position of FBI Director—Phillip Jameson.

During his career with the FBI, Jameson had cultivated a no-nonsense attitude. He was a man who brought to bear rock-steady leadership and decision-making skills and always backed up his agents. The fifty-year-old was physically fit, regularly lifting weights and jogging. He was five-feet, eleven inches tall and weighed one hundred and ninety pounds. He was bald and wore rounded, rectangular eyeglasses with thick black frames.

Jameson sat straight, reached into the pocket of his suit coat and plucked his cell phone. In the upper-right corner of the screen, the time was displayed—6:09. He typed a short text message, pressed the 'send' button and put down the phone. Picking up his desk phone, he dialed the cell number of one of his best agents, Special Agent Raychel DelaCruz.

Chapter 3: Ritz

5:09 p.m.; Dallas, Texas

Aaron Hardy reclined in a lounge chair near the outdoor pool at the Ritz-Carlton. The late afternoon sun felt good on his face and bare chest. Contemplating another dip in the pool, he flinched when his satellite phone vibrated on the glass-top table to the right. After swiping a forefinger across the screen, he typed in his password. A new text message appeared from a contact named 'Boss.' Hardy's eyebrows furled downward after he read the short message from Phillip Jameson—'GO WITH CRUZ.' *Go where?*

Still holding the sat phone, he turned his head to the left and observed the woman lying on her stomach in the chair next to him, her arms resting at her sides. She wore a white two-piece bathing suit, the strings of the bikini-style bottom tied at the hips. Her hair was dark and long, matching the skin tone and length of her legs. She was beautiful.

FBI Special Agent Raychel DelaCruz rolled onto her back and got comfortable. Her dark sunglasses blocked the sun, while it made its descent to her left. She closed her eyes and let the sun darken her body. She was Caucasian, but her mixed heritage made the color of her skin darker. She was glad she and

Hardy had been able to get away for a few days. After driving from Washington D.C. to Dallas, they had taken Saturday to rest. After a late breakfast on Sunday, they spent the afternoon at a Dallas Cowboys football game. It was mid-September and the Cowboys were hosting the Detroit Lions. Having grown up in Dalhart, a couple of hours north, she had been a lifelong Cowboy's fan. Unfortunately, since she lived and worked in Washington, D.C., finding time to attend a game had become a challenge.

Today, following some light shopping, she and Hardy had spent most of the afternoon by the pool, alternating between sunbathing and swimming. In an hour, they would be travelling to Dalhart to visit her mother. Right now, however, all she wanted was to relax and spend time with Hardy.

A moment later, she heard a familiar song playing—'Holy Spirit' by Francesca Battistelli. *I thought I silenced that.* Removing her sunglasses, she scooped the phone off the table. Since she was going to be on vacation for the next week, it seemed appropriate to change the ringtone on the device to a song by one of her favorite artists.

She tapped the screen and brought the mobile to her ear. "Special Agent Cruz." Even though her real name was DelaCruz, everyone close to her called her Cruz. She had received the name during her time in the military. Her fellow soldiers had joked with her and said that pronouncing her full name was too difficult. They shortened it to Cruz.

"Cruz, it's Director Jameson. I'm sorry to bother you while you're on vacation, but I need you for a 'pick-up and delivery' mission."

Cruz sat up and scooted further back in the lounge chair.

"One of the FBI's safe houses in Texas was breached. To my knowledge, all of the agents were killed."

She closed her eyes and put her free hand against her forehead.

"They were protecting a witness in a murder case. One agent was able to get the witness out in time, but he died a short time later."

"Where's the witness?"

"She's at an Overland Steakhouse near DeSoto. Where are you now?"

"I know the place. I'm close, maybe thirty minutes away." Cruz paused. "With all due respect, why didn't you send some agents from the Dallas field office? They could be on-scene within minutes."

"I have no idea how the safe house was breached. Only a handful of people knew the witness's whereabouts. That means we may have a leak in Dallas. I need someone I can trust to pick her up."

"I understand, sir. I'll leave right away."

"I'll send you the GPS coordinates for the new safe house. As we speak, I'm putting together a team of handpicked men to meet you there. They will take control of the situation."

"Yes, sir."

"Oh, and take Hardy with you, Cruz."

Her body stiffened. *How does he know I'm with Hardy?* She and Hardy had been dating for two months, but she had never mentioned that fact to anyone at work. "Sir, I don't think I should take a civilian into a potentially hostile situation. What if something happens and—"

"I understand your concerns, Cruz, but Hardy has proven he can handle himself." Jameson was referring to the incident two months ago that had brought Hardy and her together. Their actions had been instrumental in bringing a corrupt Senator to justice and finding the men responsible for killing Hardy's Special Operations teammates in an explosion in Washington D.C. "Besides, you need backup, in case anything *does* happen."

She protested, "Sir—"

"Cruz, take Hardy. That's an order. If there's any fallout, I'll take the heat. Call me when you get to the safe house." Jameson ended the call without giving her a chance to respond.

Hardy watched Cruz. She stared at her phone for a few seconds before her dark brown eyes settled on him; the long black eyelashes curled toward the sky, fluttering down and up when she blinked. She wanted to say something, but she was distracted. She was the most beautiful woman he had ever met. She had a long face with high cheekbones and a flawless complexion. Her hair fell below her shoulders. Looking at him with her head tilted to her left, the left half of her hair cascaded over her shoulder, covering half of the upper part of her bathing suit, stopping below her breast.

"How would you like to take a little road trip?" She swung her leg over the chair and rose to her full height—five feet, eight inches.

Hardy tipped his head backward, following her as she stood. The afternoon sun, directly behind her, silhouetted her figure. Her legs were well toned and her narrow waist complemented the gentle curves of her hips. He smiled and gestured toward the pool. "I thought we were already on a road trip."

Cruz reached to the right to grab the black cover-up, hanging over the back of her chair. She twirled the garment around her shoulders and slid her arms into the sleeves. The short-sleeved cover-up hid her bathing suit, but the hem stopped halfway down her thighs. After wrapping the attached sash around her waist and tying a loose knot, she motioned toward her phone. "That was my boss, Director Jameson. A witness in a murder case was almost killed in an attack on a safe house near here. I need to pick her up and get her to a new location."

Hardy glimpsed his cell. The text message from Jameson became clear. Though he could not tell her, Jameson wanted Hardy to assist Cruz on the assignment.

For the past two months, Hardy held a top-secret position, created by the President of the United States. He reported directly to FBI Director Jameson. His official job title was Special Agent Consultant to the Director. The President had offered the job to Hardy after becoming aware of his involvement in the incident in July that Director Jameson had alluded to, earlier, during the phone conversation with Cruz. Only a few people knew what Hardy's job entailed and she was not one of those people. She was unaware that both of them worked for the same man.

The first two months of Hardy and Cruz's relationship had been somewhat stressful. He would be gone for several days, conducting missions around the world. When he returned, he and Cruz would have a great time together, until he got a call from Jameson and the process started all over again. Hardy was given a direct order not to divulge the details of his job to anyone.

She picked up her mobile. "It shouldn't take too long, but I need to leave, immediately. Are you in?"

Hardy swung his legs to the left and stood. "I'm in. Let's go."

Chapter 4: Hotel Room

Back in her hotel room, Special Agent Cruz did not bother to take off her bathing suit. She removed her cover-up, tossed it into her travel bag and quickly dressed—tan casual pants, light blue V-neck shirt and blue leather shoes. After attaching her Glock 23 pistol and holster to her belt, she flung her shirt over the weapon, grabbed her travel bag and suitcase. Walking to the room's adjoining door, she wrapped on it with her knuckles. Hearing Hardy's voice, she entered his room.

He was standing by the bed, dressed in blue jeans, a t-shirt and black tennis shoes, holding his suitcase. She afforded herself a moment to admire his features. He was five-feet, eleven inches tall and had a muscular physique. His upper arms filled out the sleeves of the t-shirt. His light brown hair was cut short. His jaw was square and he had a chin that came to a slight point; a small dimple was centered on it. The quality that had first attracted her, however, was his eyes. They were deep blue. Peering into them, she felt as if she could see the ocean. She snapped out of the trance. "Are you ready?"

"All set." He slung her travel bag over his shoulder and they exited the hotel room, heading for the main lobby. Since Hardy had already paid the hotel bill when he arranged for a later checkout time, they hurried past the desk and through the front doors.

Cruz handed Hardy the keys to her black Dodge Charger. "You can drive." She shifted her suitcase to the other hand and fished for her phone. "I need to call Mom and tell her we're going to be getting in later than expected."

Hardy pushed buttons on the key fob. The Charger's doors unlocked and the trunk popped open. He put their luggage in the trunk, slammed the lid and got in on the driver's side. She was already dialing the number to her mother's house. Starting the engine, he put the gear selector in 'drive' and drove away.

Cruz turned her head toward Hardy. "Head south on 35E." She turned back and spoke into the phone. "Hi, Mom, it's me...I'm afraid I have bad news...No, no, we're still coming. I just have to take care of some work here and then we'll be on our way. It shouldn't be long, but I wanted to let you know, so you don't worry about us." Cruz listened.

Hardy navigated the vehicle through traffic. Out of the corner of his eye, he saw her look at him a couple of times, smiling.

"All right, Mom. I love you...we'll be there soon." She ended the call, stowed the phone in the center console and faced Hardy, a smile still on her face.

"Is everything all right? You look like the cat that ate the canary."

"Everything's fine." Her smile remained.

"What is it then?" Her infectious smile forced him to return the gesture.

"It's my mother...she's really excited to meet you." As an adult, Cruz had dated many men; however, she had never taken any of them home to meet her mother. Cruz had heard in her mother's voice the eagerness to meet him, the man who Mrs. DelaCruz had heard so much about through phone calls with her daughter.

Hardy laughed and checked the rearview mirror. "Well, let's hope I don't disappoint her." He changed the subject. "So, what are we heading into? What's the situation?"

Chapter 5: Overland

5:42 p.m.

Hardy watched Special Agent Cruz double-check the status of her pistol. "Do you have an extra one of those?" They were sitting in the Charger parked to the right of the front doors to the Overland Steakhouse. The restaurant was empty, except for the few patrons that could be seen from their vantage point. None of them matched Charity Sinclair's description. Jameson had sent a picture along with the coordinates to the new safe house.

Cruz shook her head. "You're a civilian. Plus, I want you to stay with the car, so we can leave as soon as I pick her up." She cranked her head in all directions. "I'm not hanging around here any longer than necessary."

"Are you sure that's wise? It's kind of hard to watch your back from here."

"Nothing's going to happen." She liked his concern for her safety. Being an FBI agent, she had to be tough, controlling. Those qualities did not allow her to relax, let someone else care for her needs. Time with Hardy meant she could let down her guard and not feel the need to be in charge. This situation was not one of those times. This required her to exercise her authority. She was the federal agent and the safety of the witness was *her* responsibility. "Besides, the witness is expecting *me*. If you're there, she might get spooked and run."

Hardy nodded his head. The thought of her going into the restaurant alone did not set well with him. She was unaware of why Jameson had insisted she bring him, and Hardy was not in a position to tip his hand.

Cruz exited the vehicle and stuck her head through the open window. "Keep the engine running. I'll be right back." She tapped the door with her hand and hurried toward the restaurant.

She paused at the front doors, looking through the glass. After a few moments, she swung open the glass door and entered the building.

Hardy checked the time on his watch. He was giving her three minutes to reappear or he was going in after her. She might not like it, but he did not like her going in alone, either. *Call it a compromise.*

After a minute had passed, Hardy observed three large men approach the restaurant, coming from the other way. They were dark-skinned and wearing dark suits with white dress shirts. They seemed out of place for the area this time of the day, especially such a hot day. The temperature was close to ninety degrees and they were wearing dark suits. Plus, their body language set off alarm bells in his head. His pulse quickened and his muscles tensed. His body was getting ready for a fight.

When the lead man reached around his body to grab the door handle to the restaurant, Hardy noticed a bulge under the man's jacket. Concealing full-size firearms under a suit coat was difficult. Suit coats were fitted to the shape of the wearer. Stuff two pounds of steel underneath and the result was always the same, a telltale bulge.

Chapter 6: Contact

Special Agent Cruz stood inside the front door and removed her sunglasses. She tucked one of the bows inside her shirt, letting the sunglasses hang from the neckline. Not seeing Charity in the immediate vicinity, Cruz went to the back. In the corner, sitting in a booth, she saw someone matching the description she had been given. After viewing Charity's photo on her mobile, Cruz slowly approached the booth, her FBI credentials in her hand.

Charity rested her forehead on her crossed hands. Sensing someone was standing near her, she lifted her head. Her eyes were drawn to the badge in Cruz's hand and she relaxed when she saw the letters FBI.

"Charity Sinclair?"

"Yes, that's me."

"I'm Special Agent Raychel DelaCruz. Director Jameson sent me." She spotted the scratches on the woman's arms and legs. "Are you hurt? Do you need any immediate medical attention?"

Charity held out her arms in front of her, examining the red lines. Inwardly, she laughed. She looked as if someone had used her for a piece of paper. "No, these are just scratches from tree limbs." She pointed over her shoulder. "I walked through the woods back there to get here. I'm fine."

Cruz motioned. "We should get going, Miss Sinclair."

Charity nodded and stood.

The two women walked toward the front doors, Cruz in the lead. Rounding the last booth, they stopped. Cruz grabbed Charity's right arm, ready to push or pull her in whatever direction was necessary.

Her voice cracking, Charity put her fingers to her lips. "Oh, no, they found me." Blocking their way out the front were three men in dark suits. She recognized the one in the middle. She had caught a glimpse of him when the agent had escorted her out of the safe house. He was the one who had shot the agent who saved her life.

"Stay calm." Cruz's eyes shifted left and right and back again. She sized up each man, determining which one was the most dangerous. The only way out of the restaurant was through the front door. The man to her right was blocking the way to the exit at the back of the restaurant. Even if she drew her pistol first, taking out three men without being shot was a tough act. Plus, she had Charity's safety to consider. Her eyes continued to scan the men and the immediate area, searching for another option.

"Special Agent Cruz of the Federal Bureau of Investigation, I believe." The man standing in front of her took off his sunglasses and held them up to the light, checking for smudges.

She faced him. He had an arrogant demeanor and was extremely calm. He appeared to be Latino and wore a dark gray suit, white dress shirt and shiny black shoes. His forehead was perspiring. The man smiled and removed a white handkerchief from the front pocket of his trousers before rubbing his cloth-covered fingers over the lenses of the sunglasses. Afterward, he used the handkerchief to wipe the sweat from his face.

"You're wondering how I know your name, no." He tucked his sunglasses inside the left breast pocket of his jacket and folded the handkerchief before returning it to his trouser pocket. "We, Latinos, are not stupid like you Americans think we are. We have our intelligence sources, too." He pulled back the lapels of his jacket and slid his hands inside his trouser pockets. He lowered his head, but raised his eyes toward Cruz. "I'll make you a deal." He tipped his head toward the back corner. "If you go over there, sit down and have yourself a cup of coffee, I promise not to kill you."

Charity's fear came through her trembling arm. Cruz gave her a sideways glance and shook her head, reassuring her witness that the man's offer had no traction.

"I'm a reasonable man. There's no reason for *both* of you to die, today." He motioned toward the men on either side of him. "Do you *really* think you can outdraw three of us?"

If she drew her weapon, she could get two of them, but not the third. The scene before her was starting to move in slow motion. She was trying to come up with a plan that would give her and Charity the best chance for survival. Pushing her witness to the floor and drawing her weapon would save a second. A second was a lot of time in a gunfight.

301

Since the man to the left was closest, he would get the first bullet. Gray Suit would be last; he still had his hands in his pockets and he would take a split-second longer to reach his gun. Flexing the fingers of her right hand, she visualized the moves she would have to make. Chairs scraped across the floor and patrons scurried away. The kitchen staff ran toward the back door. At first, Cruz thought the people had seen the pending fight. A familiar deep voice from behind the man in the dark gray suit told her otherwise.

"The real question is do you *really* think you can outdraw a man who has a rifle pointed at your back?" Hardy had an MP5 rifle, swinging it back and forth, pointing the muzzle at each one of the men. Back in Washington, D.C., when Hardy put the suitcases in the Charger's trunk, he had noticed a black duffle bag. He knew it was a cache of weapons and gear. Everyone in the industry had one.

"And, you must be the one named Hardy." Gray Suit turned.

"Not so fast, slick." Hardy raised the MP5 and aimed it at the man's head. The man stopped. "Now, slowly take your hands out of your pockets. And, if I see anything in them, you won't see *anything* ever again. Comprende, Amigo?"

The man showed his hands and chuckled. "You Americans butcher our language." He shook his head. "Now, I suppose you're going to call this a 'Mexican standoff.'"

Hardy ignored the man.

"You won't make it out of here alive. My men will be waiting for you outside. They will gun you down the minute you step through those doors."

Hardy knew the man was bluffing. "Since you like deals so much, here's one for you. From now on, every time you speak I put a round in the back of your knees. Open your trap enough times and you'll never walk again. It's your choice...stop talking, or you stop walking. Now, one at a time, I want you to remove your *pistolas* and throw them on the floor." Hardy aimed his rifle at the man on the left. "Starting with you big fella."

Gray Suit saw that Hardy and Cruz, now holding her weapon, were focused on the same man. He saw an opportunity to save his own life. Without moving his head, he caught his henchman's gaze. He gave him a barely perceptible nod of his head and the man on the left threw open his suit coat.

Hardy pressed the trigger and the MP5 barked three times; the rifle was set to 'three-round burst.' All three bullets found their target. A split-second later, Cruz fired three rounds at the same man. He spun around and landed on a small café table. The table toppled over and the man spilled onto the floor. Before Hardy could bring the rifle back, Gray Suit had grabbed the barrel and driven it downward. Three more rounds let loose, ricocheting off the floor.

Cruz swung her pistol to her left and shoved Charity to the floor. The second henchman fired his weapon. Cruz dove on top of Charity, while firing several rounds at him. Of the five bullets that hit the mark, the second one was the most important. That bullet had entered through the man's mouth, shattering his teeth and severing his spinal cord. He crumpled to the floor.

Two men down, Cruz found Gray Suit. Through the legs of tables and chairs, she saw him and Hardy struggling for control of the rifle. There were too many obstacles in the way to take a clean shot. The man kneed Hardy in the ribs. Three rounds fired from the rifle and three holes appeared in the ceiling. Cruz stayed on top of Charity, protecting her witness from stray bullets.

Gray Suit jerked backward on the rifle before pushing forward with all of his might. The sudden change in direction was too much for Hardy. He lost his balance and fell backward, landing hard on the floor. Three rounds shot out of the rifle's muzzle before the man came down on him. Both men lay on the floor. Neither one was moving.

Cruz shouted, "Hardy," getting to her feet. Not looking at her witness, she shot a finger in Charity's direction, "Stay down," and moved around a table. Standing next to the commingled arms and legs of Hardy and the attacker, she saw Hardy's face. His eyes were staring at the ceiling and his mouth was slightly open. During her career, she had seen death up close. The faces of the dead had one thing in common; they were void of all expression. Hardy had that look. Cruz felt her throat closing and her stomach muscles convulsing. Her pistol felt as if it weighed a hundred pounds. The only thing heavier was the lump in her chest. She knelt next to Hardy.

A fraction of a second later, he coughed and expelled a long breath before taking a huge gulp of air. He coughed again and rolled the body to the left; the wooden handle of a steak knife protruding from of the corpse's chest. A growing circle of blood stained the white dress shirt.

As he fell, Hardy had grabbed the knife from one of the tables. The man came down on the blade, while his knee rammed into Hardy's groin. Still coughing, he reached for Cruz.

"Thank God." She wrapped his arm around her shoulders and helped him stand. "I thought you were dead."

He bent over and cradled his smarting testicles. "Right now," his chest heaved, "I think I'd prefer that."

"Shall I rub it? Would that help?"

He rose to his full height, a devilish grin spreading across his lips, while his mind went to a far off place. He ogled her out of one eye, his half smile still present. "Yes...and no."

She patted his chest. "Down boy...I was kidding. Are you okay to stand?" He frowned before nodding his head. "Good. I'll get Charity and we can get out of here."

Hardy picked up the MP5 and removed the magazine—two rounds. He put the magazine back in and pulled back on the bolt, until he saw the rim of a nine-millimeter case. *Three rounds left.*

Cruz returned with Charity and the three of them left the restaurant. Cruz hurried around the front bumper of the vehicle. "Charity, get in back and stay down." She climbed into the driver's seat. Once Hardy was inside, she jammed her foot down on the accelerator and the tires squealed. Smoke rose into the air and two black lines appeared on the pavement behind the Charger's spinning tires.

Cruz pressed buttons on the Charger's built-in GPS navigation screen. She had entered the safe house coordinates from Director Jameson on the way to the restaurant. Confirming they were going in the right direction, south on 35E, she adjusted the rear-view mirror to see Charity. "We're on our way to another safe house. Hang in there, Miss Sinclair." She glanced at Hardy, who was cupping his... "How are your—" she shook her head, "*you* holding up?"

"I'll be fine." He maneuvered the MP5 rifle and managed a brief smile. "Don't worry. You still have a *future* with me."

Blushing, Cruz glimpsed the rifle. "Lucky for us, you found my secret hiding place."

Chapter 7: Safe House

6:04 p.m.

Director Jameson had provided the coordinates to a safe house south of Lancaster near Bear Creek. The house, a short drive from the Overland Steakhouse, was at the end of a long dirt driveway and surrounded by trees. The nearest tree line was no less than fifty meters from the house, so the occupants had a clear line of sight in all directions. Special Agent Cruz steered the Charger toward the two-story house, the roof's pitch almost flat. The window shades were closed. The exterior of the house was worn, the paint peeling and faded. Sections of siding hung at angles. It was evident the house had seen better days.

She checked the GPS.

Hardy read her thoughts. "Are you sure this is the right place?" He surveyed the house and the surrounding terrain. Tall weeds flanked the Charger. The brown grass had not been mowed in weeks. Dropping a match or flicking a cigarette would have started a forest fire. An old sedan was parked out back. The tires were flat and the driver's door, along with the windows, was missing. Weeds found their way into the shell of what at one time had been a nice car.

Cruz stepped on the brake pedal. "The GPS says we're here."

Hardy put a shoulder to the door. "Well, let's hope we're all current on our tetanus shots." He got out and ascended the stairs that led to the front porch.

Cruz joined him; Charity was two paces behind them.

"Uh...how do we get in?" He eyed the solid steel door with no doorknob.

Cruz ran her fingers around the bottom of a mailbox attached to the side of the house. Finding what she was looking for, she pushed up and the right side of the mailbox popped open. A numeric keypad had been built into the siding. She pressed numbers, corresponding to the security code Jameson had sent, and hit 'enter.' A sound similar to briefcase latches releasing—only louder—was heard and the heavy door opened a crack.

"Cool. You FBI people have the neatest gadgets."

Cruz and Charity exchanged a glance. *Men and their toys.*

He shoved the door the rest of the way open. The house was dark, but a faint light came from around the window shades. Feeling for a switch on the wall, he slid his hand upward and three lamps lit the room. Judging by the condition of the exterior, Hardy had expected the inside to be a mess.

The living room was nicely decorated. To the left, a stone fireplace with a flat-screen television was mounted above the opening. The fireplace faced a large wooden coffee table to his right. The table was surrounded by sectional sofas, arranged in the shape of a 'U.' Behind each sectional, a sofa table supported a lamp. In the far right corner, another flat-screen television, two straight back lounge chairs, two ottomans and a coffee table—complete with a video game console—formed a cozy gaming area.

Hardy advanced further into the room, admiring the hardwood flooring. Letting out a low whistle, he said, "Very nice." A wooden staircase, accessed from the right side of the fireplace, rose to the second floor. The staircase passed in front of the chimney on a diagonal.

Cruz slipped past him and headed straight for the kitchen at the back of the house. Passing the dining area, she noted the large oak table surrounded by six solid wood chairs. The kitchen cabinets, baseboard trim and flooring were also made of hardwood and stained a dark color.

While she continued to inspect the kitchen, Hardy walked past the fireplace and made a button hook. "I'm going to check out the upstairs."

He did a 'one-eighty' at the top of the stairs, his fingers dragging across the rough stones of the chimney and walked down the upstairs' hallway. He leaned over a wooden railing to the right and could see most of the main floor.

Four doors were lined up on the left side. The first and last one led to bedrooms, each room set up the same—bunk beds against the left wall and a flat-screen television on the wall across from them. A desk and chair in one corner and two dressers in the opposite corner rounded out the floor plan.

The second and third doors led to bathrooms. The left bathroom had the sink, toilet and shower against the right wall. Shelves holding towels, washcloths, bathmats and toiletries were on the left wall. The right bathroom was a 'mirror-image' of the left.

Hardy descended the stairs and saw Charity rummaging through the refrigerator. He veered left and checked out the two rooms on the first floor. One was a bedroom, arranged like the others, except with a queen size bed, and the other was a third bathroom. *Can't have too many bathrooms, I guess.*

A duffle bag slung over a shoulder, Cruz entered the back door and dumped her suitcase on the kitchen floor. She poked a finger at the luggage and glanced at Charity. "You should be able to find some clothes in there that fit."

"Thank you." Charity closed the refrigerator and picked up the suitcase. "There's not much to eat." She took a bite of a juicy Jonagold apple and wiped her mouth with the back of her hand. "I'm," she chewed and talked, "going to take a hot shower."

"You have your choice of two upstairs," Hardy jerked a thumb behind him, "or one down here."

Charity sunk her teeth into the apple and sloughed upstairs, the suitcase bouncing off her leg with every other step.

Cruz slipped the duffle bag off her shoulder, dropped it onto the dining room table and unzipped it. "I parked the car around back, so it wouldn't be seen from the road." She fumbled around inside the bag before handing Hardy two full magazines for the MP5. After clipping a double-magazine pouch—two full pistol magazines inside—to her belt, she slid the zipper on the duffle all the way to the right and faced Hardy, who had already inserted one of the magazines into the rifle and was shoving the second into the back pocket of his jeans. The hiss of water sounded from the upstairs shower.

Hardy set the rifle on the table and pulled out a chair. "How long before someone from your agency shows up?" He sat and let out a sigh. "And, how did that guy know my name?"

Cruz shook her head. "He knew mine, too." She put her cell phone to her ear and ran her fingers through her hair. "Whoever he was, he seemed—" she stopped talking to Hardy and spoke to the cell. "Director Jameson, it's Cruz. We're at the safe house. The witness is secure. How far out is your team?"

"They're airborne and should be on-site in ninety minutes."

She caught Hardy's eye and mouthed the words 'ninety minutes.' "We were almost too late."

"What do you mean?"

She relayed the events to Jameson. "How many people knew the witness was at the restaurant? Unless those men followed Charity, how could they have gotten there so fast?" She paused. "Who was with you when you called me?"

Jameson was lost in his thoughts.

311

"Sir, are you still there?"

Jameson shook his head. "I'm here. I was alone in my office with the door closed. I contacted nobody, except the men who are on their way to you right now."

"Then my question still stands. How did they know the witness was at the restaurant?"

"I don't know, Cruz, but I plan to get to the bottom of this."

"In what case is our witness testifying? Who's being charged with murder?"

"Hector Gutierrez," said Jameson.

"You mean the Mexican mafia crime boss?"

"Yes. A prostitute was killed in a hotel room in Texas, near the border. Miss Sinclair was staying at the same hotel. She is very...*proficient* with computers. While she was working with her laptop, she gained access to the hotel's security cameras and witnessed the murder."

"I'm assuming that when you say she *gained access,* you mean she hacked the system." The shower stopped running and her eyes shifted upstairs. "Why didn't she go to the police?"

"She did. By the time the police arrived, the security footage had been corrupted. That's when the FBI got involved and put Miss Sinclair in protective custody."

Cruz put her fingers to her lips. "So, the FBI is attempting to prosecute a man based on a woman witnessing a murder through security footage that is now corrupt. I'm not a lawyer, but that sounds like quite a stretch."

"It is, but if we can get this charge to stick, then we can take one more criminal out of the equation. It's worth a try."

"Where's Gutierrez, now?"

"He's in federal custody, waiting for his trial."

"Then, it's safe to say that the men who broke into the safe house and the men who were at the restaurant are working for Gutierrez."

"It's a very good chance. I'll call you when I get more. I think it's also wise to keep our phone calls to a minimum. We don't know how they're getting their information, so watch your back, Cruz." Jameson ended the call.

Chapter 8: SS7

Special Agent Cruz set the mobile phone on the table. "The Director doesn't know how they knew where to find Charity. He says he was alone in his office when he called me." She ran her fingers through her hair, flipping the locks backwards when she got to the back of her head.

"They didn't follow her to the restaurant." Hardy was fiddling with the MP5 rifle. "They came from down the street and didn't appear to have been walking all that long." He tapped the rifle's stock with his middle finger. "No, they were parked down the street from the restaurant. I'm sure of it. They had inside information on Charity's location. They *knew* she was there."

Cruz leaned forward and showed him her palms. "What about the man who knew our names? How would he have gotten that information? Jameson told no one...No one was with him when he called. What if—"

"There's another possibility."

Hardy and Cruz tipped their heads back.

Charity was standing near the upstairs handrail. She had a large white bath towel wrapped around her body. Near her left armpit, the ends of the towel overlapped and rolled inward. The towel left a good portion of her body exposed. From their vantage point, both Hardy and Cruz could see Charity's entire left leg up to her waist. Her head was cocked to her right and she was holding a second towel in her hands, rubbing her hair as it hung down. The vigorous drying motion threatened to release the towel, barely clinging to her body.

Hardy could feel his cheeks getting warm. "What do you mean?" He saw Cruz in his peripheral vision, her eyes shifting from him to Charity.

"I'm sorry. I didn't mean to eavesdrop, but I overheard your conversation and it got me thinking." She stuck a finger in Cruz's direction. "Agent DelaCruz, you said that—"

"Please call me Agent Cruz."

Charity smiled and went back to drying her hair. "Agent Cruz, you said that Director Jameson was alone in his office when he called you." Her eyes shifted to Hardy. "And, you're certain those men didn't follow me to the restaurant. I agree. No one was on the road when I got out of the car and walked into the woods. I could've gone in any direction, yet those men showed up at the restaurant too quickly. So, I'm thinking somebody was listening in," she pointed at Cruz, "on your conversation with Jameson, Agent Cruz."

"I'm not following you." Hardy pointed across the table. "She said that Jameson was alone with the door *closed*. How can someone be listening?"

Charity tilted her head backwards and shook it a few times, her hair swinging back and forth like a clock pendulum. "I mean electronically." She threw the towel over the railing and ran her fingers through the full length of her hair several times. "Someone

315

could have been listening to your conversation over the Internet. I'm assuming either you or Director Jameson used a cell phone during the call, am I right?"

Cruz nodded. "He called me on my cell from his office line."

"I'm sure Mr. Jameson has a cell phone of his own, too. And, it is most likely near him most of the time. So, those people could have been listening to the conversation through either one of those devices."

His arms folded over his chest, Hardy cupped his chin. "How's that possible?"

"Cell phones today are like supercomputers. There is so much technology in them they rival laptops. People don't think of their cell phones as computers, so they don't take precautions to safeguard them." Charity leaned forward and rested her forearms on the railing before crossing her feet at the ankles. "Even if they did, there's a little known thing called SS7."

Hardy looked at Cruz; she shrugged her shoulders.

"Yeah, not many people are aware of it. SS7 is the crux of the problem. Billions of communications pass through it every day. It's crucial in allowing mobile phones to roam. Experienced hackers know how to exploit SS7 and can do everything from listening to live conversations to spying on people through a phone's camera and even activating the device's microphone."

Cruz sliced her fingers across her neck. "What if the power was killed...shut the phone off?"

Charity cocked her head. "Who does that? Besides, the mobile network is independent from the GPS chip and knows where the phone is at all times."

Hardy stared at Cruz's phone. "What does it take to gain access to someone's phone?"

"Not much, really," replied Charity, slowly shaking her head. "It could be something as simple as the phone's number."

Hardy snatched Cruz's phone and stood. He dropped it onto the floor and smashed it under his foot, sending pieces in all directions.

Cruz sprang from her chair. "What did you do that for?"

Hardy pointed at Charity. "Get dressed. We're leaving." He pointed at the remnants of Cruz's phone. "Jameson called you on that and told you," he motioned upstairs with his head, "where she was. Jameson also sent you the coordinates to this place via that phone. This safe house may have been compromised already. We can't stay here any longer." He jerked a thumb. "If what she says is true, then those men may be tracking us through *your* communications."

Cruz stared at the plastic parts. *Son-of-a-gun...he could be right.*

"Think about it, Cruz. How did that man at the restaurant know our names?" Hardy felt a vibration in his left front pocket. He stuffed a hand into the pocket. "These people have been ahead of us the

317

whole time. Your phone may have been their tracking device." He glanced at his phone—'Boss.'

Cruz pointed. "You can't take that. What if they've hacked yours as well?"

"Trust me, *no one* can hack this." He had a state-of-the-art piece of technology two generations ahead of anything on the market. Given to him by Director Jameson, Hardy's mobile was a satellite phone. Looking like any other ordinary cell phone, it was anything but ordinary, capable of getting a signal in places where normal phones could not. The GPS tracker was accurate to within a block of his location. "Hardy."

"Hardy, it's Jameson. You've got to shut off Cruz's phone. We think they may have hacked into my cell and—"

"We know. I've destroyed it and we're getting ready to leave this place. We can't stay here."

Cruz made eye contact with Hardy. "Who's that?"

He went back to his conversation. "What are you calling me on, sir?"

"Don't worry. I'm on my sat phone. They can't hear us."

Cruz heard Jameson's voice. "Is that Director Jameson?" *Why is he contacting Hardy?*

Chapter 9: Crossfire

Hardy whipped his head around and darted to the front window. He drew back the curtain. "It's too late, sir. They've found us. We've got to go *now.*" Hardy disconnected the call and jammed the phone into his pocket.

Having joined him at the window, Special Agent Cruz eased back the other curtain. Three vehicles were lined up at the tree line, facing the house. She counted twelve men fanning out and approaching the house. "Even if we could get to the Charger in time, they have the only escape route blocked."

Hardy spied the sectional sofas. "Give me a hand." They slid one sofa in front of the front door and dragged the other two to the window. Tipping them on end, they leaned them against the window. "That should slow them down."

Running into the dining area, he hauled—Cruz pushed—the heavy wooden kitchen table toward the back door. Hardy joined her and they lifted the table and let it fall against the door. "That's all we can do. Let's go." He raced toward the stairs. Cruz grabbed her duffle bag and followed.

Charity was standing at the top, dressed in Cruz's clothes—shorts, t-shirt and tennis shoes. "What's going on? Aren't we leaving?"

Hardy jabbed his forefinger over her shoulder. "Change of plans—we need to shelter in place. Get to the bathroom." Stopping and pressing his body against the handrail, he grabbed Cruz's arm and pulled her past him, "Get her to safety," before bounding down the stairs.

"Where are you going?"

"I forgot to get the lights." Hardy moved from lamp to lamp, breaking each bulb. The main floor was in near darkness. With the lights out, they were on a more level playing field. Hardy's team knew the layout, but the opposing force did not. He took the stairs two at a time and joined the women in the bathroom.

Hardy threw back the shower curtain and motioned toward Charity. "Get in the tub and lie down. It's not perfect, but it might help stop bullets." He helped her into the tub and held her arm, while she got on her belly. "Make yourself as flat as possible."

Cruz drew and checked the status of her pistol. "How are we going to play this?"

Hardy motioned toward the stone chimney. "You take a position behind the chimney." He tilted his head toward the opposite end of the hallway. "I'll be over there." He made an 'X' with his forearms. "We'll set up a killing field and get them in the crossfire. We need to maintain the advantage of height and keep them on the first floor."

Hardy ran to the end of the hallway, while Cruz knelt by the chimney. He wanted to ask her how long before her men arrived, but he knew the answer—*too long*. His phone vibrated. "We're kind of in the middle of—"

Jameson cut him off. "The team I sent will never make it in time. We're going to plan 'B.' Backup will be there in ten minutes."

Hardy crouched and got as low as possible. "I'm not sure we have ten minutes, but copy that." Changing the rate of fire on the MP5 to single-shot, he spied Cruz. "Okay, let's make every shot count."

Chapter 10: Cover Me

They did not have to wait long for the armed men to begin their assault. Glass broke at the front and back of the house. The sofa nearest the front door crashed into the living room. Two men entered through the window.

Hardy waited until the first man was inside. He fired three times and the man dropped to the floor, his leg hanging on the windowsill. The second man had one foot inside and could not back out soon enough. Hardy shot him twice in the head. The man's body went limp and lay over the windowsill. Gunshots sounded to the right.

Special Agent Cruz fired on intruders at the back of the house. One man came in through the window over the kitchen sink. She shot him twice. When he did not go down, she fired two more times and he dropped onto the sink, his body sliding over the edge and landing on the floor. A barrage of gunfire came from the kitchen window. Chips from the stone fireplace flew in all directions and Cruz took cover, pressing her back against the chimney.

Gunfire came from the window in the living room. Bullets punched holes in the wall above Hardy's head. He dropped to the floor, got into a prone position and returned fire. The bolt on his rifle locked open. Jettisoning the spent magazine and yanking a fresh one from his jean pocket, he jammed it into the rifle and released the bolt. "How we doing over there, Cruz?"

She leaned out and saw a man inside the kitchen and a second one jumping off the sink. Not having enough time to acquire a sight-picture, she extended her weapon and fired several times before the men disappeared from sight. Getting Hardy's attention, she pointed two fingers at her eyes before holding up those fingers and motioning toward the main floor.

Hardy nodded and ran toward her in a low crouch. Back to back, they leaned against the chimney. He peered around the corner and had a clear view of the front window. Focusing on the wall facing the top of the stairs, he saw light from the kitchen window shining on it. Shadows danced on the pale-colored surface. The dark images moved, growing bigger. He held off as long as he could before pivoting his body around the chimney. His rifle up, he pressed the trigger six times, sending three bullets at each man.; the first one fell forward, while the second clutched his chest and toppled over backwards, his rifle discharging when he landed. Pivoting back behind cover, Hardy saw a man attempting to enter through the front window. He took careful aim and pressed the trigger once. The attacker disappeared from sight. Incoming rounds slammed against the chimney, which did not afford much protection for two people. Cruz's body was pressed against Hardy's back. He ejected the rifle's magazine. *Eight rounds left.*

Cruz spun around and fired, until her weapon's slide locked open. More men climbed through the kitchen window. Tapping the magazine release button on her pistol, while slipping her fingers under her shirt, she grabbed a full magazine and elbowed Hardy. She held up the magazine, "Last mag," before inserting it into the pistol and running the slide forward.

By his count, Hardy had killed four or five attackers. "How many have you shot?"

"I got at least two. There are more inside the house, now."

Hardy watched the wall at the top of the stairs for shadows. They were low on ammunition and there were still a half-a-dozen armed men nearby. His sat phone's speaker squelched. A deep and muffled voice bellowed from his pocket. "Shepherd, this is Bigfoot. Do you copy—over?" Shepherd was Hardy's call sign.

Cruz spun her head around. "What was that?"

Hardy dug out his phone. "Bigfoot, this is Shepherd. I hear you loud and clear—over."

Cruz stared at Hardy. *Shepherd? Bigfoot?*

"Shepherd, be advised AR-1 has a fix on your position. We're two minutes out. What's your situation—over?" Bigfoot was the call sign for Tom Henderson. He was the leader of AR-1, an assault and rescue team created by Director Jameson to provide support for Hardy when he was on missions. Jameson had dispatched AR-1 soon after getting the call from Charity. The team had been conducting

324

training in Little Rock, Arkansas and he wanted the team close in case they were needed.

Bullets came through the second floor hallway, sending faint beams of light toward the ceiling. Cruz drove her body harder against Hardy, nearly pushing him beyond the cover of the chimney. "They're firing through the floor." She leaned out and fired over the railing.

"We're on the second floor. OpFor,"—opposing force—"is on the main floor, all heavily armed." More bullet holes appeared in the floor; one a few inches from Cruz's leg. Hardy yelled above the gunfire. "We're pinned down and running out of ammo—over."

"Roger that, Shepherd. We're coming to you—over."

Hardy jammed the sat phone back into his pocket, spun out from the chimney and emptied his rifle at the first floor figures. One man ducked into the bathroom, while a second took cover in the main floor bedroom. A third dove to the floor, but Hardy doubted the man had been struck by a bullet. He reeled around and rammed the last magazine into the rifle; a partial—two rounds left. Cruz and he did not have the two minutes AR-1 needed to get there. He spotted Cruz's duffle bag on the floor. Kneeling, he rummaged through its contents. Grabbing a road flare, he rushed past her. "Get ready to cover me."

Hardy went into the first bathroom and re-emerged with several folded bath towels. He ignited the road flare and held it up to a towel. "Cover me." Cruz moved to the corner of the chimney, nearest the stairs. One by one, he lit and tossed the flaming towels over the railing, hoping the fireballs would dissuade the attackers from coming up the stairs. Adding to the blaze, Hardy tossed the road flare over the railing.

Cruz and the first floor gunmen exchanged gunfire, stone chips spitting at her face. Taking cover behind the chimney, she felt a sharp pain on the right side of her stomach. Her back to the chimney, she closed her eyes and crinkled her nose. The pain shot up the right side of her body. Her stomach was on fire. Hardy approached and she held up her empty weapon. "I'm all done." Her arm fell to her side and the weapon slipped from her grasp.

Moving around her, Hardy relinquished his rifle. "You've got two rounds." He withdrew his Cold Steel Recon 1 tactical knife, locked open the blade and assumed a fighter's stance at the corner of the chimney. Crouching, he squeezed the knife. *Come and get some, you son's-of—*

Chapter 11: Neutralized

Smoke from the smoldering towels rose toward the ceiling. The smoke alarm above the first bathroom door wailed. Blocking the ear closest to the alarm, Hardy heard what sounded like suppressed weapon's fire. A few moments later, his phone vibrated and the speaker crackled. He retrieved the cell. "This is Shepherd. Say again—over."

"Shepherd, this is Bigfoot. All targets have been neutralized. Your path is clear. I repeat—all targets neutralized. The structure is clear—over."

"Copy that." Hardy hurried to get Charity. The two of them were greeted by the sights, sound and smells of heavy, but dissipating smoke and a blaring alarm. Escorting Charity toward the stairs, he saw Special Agent Cruz. She had slid down the chimney and was sitting on the floor, covering her stomach. He knelt. "What's wrong?"

She raised her head and peeled back her hand; it was covered in blood. There was a circular stain on her light blue shirt, growing larger. "I thought it was a sharp stone." Her head dropped and she examined her wound.

Hardy screamed into his phone. "Man down, man down, I need immediate medical attention on the second floor." He ran back to the bathroom and returned with two bath towels. He pushed aside her hand and pressed a towel against the wound.

Cruz screamed and arched her back. She grabbed Hardy's forearm, her fingernails digging into his arm. He felt the pain, but never moved. Her body convulsed and her head rocked backwards, bouncing off the chimney. Hardy cradled her head with his free hand. Her breathing was labored and every breath of air sent new waves of agony up her right side. "Damn it. Where's that medic?" he bellowed. Seconds later, Tom Henderson and Eva Draper appeared.

Draper, the team's medical specialist, skirted by Henderson and dropped to both knees on Cruz's left. Draper was short, standing five-feet, three inches tall and weighing a little over one hundred pounds. Her black hair was cut short, stopping at the neck. The bangs of her hair covered her forehead, ending at the top of her eyebrows. She was twenty-seven-years-old, but her facial features made her look as if she was in her late teens. She had grown up and spent her entire life in Michigan, Hardy's home state. The two of them had connected from their first conversation, talking about all things related to Michigan. Like Hardy, she was a die-hard fan of the Detroit Lions and they had had numerous conversations about the team and its prospects at a winning season this year. Right now, however, the only thing on Draper's mind was Cruz. "Where is she hit?" Draper bobbed her head back and forth, searching for wounds.

"Stomach, right side," Hardy replied. "I've had pressure on it. There's a lot of blood."

328

Draper shuffled to the left and straddled Cruz's leg. She reached for the towel Hardy was holding, "Move," and pushed.

Hardy did not budge.

The medical specialist faced him. He was staring at Cruz. Draper leaned forward and got his attention. Knowing this was difficult, she employed her best soothing voice. "Let go, Hardy. I've got it from here."

Henderson put a hand on Hardy's shoulder. "Come on, let Drape do her job." He reached under Hardy's armpit and pulled him to his feet. Hardy could not have resisted Henderson's strength even if he had tried.

Tom Henderson stood six-feet, three inches tall and weighed two hundred and thirty-five pounds of solid muscle. He was thirty-six-years-old and had spent half of his life in the service of his country. The hair under his helmet was dark; patches of gray peeked out. His facial features matched his wide frame. His eyes were set far apart and his nose was broad; a full, handlebar mustache lay beneath it. He was proud of the mustache and could be seen stroking it with his fingers at every opportunity.

Draper examined Cruz. "She's lost a lot of blood. I see an exit wound on her back, so I think the bullet went straight though. I can't tell if any major organs have been hit. We need to stop the bleeding and get her to a hospital ASAP."

Henderson brought a radio to his mouth. "This is Bigfoot. We need that bird back here, now! We have an injured soldier that needs immediate medevac. Do you copy—over?"

A voice from the radio: "Copy that. We are coming in now on the south side of the structure—over."

Hardy faced Charity and pointed. "Go with him." He spun his head toward Henderson. "Where's Ty?" Hardy was referring to the last member of AR-1, Tyler Pendleton.

"He's outside, watching our backs."

"Good. Get everyone ready to go. I want to lift off," he gestured toward Cruz, "as soon as she's on board."

Henderson grabbed Charity's hand and led her toward the stairs. "Copy that." Over his shoulder: "The stairs are clear. You have no obstructions to the chopper."

Hardy knelt next to Cruz. She plopped her hand onto his thigh and he slipped his hand under it, squeezing gently. She lifted her head. Her eyes were barely open, her eyelids fluttering up and down. She mumbled something. He leaned closer and put his ear to her mouth.

"Who...who are...these people? Jameson, why did he...call...you?" Her chest rose and fell. The spent oxygen barely made it to Hardy's cheek. "I swear...I don't think...I know you...at...all."

Hardy closed the distance between them—their cheeks touching—and slammed shut his eyes. A six-inch knife had been thrust into his heart. At that moment, he wanted to tell her everything, everything about himself—his job, his family, his likes and dislikes, his favorite color, his favorite food. He wanted to tell her those things every other couple shared when they were getting to know each other. Putting his lips to her ear, he opened his mouth to speak. Bound by an oath to the President, he shut his mouth. The oath kept him from sharing what he did for a living. The oath was tearing him up inside, threatening to destroy his relationship with possibly the only woman who could understand him.

Cruz's head slumped forward and Hardy held her face in his hands. "Cruz, talk to me...Cruz."

Draper put her fingers under the woman's chin. "It's okay, Hardy. I have a pulse, but we need to move, now!" She collected her medical supplies and stood. "Hardy, let's move."

He snapped to attention, sliding his right arm under Cruz's knees and his left arm under her back. Lifting her from the floor, he hurried toward the stairs. Her head hung down. He brought his left elbow up and her head came forward, coming to rest on his shoulder. With Draper in the lead, making sure there were no obstacles in his path and providing support in case he lost his footing, Hardy carried Cruz down the stairs.

Once outside, Henderson and Draper took Cruz and put her into the aircraft, while Tyler scanned the area for threats. Hardy climbed inside and got on the floor next to her. When Draper, Henderson and Tyler were aboard, the Bell 412EP helicopter lifted off. Banking right, the aircraft headed for the hospital.

Hardy cradled Cruz in his arms, whispering in her ear. Even though the noise from the aircraft's rotors and engine drowned out his words, everyone suspected what he was saying. Draper leaned forward and placed a hand on his shoulder.

Chapter 12: Baylor

The helicopter touched down at Baylor University Medical Center in Dallas, Texas. Henderson had contacted Director Jameson, who made a few calls and had a team of doctors and nurses standing by on the roof. They quickly got Special Agent Cruz on a gurney and examined her on the way to the operating room. Doctors determined she needed immediate surgery.

While Cruz was wheeled to the operating room, Doctor Raj stayed behind. He spoke in a thick Indian accent. "The surgery could take up to three hours, depending on what I find when I open her up. As soon as I know more, I'll let you know." He turned to leave.

Hardy put a hand on the doctor's shoulder. "Is she going to be all right, doctor?"

"It's too early to tell." He removed the hand. "I need to get prepped. Leave your contact information at the front desk." He disappeared behind the double-doors before anyone had a chance to ask more questions.

Hardy stood with his hands on his head, fingers interlocked, facing the slowly closing double-doors. He watched the doctors and nurses take the gurney—and Cruz—out of his sight.

Charity and the members of AR-1 had gathered around him. Several moments passed before Draper stood alongside Hardy and put her hand on his lower back. "She's going to be okay, Hardy."

Hardy dropped his hands and made eye contact with everyone. When he came to Charity, he stopped and stared. He could nothing for Cruz, but he could fulfill her duty to the witness. "Miss Sinclair, we're going to move you to a safer location. I'll contact Director Jameson and get another safe house lined up for you." He turned his head toward Draper and gestured toward Charity. "Draper, I want you to—"

"The hell you are," said Charity, raising her voice and interrupting him. All eyes focused on her. She pointed at the doors. "Twice, that woman risked her life to save me. I'm not going *anywhere*, until I know she's going to be okay. I owe her at least that much."

"This isn't open for debate, Miss Sinclair. Your safety is my responsibility now and I make the decisions. And, I say we're moving you."

Charity put her hands on her hips and glimpsed him from head to toe. "I can see you're a man who's used to getting his own way—that's fine with me. In this case, however," she poked her forefinger into Hardy's chest, "you will *not* be getting your way." She jerked her thumb at her chest. "You will *not* be ordering me around. And, if you try to remove me from this hospital," she moved her right foot back, transformed her hands into fists and brought them to her chest, "you may succeed, but I *guarantee* you I will not go quietly." Still in a fighting stance, she gestured toward Henderson and his team. "Besides, how much safer can I get with all of you around me."

Hardy's mouth fell slightly open and his eyebrows went up. After a few seconds, he lowered his head and his nostrils flared. His fingernails dug into his palms. She was right. He was used to getting what he wanted. He had been in positions of authority for many years and no one had spoken to him that way. If Charity had been a man, she would have been picking her teeth off the floor. Since she was a woman, however, he could not correct her insolence with his fists. He glimpsed Henderson and Tyler.

Raising their hands in surrender, they stared at the floor and shook their heads. Hardy moved on to Draper, who poorly hid a small grin.

"Don't look at me. I'm on *her* side."

Coming back to Charity, Hardy's eyes narrowed before he unclenched his fists. *What am I doing?* He was not going to hit a woman.

"She has a point, Hardy." Draper made a circular motion with a finger. "There's no safer place for her than with those who've already killed to defend her."

Not feeling up to arguing, he threw up his arms. "Fine," he grunted, departing from the group. "Have it your way." Over his shoulder: "For future reference, the next time you plan to hit someone, you might want to make a *proper* fist." He disappeared down the hallway.

Charity glanced at her hands. They were in the shape of fists, but she had her thumbs tucked under the rest of her fingers. If she had thrown a punch, she would have most likely dislocated or broken her thumb.

"Come on, slugger." Draper wrapped an arm around Charity's shoulder. "Let's get some coffee. We've got a few hours before we know anything."

Chapter 13: Tick, Tick, Tick

Aaron Hardy found a small waiting room void of people. He sat in a cloth chair in the far corner. Resting his elbows on his knees, he leaned forward and buried his face in his hands. He remained in that position for several minutes. The room was quiet, except for the second-hand on the wall clock above him. Each time the second-hand moved, it made a sound—tick...tick...tick. The noise would have been maddening for most people. Hardy focused on the consistency and matched his breathing to the beat. He was thinking of many people and things—Special Agent Cruz's health and his relationship with her, Miss Sinclair's safety, Jameson, his job and Gutierrez, the s.o.b. responsible for all of this. His mind was unable to concentrate on a specific one.

With his fingertips, he rubbed his eyes before transitioning to his temples. He needed to call Jameson. Right now, his nerves were raw and he was concerned about what he might say to him. On some level, Hardy held Jameson responsible for Cruz's condition; however, on a deeper level, he knew his emotions were getting the better of him. She was a federal agent. She was performing her duty. Gutierrez was ultimately liable. He was the one who started this, forcing Charity to go into protective custody. His men carried out the attack on the safe houses. Yes, Gutierrez was the one on whom Hardy wanted to unleash his anger.

His thoughts went back to Cruz and the look in her eyes before she lost consciousness. She did not trust him anymore. At the very least, she was losing faith in him. That was almost too much to bear. His phone vibrated a few minutes later. He leaned back in the chair and stuck his hand inside his pocket. He knew it was Jameson before he saw the phone's screen. He gave himself a mental pep talk and finished by saying aloud, "Keep it together, Hardy." He put the phone to his ear. "Hardy."

Chapter 14: Justice

"Hardy, this is Jameson. What's the word on Cruz? How's she doing?"

"She's in surgery. The doctors were unsure of her injuries and said it could take up to three hours before the surgery is complete. They'll let us know as soon as they know more." Hardy put his hand to his forehead before running his fingers through his hair. He sat straight in the chair and put his hand on the armrest.

The line was quiet for a few seconds before Jameson spoke. "She's tough. She'll pull through."

Hardy squeezed the armrest tighter. The veins in his arm stuck out. "You smug, arrogant jackass—you don't give a damn about her. You only want to know when you can have her back in the field. It's *your* fault she's here in the first place." That was what Hardy wanted to say. His reply came in a monotone voice. "Yes, she will."

"Hardy, I've got bad news. I've been informed by the Attorney General that the government has decided not to pursue the case against Gutierrez."

"What," said Hardy, rising from the chair? "They can't do that."

"I'm afraid Gutierrez has already been released from federal custody. He got on a plane headed for Mexico."

Hardy could not believe what he was hearing. He made a fist with his left hand and reared back to punch the wall. He caught himself. "What about those agents who lost their lives at the safe house? They were *your* agents."

"Hardy—"

"What about Cruz," continued Hardy, glimpsing his hand, still stained with her blood? "She took a bullet to protect *your* freaking witness?" His mind had queued up the word *freaking*; however, the word that slipped past his lips was something else. "She was following *your* orders and now you're giving up. You put her in harm's way and now you are abandoning her."

"Agent Hardy," shot back Jameson, "You need to calm down and—"

"Don't tell me to calm down. I'm the one who's *here*. I'm the one who's dodging bullets. I'm the one having to carry Cruz to a helicopter and watch her being wheeled away for surgery. I'm *not* the one playing politics in Washington, however, while good agents are losing their lives." As soon as the words left his mouth, Hardy knew he had crossed the line. His temper had taken over and he could not take back what he had said. He bordered on insubordination.

"Damn it, Hardy, that's enough," shouted Jameson. His voice came through so loudly that Hardy removed the sat phone from his ear. "Now, I order you to shut your mouth and listen to me. I give the orders and you listen. Is that clear, Agent Hardy?"

Hardy opened his mouth to tell Jameson what he could do with his orders, but remained silent.

"I said is that clear?"

"Perfectly," replied Hardy through clenched teeth.

"Good." Jameson took a few moments to get his anger under control. "This matter with Gutierrez is complicated and I don't have the time to explain it to you. The decision to let him go was not my call to make. I don't agree with it, but there's nothing I can do about it."

"You could have used—"

"Hardy," said Jameson, his voice rising. "Just because I don't agree with the decision to let him go, doesn't mean my hands are tied in the matter."

Hardy felt a glimmer of hope. "I'm not following you."

"We've been tracking Gutierrez's plane since it took off. It landed in Mexico. We have an asset in the country who has confirmed that Gutierrez is currently at a small villa just over the U.S. border. Our asset believes Gutierrez will be at the villa for another two hours, maybe three. We only have a small window of opportunity."

Hardy switched the phone to his other ear. "What are you saying?"

"I'm saying I have a jet waiting on the tarmac at Dallas/Fort Worth all gassed up and ready to go. Once you're aboard, I'll send you the details. You'll have free reign to do whatever is necessary to bring Gutierrez to justice. Take Henderson and his team along for support."

Hardy stood still, thinking. He wanted justice for Cruz, but how could he leave her? He wanted to be the first one to know when she was out of surgery. He wanted a familiar face there when she opened her eyes. In any other circumstance, his decision would have been certain and immediate. His thoughts scattered when he heard Jameson's voice.

"The clock's ticking, Hardy. What's it going to be?"

Chapter 15: Tango Down

8:51 p.m. (local time); Mexico—just over the United States border

The sun had set more than an hour ago, but the air remained humid. Hardy could feel the sweat beads on his forehead. He looked toward the sky. A half-moon provided enough light to make out the figures moving back and forth around the perimeter of the small villa. He had agreed to lead this covert incursion into Mexico on the condition that Draper remain at the hospital and watch over Charity and Special Agent Cruz. He requested regular updates on her condition via text messages. Jameson had arranged for a team of trusted agents to see to Charity's safety.

"Three tangos down—over." Henderson had made three long-range shots from his vantage point on a small hill, two hundred meters away from the northeast corner of the villa. His specialty was long-range sniping and Hardy was convinced Henderson was the best. "You're clear to proceed."

"Copy that." Hardy motioned it was time to move out. Crouching, Hardy and Tyler ran to a row of hedges fifty meters away from the southwest corner of the structure. They located the two sentries guarding the front door and sent two silenced rounds from their MP5 rifles toward each man. The men dropped. Hardy and Tyler sprinted to the villa and took positions on either side of the front door—Hardy on the left, Tyler on the right. They waited for Henderson's update. Hardy gripped his rifle tighter. *Come on, Big Man. Give us a report.* If any one of the remaining men emerged, Hardy and Tyler would be forced to shoot him, exposing their presence and losing the element of surprise. Hardy's earpiece crackled.

"Bigfoot is in position—stand by." A few seconds passed, while Henderson peered through the scope on his sniper rifle. "You have six confirmed targets and three potential targets on the first floor, concentrated in the center of the room—over."

"Copy that." Hardy signaled to Tyler and readied his rifle.

Tyler pushed open the door.

The structure was small and simple. Three couches were grouped together in a 'U' shape in the center. A chandelier above the couches was lit, but a few bulbs were missing. Two large windows took up most of the wall space on the east and west side. A staircase was located on the east wall that led to an upper level walkway running east to west. On the north side of the walkway were three doors. Beneath the staircase, on the east wall, was a closed door. At the far end of the main floor was a kitchen area.

Hardy advanced into the room and moved right. Tyler followed and went left, flanking the house's occupants. Six men were sitting on the couches, while three topless women danced on the floor between the couches. The women stopped dancing and the men stopped ogling and turned their attention toward Hardy and Tyler. The women, having been around men with weapons, were not surprised by the tactical team's entrance. Seeing the rifles, the smiles on the men's faces disappeared.

Tyler was the first to engage. He let loose a volley of suppressed weapon's fire at the two men on the right couch. They never got to their feet. Their heads tilted backwards, hitting the headrest.

Hardy moved right and discharged his rifle at the two men on the couch nearest the front door. Each trigger press sent a three-round burst. Like the two on the right couch, the men remained in a seated position, as they expired from gunshot wounds to the back of the head.

The final two men on the far couch—opposite the three women—were more difficult to put down. Hardy did not want the women to become collateral damage. Secretly, he hated that term. In his mind, if a mission was properly planned and executed, there was no collateral damage. That occurred when people got careless. Moving further and further, he cleared the last woman and dropped the man on the right, who had stood, only to fall backward into a seated position when Hardy's bullets ripped open the man's shirt. The women screamed and dove for the floor. The last man alive grabbed a handful of one woman's black hair before she could hit the floor. He put the muzzle of his pistol against her right temple. She tried to scream, but only produced a whimper.

The man's head darted out from behind her, alternating from one side of the woman's head to the other. He stepped back, but his knees hit the sofa, impeding his rearward movement.

Tyler advanced, while Hardy transitioned to his suppressed pistol and crept closer. Their weapons were pointed at the man's head each time he appeared from behind the woman. When Tyler was within arm's reach, he stopped.

Glimpsing his teammate, Hardy clenched the pistol tighter, drew in a short breath and let out half. Timing was crucial for the next move. A woman's life depended on a precise combination of Tyler's speed and Hardy's accuracy. *Come on. Show me your beady little eyes you son-of-a—*

The skittish head jutted out toward Hardy, the left eye lining up perfectly with Hardy's front sight. Striking like a coiled snake, Tyler leapt forward. Hardy fired one round. Twelve hundred feet-per-second later, the 9mm bullet found its target, as Tyler clutched the man's gun hand and jerked the pistol toward the ceiling; the weapon discharged before he could wrench it from the limp hand. The lifeless body and the terrified, screaming woman collapsed onto the floor. The women were shaking and crying, but unharmed.

Holstering the pistol and grabbing his rifle, Hardy motioned for Tyler to open the door under the staircase. "We are no longer silent. Move forward and assault—over."

"Copy that," confirmed Henderson.

Hardy kept his rifle trained on the door, while Tyler opened it and stepped back, allowing Hardy to enter and clear the room. He re-emerged and headed toward the staircase, swapping out the partially spent magazine in his rifle for a full one.

The two men crept up the stairs. At the top, Hardy signaled and Tyler kicked in the first door. They cleared the room and moved on to the second one, repeating the process. Exiting, the doorframe above their heads came apart, sending splinters into the air. They backed up and took cover. "Bigfoot, this is Shepherd. T-Rex and I are on the second floor, taking fire. The shooter's on the main floor. What's your position—over?"

Before Tyler joined the team, his call sign had been T-Man; however, he changed it to T-Rex when he discovered Henderson's call sign was Bigfoot. Since Tyler was six-feet, four inches tall and outweighed Henderson by at least twenty pounds, Tyler had to have a name that reflected his larger physical stature. It was a classic 'mine is bigger than yours' scenario.

Getting no response, Hardy was about to re-issue the command when three shots from Henderson's Smith and Wesson M&P pistol, chambered in 45 auto, filled the villa.

"This is Bigfoot. One of you needs to spend some time on the shooting range. Thanks to me, your tango is down *for good*. You are clear to proceed—over." One of the men Hardy had shot had still been alive.

"Copy that, Bigfoot." Hardy and Tyler positioned themselves near the last room. Hardy nodded his head and Tyler put a boot to the door; it flew open, slamming against an inside wall.

Hardy entered the room and darted left, while Tyler went straight along the right wall. Three half-naked women were sitting on a huge bed against the far wall. The bed was almost the size of two king-size beds. They were huddled together near the headboard, covering their bodies with bed sheets, blankets, pillows, whatever they had grabbed. The room was smaller than the first two and the bed took up most of the floor space. There were no windows and no place for someone to hide, except under the bed; Tyler checked it, stood and shook his head. Hardy inspected the entire room, his head pivoting in all directions. He studied the women. They were afraid, but their body language was sending other signals, too. At different times, each woman shifted her eyes toward the wall behind Hardy before coming back to him. It was subtle, but he noticed it. He turned around and examined the wall. There was nothing special about it. Taking a few steps backward, he made mental calculations of the room's size. Even though it was smaller, it appeared to occupy the same amount of cubic feet as the other bedrooms.

After walking to the door and inspecting the wall, Hardy raised his hand and motioned toward the wall. Tyler hefted his rifle. Hardy fired down the length of the wall, while Tyler sprayed it from the side, until their weapons ran dry.

Hardy strode the length of the wall, swapping magazines. He spotted something at the far end. Stopping and examining the section, which appeared to be a thin, moveable panel, he glanced at Tyler and slid the panel to the left, revealing a secret hiding place. Hardy clicked the flashlight mounted to his rifle. The immediate area was clear. He took a step forward and pointed his rifle down the narrow cavity. Halfway down, a man lay motionless. Hardy advanced, his rifle trained on him. Standing next to the corpse, he recognized it as the former Hector Gutierrez, the man's bare chest covered with bullet wounds. Lifeless eyes stared back at Hardy. *That was for Cruz.* Making sure he accomplished the mission, he put one round into the head, "And, that's for me," before pivoting and leaving the room.

Henderson had joined them and was standing next to Tyler. He tilted his head back and raised his eyebrows. "Did we get him?"

Hardy nodded. "Eagle, this is Shepherd." Eagle was the call sign for the helicopter that had dropped them near the villa. "Mission accomplished—we will meet you at the rendezvous point in twenty minutes. Do you copy—over?"

"Copy that, Shepherd. We will be waiting your arrival—over."

Twenty minutes later, safely aboard the helicopter, Hardy took out his sat phone and sent a text to Draper. Ten seconds later, she responded. *She's out of surgery and in post-op recovery. Still haven't heard from the doctors.*

Chapter 16: Waiting

11:02 p.m.; Baylor University Medical Center, Dallas, Texas

Hardy rounded the last corner and made a beeline for the room where Draper had said she and Charity were waiting. Henderson and Tyler were a step behind. Barging into the waiting room, Hardy looked for Draper. "Where the hell is she?" He wheeled around and nearly collided with her.

"Come with me." She grabbed a handful of his shirt and yanked. "A nurse escorted Charity and me to a consultation room. She said the doctor would be with us, shortly."

"So, any word on how the surgery went?"

"No." She led him into the consultation room.

Small and minimally furnished, it was evident the room was only meant for short conversations between doctors and family members. Charity was sitting at a small table—the only table—facing Hardy. There was a chair next to her and another opposite the table. She stood and offered him her seat.

Hardy waved her off and motioned for her to sit. "How are you doing?" Charity appeared tired, worn out. The day's events had taken a toll on her. "Have you managed to get some sleep?"

She regarded him. After everything he had experienced, he still had the decency to inquire about someone else's well-being. His face was haggard and the lines on his forehead were set deeper. Wherever he had been for the last couple of hours, it was obvious he had not gotten any rest. She flashed a smile. "I'll be fine. Don't worry about me."

Hardy nodded and turned around when the doctor entered. "How is she? Is she going to be all right? When can I see her? What about—"

The doctor raised a hand. "Hold on." He pushed the door, but jumped back when a meaty hand prevented him from closing it.

Henderson and Tyler forced their way inside.

Doctor Raj pushed back. "I'm sorry, but this room is for family members only. You'll have to—"

Hardy put a hand on the doctor's shoulder. "It's okay, doctor. They're with me."

The tiny space became smaller with the addition of two people, two large people.

Doctor Raj slid out a chair. He was a short man with a thin build. He was in his mid-forties. His skin was dark and his hair was black. A pair of wire-rimmed eyeglasses rested on a small nose. He was dressed in light blue scrubs and was still wearing a cap from surgery. Tied around his neck, a surgical mask rested on his chest; the untied strings of the mask swayed back and forth when he moved. After sitting across from Charity, he swiped the cap from his head and tossed it onto the table.

Hardy motioned for Draper to take the last chair. She shook her head and pointed. He could tell there would be no negotiating with her. Plus, he was exhausted and welcomed the time off his feet. "Thanks." Draper stood next to him, while Henderson and Tyler moved around the doctor and stood behind Charity. Everyone faced the doctor.

Before Doctor Raj spoke, he slowly moved his head from left to right and examined each person. During his time in medicine, he had met with many people to discuss operations. These people, however, were most unusual; three men and one woman wearing black tactical clothing and combat boots, looking as if they had just come off the battlefield. Lastly, he spied Charity and her minimal clothing. She seemed different from the others. "How are you related to the patient?"

Hardy was direct. "She's a *very* close friend. Now, tell us how she's doing."

Raj's eyes settled on Hardy and assumed him to be in charge. "All right, let me first say that the surgery went very well, and she is out of post-op, resting in her room."

Hardy relaxed a little. *Good news.*

"When I got her on the operating table, I saw there were two entry wounds, extremely close together. They were touching, in fact. However, there was only *one* exit wound. Knowing it was very unlikely that both bullets would have exited the body in the same spot, I took a closer look and found a bullet lodged near her lung. I was able to remove it and there were no signs that the bullet had fragmented. I believe it was in one piece."

Hardy leaned forward. "So, she's going to be all right."

The doctor removed his eyeglasses and set them on the table. He rubbed the indentations left by the nose pads. "One of the bullets nicked her kidney."

Hardy arched his eyebrows. His stomach muscles contracted. *Bad news.*

"I was able to stitch up the kidney, but I'm concerned about an infection. The entry wound had a lot of debris in it."

Hardy and Draper looked at each other. They had worked on Cruz at the safe house, trying to get her bleeding under control. Did they cause the infection?

"Now, I understand that whoever stopped the flow of blood did so with whatever materials available." He pumped his hands. "Don't get me wrong, if that wound had been left alone, she could have died before even making it here. That was a good field dressing; however, at this point, there is a risk of infection. I have started her on some antibiotics and she's heavily medicated to help her body fight. Rest is the best thing for her right now."

Hardy stood. "Can I see her?"

Raj shook his head. "I'm afraid not, son. She won't open her eyes for at least twelve to eighteen hours. As I said, she's on some strong medications." He stood and eyed Hardy. "The only thing we can do is wait." He took another glance at the others, especially their attire. "I presume your friend is a soldier?"

Hardy's mind was a million miles away. "What?" He shook his head. "I'm sorry. Yes, she's FBI...an FBI agent."

"Good. That fighting spirit can only serve to help her get better." The doctor opened the door. "If you have any questions, I'll be around. Just tell one of the nurses."

Everyone thanked the doctor before he left.

Hardy stared at the open doorway. The room was quiet, except for the usual hospital noise at the nearby nurse's station. He ran his fingers through his short hair and vigorously scratched the top of his head. Glancing at the members of AR-1, he waved a hand. "You don't have to stay here. Go get a hot shower and some rest. You heard the doctor. There's nothing we can do for the next eighteen hours." He took a couple steps toward the door. "I appreciate—" Draper grabbed his elbow. He glanced at the hand before making eye contact.

"We're not leaving you, Hardy." She tilted her head toward Henderson and Tyler. "That's not how we do things."

"We don't," said Tyler, "leave a man—or in this case, *a woman*—behind."

Hardy cranked his head toward the voice.

Henderson locked eyes with Hardy. "Damn straight we don't."

Hardy pursed his lips and nodded. "Thanks." He shuffled through the doorway. "I need some air."

Chapter 17: Penland

Hardy roamed the hospital hallways for the next half an hour. Lost in thought, he passed by nurses, doctors and people visiting family members and friends. He glanced inside rooms and saw patients lying in beds. Loved ones were gathered around the bed. Some were crying. He kept walking, not wanting to contemplate a similar scene with him and Special Agent Cruz.

He turned a corner, his mind replaying the images of her being taken away for surgery. He had no idea how long he had been walking, but when he stopped and looked up, he was standing at the door to Penland Chapel. He stared at the door for a full minute, breaking away to glance up and down the hallway. *What the hell.* Opening the door, his heart beat faster and his body temperature went up. Mustering the courage to take the first step, he slipped inside and closed the door behind him. As soon as the latch caught, he seemed shut off from the rest of the world.

For a few moments, he stood by the door, unsure if he was scrutinizing the chapel, or the chapel was scrutinizing him. He chose a chair in the back corner, crossed his legs and leaned back. A split-second later, he put both feet on the floor and sat erect, not knowing if his posture was disrespectful. He folded his arms over his chest and

stared straight ahead. *Maybe this was a mistake.*
Places like these made him feel awkward. They were
tolerable with others around, but being alone was
nerve-racking. The silence seemed to shine a
spotlight on his soul, his closely guarded inner
thoughts.

He got up to leave, but stopped and sat again.
Where am I going to go? He had nothing to do, but
wait. Being a man of action, Hardy hated to wait.
Waiting made him feel powerless, unable to achieve
results. Minutes later, he held his head in his hand.
His body shook and his broad shoulders rocked up
and down, matching his labored breaths. He wiped
his face and rubbed his hands together. "Get it
together, Hardy," he whispered. He took a deep
breath and slowly exhaled.

"God, you know I'm not a religious man." Hardy
shook his head. *What am I doing? I've got no
right...*he paused... *Where am I going to go?* "God,
you know the things I've done. I have no right to ask
you for anything." Washing his hands down his face,
he sniffed. "Still, I don't know what to do. I don't
know where to go. I'm at the end of my rope."
Hardy thought of his teammates, killed in the
explosion two months earlier. "I don't know if I can
take another loss. Please help Cruz pull through.
Please, don't punish her for what I've done." His
head slumped and he closed his eyes. Thoughts and
images rushed through his mind. He could not
process them or control their coming and going.
Fatigue made it difficult to concentrate. Several
moments passed. All he could do was let his

thoughts take him wherever they wanted him to go. In the midst of the mental chaos, he prayed repeatedly, "Please, God, save her." Time seemed to stand still and the mental confusion subsided. He slouched in the seat, his body perspiring.

Ten minutes later, the door opened.

"Hardy," said Draper, "we've been looking all over for you. Cruz woke up ten minutes ago."

"What," he said, standing?

"Yeah, she just opened her eyes and said your name. A nurse was with her at the time. She—"

"She woke up ten minutes ago and you're only now telling me." He charged out of the chapel.

"Well, excuse me." Draper held up her hands and glanced around. "This isn't exactly the first place I'd expect to find you." She followed him out of the chapel.

Chapter 18: Peace

A nurse held up her hands. "I'm sorry, sir, but I can't let you in there."

Hardy reached for the doorknob. "Is she awake? I want to see her."

She intercepted his hand. "I have strict orders. No one is to go in there without the doctor's permission."

"Okay. Get the doctor's permission." He eased her to the side. "I'll be in here when he comes."

Pushing past Henderson, who stood next to the nurse, Doctor Raj forced his body between Hardy and the nurse. "What's going on here?"

"I was told she asked for me." Hardy pointed at the door with his forehead and his voice grew louder. "Now, I want to see her."

Hearing the commotion, two nurses cranked their heads around and stared at the group. One picked up a phone and dialed security.

"I understand how you feel, but I must re-iterate how important it is for her to get her rest. This is not about *you*, sir. It's about the well-being of the patient, *my* patient." He grabbed Hardy's hand, which was still on the doorknob. "Now, please—"

"For crying out loud, Doc," Henderson jutted his chin toward the door and the woman on the other side, "She asked for him." He made the 'peace' sign. "Just give him two minutes in there. Two minutes isn't going to hurt her."

Doctor Raj studied Hardy for a few seconds before holding up his index finger. "You've got *one* minute." He stepped back and motioned toward the nurse, who set the phone back in the cradle.

Not giving the doctor the opportunity to change his mind, Hardy sneaked into the room and slowly closed the door. He tiptoed to her bed, picking up a chair on the way. Careful not to make a sound, he sat and stuck his arm between the slots on the bed's handrail. Holding Cruz's hand, he stroked her hair and pushed the locks away from her face. She tightened her grip on him. Her eyes fluttered before opening. He folded his hands around hers, careful not to dislodge the IV. "Hey there," he said, smiling. "I'm here."

Even though she had been given a strong dose of medication, Cruz recognized him. She returned a feeble smile. There was an intubation tube down her throat and two plastic oxygen tubes in her nose. She tried to speak, but her throat was sore and it hurt to talk. She coughed and let out a groan.

"Shhh, that's all right. Don't speak." He patted her arm. "Charity is safe. You accomplished your mission. The doctor said the surgery went well." He omitted the part about the possible risk of infection. She did not need that on her mind. She only needed to focus on getting better. He leaned closer. She seemed relaxed, almost at peace. He assumed it was the medication. "Everything is going to be all right.

You just need to take it easy." She closed her eyes, but her grip remained strong.

The doctor had given him one minute and he had stolen another four. Her chest rose and fell with each breath. Combing her matted hair, he felt her hand go limp. He held on. His thoughts turned to his prayer—his *words*—in the chapel and the timing. Ten minutes *after* asking...God...for help, Draper entered the chapel and told him Cruz had opened her eyes and called his name ten minutes *earlier.* Hardy lowered his head. *Is it possible that...* He was still holding her hand, contemplating the connection when someone, the nurse placed her hands on his shoulders. His head shot upward.

"Please, sir, it's time for you to go and let her sleep." She kept her hands on his shoulders, until he rose from the chair and slid his hand through the bed's railing. He wanted to stay, but he understood it was best for her if he left.

Turning around, he had a strange feeling of calmness wash over him. He looked back at Cruz. He did not know how, but at the very depth of his being, he knew she was going to be all right. A smile crossed his lips and he left the room, his mind and heart at peace.

Chapter 19: Surprise

September 20th, 7:37 a.m.; Baylor University
Medical Center, Dallas, Texas

"She's still kind of out of it from all the medication, but the doctors say she's steadily improving." Hardy strolled down the hallway at the hospital.

"That's good news." Draper and the rest of AR-1 had stayed with Hardy, until he had received news from the doctor that Special Agent Cruz's risk of infection was extremely low; she was recovering quicker than expected. The team left to finish their training in Little Rock. Since leaving the hospital, Draper had called Hardy every morning at 7:30 to check on Cruz's condition. "Give it time. She's going in the right direction. From what you've told me about her, she's tough and will beat this."

"Thanks Drape." Hardy stopped in the hallway. "Listen, I want to thank you again for what you did for Cruz...treating her at the safe house, staying behind to be with her. I know you wanted to be a part of that mission in Mexico, but I needed to know that someone was going to be here for her."

"You're welcome. I'd do it all over again...for you *and* for Cruz." Draper paused. "Maybe someday we can all get together for dinner and have a proper introduction—*your* treat."

Hardy laughed. "I'd like that." The smile faded. He knew as long as Cruz was not privy to what he did for a living, he could never introduce her to AR-1.

"Take care, Hardy. I'll talk to you, soon."

"Thanks, again, Draper." He disconnected the call and slipped the phone into his pocket. Approaching the nurse's station, he smiled at a middle-aged woman with short blonde hair. She stood and came around the desk.

"Good morning, Aaron." Janet sidestepped him and headed down the hall. "Did you get a good night's sleep?"

Hardy had practically lived at the hospital for the past three days. Most of the nurses had gotten to know him on a first-name basis. Last night, Janet had arranged for him to sleep in an empty room down the hall, so long as he did not make too much of a mess. Hardy had gladly accepted the offer. It was the first time he had been able to get some quality sleep. This morning, he felt refreshed and full of energy.

He fell in step behind her. "Yes, ma'am, I did. Thank you again for getting me that room. I promise I left it exactly the way it was."

"You're in for quite a surprise, I think." She knocked on Cruz's door before opening it slowly and poking her head inside. "Knock, knock." She walked around to the far side of the bed.

Entering, Hardy's eyebrows arched. Cruz's mechanical bed formed the letter 'L' and she was sitting. The intubation and oxygen tubes were gone, but the IV remained. Her long dark hair, which had been greasy and plastered to her head was clean and brushed, falling to the sides of her shoulders and stopping below her elbows. Coming closer to the bed, he noticed she was not only awake, but also alert; her eyes were sharp and focused. Even though he had spent the past three days with her, she had been sleeping most of the time. When she was awake, the medication had made her groggy. At those times, Hardy had wondered if she even knew he was there.

"How are you feeling?" Janet asked, swiping her badge across a computer keyboard.

"A little tired," said Cruz before turning toward Hardy and the bouquet of flowers in his hand. "I'm hungry, too. Is there any chance I can get something to eat?"

Janet smiled. "Absolutely," she said. "That's a good sign, dear." She went back to the screen, punched a few more keys and clicked the computer mouse several times. "First, we need to get you up and moving. I was just getting ready to take you for a walk." She looked at Hardy. "I think I found someone who might want to take my place, however."

Cruz cocked her head and gestured at the flowers. "What do you have there?"

He stepped forward and handed them to her. "These are for you." He glanced at a glass vase of flowers on her tray table. "But, I see someone else got here before me."

She took the flowers from him and smelled them. "Yes, Charity was here earlier. She wanted to

363

see how I was doing before she went back home." Cruz gave the flowers to Janet, who was waiting to take them. "She's such a sweet person, isn't she?"

Hardy's mind formed a picture of Charity, a determined look on her face, fists up and ready to punch him for wanting to move her to a safe location. "Yeah, she's a sweetheart all right."

"Okay, let's get you on your feet." Janet slipped a pair of pink socks on Cruz's feet and helped her stand.

Cruz looked over her shoulder and flicked her eyes downward. "Will you do the honors?"

Hardy overlapped the gown and tied the strings together, covering her bare butt.

"Now, remember," said Janet. "Take it slow and don't go too far. You don't want to tear your stitches."

Janet, with Hardy's assistance, helped her patient get to the door. At the nurse's station, she let him take over after another word of caution about the stitches.

Cruz curled her arm around his elbow and took small steps, careful not to overextend her gait. She still had many questions for him. What did he do for a living? What happened at the safe house? Who were those men he was talking to on the phone? The details of the incident at the safe house were foggy and she wanted answers to her questions. Right now, however, she was simply enjoying walking with him, arm-in-arm.

Fifteen minutes later, she was back in her bed, tired, but still feeling good. She placed an order for breakfast. When it arrived, she ate every morsel. Janet had put the flowers from Hardy in another vase and set the vase on the opposite side of the room.

Hardy had kept the conversation to safe topics, not wanting to broach the subject of the safe house events. She needed to heal, not dredge up memories he could not explain. There would be plenty of time to discuss that issue. Besides, she had been somewhat aloof with him and he sensed she had been thinking about the same thing. As much as he may have wanted to tell her everything, he could not defy a direct order from the President. Hardy came around to the left side of her bed and pivoted the tray table ninety degrees to give her more room. Sitting down, there was a knock at the door and Director Jameson entered. "Hello, Agent Cruz."

Director Jameson was dressed in a black suit, white dress shirt and a red tie with black diagonal stripes. A gold tie bar held the tie in place. His black shoes—perfectly polished.

"Director," said Cruz, digging her palms into the mattress and trying to push her body further up the bed.

Hardy pushed himself to his feet. "Sir."

Jameson waved a hand at them. "Please, as you were," he said, striding past the foot of the bed and taking a position beside her bed. Hardy remained standing. "How are you feeling?"

She did not want to get into the specifics. "Good, I'm feeling good—a little tired, but good."

Jameson nodded his head, pleased to hear the news. He shot a glance at Hardy, but remained silent.

Hardy stared back at the man. Dallas was a long way from Washington and it was a little odd for the FBI Director to come this far to inquire about her health.

Jameson spotted the vase. "Nice flowers."

Cruz squirmed. "Charity brought them in before she left this morning."

"That was nice." He grabbed a chair from the corner. Pushing the tray table further away, he placed the chair as close as he could to the bed, removed his suit coat and laid it across the chair's back. Sitting and facing Cruz, Jameson leaned back and crossed his legs before resting his arms on the chair's armrests.

Cruz glanced at Hardy; he was sitting. She turned her head back toward her boss.

There was more silence, as Jameson focused more of his attention on Hardy than her. Jameson picked a piece of lint from his pants and let go of it, watching it float to the floor. He lifted his head and locked eyes with her. "Cruz, I have something to tell you about Mr. Hardy. Do you feel up to hearing it?"

The muscles in Hardy's arms and chest tightened. His eyes moved toward Cruz.

She met Hardy's gaze before whirling her head back toward Jameson. "Of course, sir." Even though she was feeling a bit tired, she did not want to say 'no' to her boss, especially since Hardy was the topic of the conversation.

"Good." Jameson rested his elbows on the chair's armrests and brought his fingertips together. "What I'm about to tell you is highly confidential and must not leave this room. Is that clear?"

She slowly nodded her head. "I understand, sir." She glimpsed Hardy, who looked as if he was bracing for a car accident. *What's going on here?*

"Special Agent Cruz, Mr. Hardy works for me," Jameson waited a beat, "and for the President of the United States."

Cruz's jaw dropped open. "Excuse me, sir?"

Jameson spent fifteen minutes explaining the details of Hardy's coming to work for the President. She had glanced at Hardy several times. Each time she looked at him, it seemed as if she was on a date, more precisely, a speed date. The bits and pieces about his life, and who he was, were racing toward her. In the end, the information overload was worth the stress. When Jameson finished, she stared at Hardy. The questions and doubts that had plagued her were gone. The truth was out there. She stretched out her hand and he took it.

"Now you know," Jameson continued, "*why* I wanted you to take Hardy to pick up Charity, as well as why I couldn't tell you the reason." Jameson nodded at Hardy with his forehead. "His employment activities are a matter of national security. As such, only a few individuals have access to that information."

Hardy maintained her gaze. She smiled. Her face softened. They would be okay. Jameson had divulged Hardy's secret, freeing him to pursue a

367

normal relationship with her. He chuckled to himself. *Normal.* Whatever that was going to be, he planned to make it work.

Jameson stood, put on his suit coat and returned the chair back to its original place in the corner. Straightening the lapels of his suit coat and pulling on his shirt cuffs, he eyed his agents, holding hands. "I can see that the two of you have a relationship that goes beyond the professional realm."

Both of them pivoted toward their boss.

He pointed a finger at them. "What you do in your personal time is none of my business; however, if I suspect that your personal relationship is affecting your work," he paused to add emphasis, "It will *become* my business. Am I clear?"

Cruz nodded. "Yes, sir."

"Crystal," said Hardy.

Jameson adjusted his suit coat. "Take as much time as you need to get better, Cruz. Then, take a couple extra days for yourself. I have already assigned other agents to your cases, so don't worry about that. Just let me know when I can expect you back at work."

"I will, sir."

"If you don't mind me asking," Hardy said, standing, "How did you get the President to agree to bring Cruz on board? I thought my job was on a need-to-know basis."

Wrinkles formed on Jameson's forehead. Gazing at the end of the mattress, he drew back the lapels of his suit coat and slipped his hands inside his trouser pockets. "The President doesn't know yet."

Hardy's eyes widened.

"I haven't quite figured out how I'm going to tell him." Jameson withdrew his left hand and waved it in front of his chest. "But, that's my problem." He lifted his eyes and regarded his female agent. "After all you've done for your country, Cruz—*and me*—I thought you deserved to know the truth." He stood erect and maintained eye contact. "You took a bullet for your country, Cruz, protecting a witness." The words triggered the phone conversation he had with Hardy and a sliver of a grin passed over his lips. He glanced left. "Or, as Mr. Hardy so eloquently stated it..." Jameson waved a hand and came back to Cruz. "Anyway, I'm sure my suffering the President's anger won't be as bad as what you've endured."

"Thank you, sir. I appreciate that."

Jameson got Hardy's attention. "That was nice work in Mexico. With Gutierrez and his son out of the picture, Miss Sinclair should be safe now." The man Hardy had killed with the steak knife was the only son, and blood relative, of Hector Gutierrez. "The Gutierrez Cartel will have a difficult time regaining its power any time soon." Jameson included Cruz. "If it were not for your efforts, she would not be alive today. Both of you...good work."

"Thank you, sir," Cruz said before adding, "Did you ever find out how they were tracking us?"

"Not exactly, but we think it was most likely through my cell phone. Once they gained access to it, they knew everything we were doing. As a result, new security protocols have been implemented throughout the agency, including updating the encryption on every agent's phone. I'm just relieved there wasn't a leak in the agency. That would have been worse." Jameson wished her well again and left the room.

Hardy turned toward Cruz. She was grinning. One eyebrow was slightly higher than the other one. Hardy had seen the look on a few occasions. She had something to say, something cute or funny.

"So," she began, dragging out the word. "Do I call you *Shepherd*, now?"

Hardy chuckled and lowered the handrail on her bed.

She scooted over to make room. "Or, do you have some sort of secret agent number I'm supposed to use? Tell me. I've never known a secret agent man before."

Taking care not to bump her, he climbed into the bed. *Wow. She's going all in on this.*

Cruz pressed him. "So, what's the story behind the name?"

Lying next to her, he leaned back and put his left arm around her shoulder. She lowered her head onto his chest. He tucked his right hand behind his head and stared at the ceiling. *This is nice.*

"Are you going to tell me, or what?" She poked him in the stomach.

"I like German Shepherds. When I was a child, my parents had German Shepherds as pets. During my time in the military, I worked with them, too. They're intelligent and loyal animals that would defend the ones they love, even if it meant losing their own lives." He lowered his eyes to look at her

370

and breathed in the scent of her hair. "Most people expect to hear a heroic story of how I saved my team from the enemy or something like that." He looked up again. "It's a very boring story, actually."

Cruz tilted her head back to see him. "I like it." Thinking of the qualities he had used to describe the German Shepherd breed of dog, she added, "And, I think the name fits you, *perfectly*." Touching a forefinger to his cheek, she turned his head toward her and kissed him. A few seconds later, she laid her head on his chest.

Hardy squeezed her shoulder and kissed the top of her head. *Yes, this is very nice.*

IF YOU ENJOYED

The President's Man,

Please post a review

on Amazon.

Thank you.

Thank You

Thank you for purchasing and reading the first three installments of the Aaron Hardy series. I hope you enjoyed reading them as much as I enjoyed writing them. Please visit your favorite bookseller and leave a review for The President's Man.

Reviews are extremely important to authors. Your comments help us understand what our readers are thinking and feeling about our work. Your review also helps others in the purchasing process. More purchases means others are enjoying our work and want us to write more books. Your thoughts are critical to our success and the availability of good fiction.

I hope you're looking forward to the next book in the series, Patriot Assassin. Keep reading for a sneak peek.

Sincerely,
Alex J. Ander

Other books by Alex Ander:

Aaron Hardy Patriotic Thrillers:
The Unsanctioned Patriot (Book #1)
American Influence (Book #2)
The London Operation (Book #2.5 – FREE...
...Details in every Aaron Hardy ebook)
Deadly Assignment (Book #3)
Patriot Assassin (Book #4)
The Nemesis Protocol (Book #5)
Necessary Means (Book #6)
Foreign Soil (Book #7)
Special Agent Cruz Crime Dramas:
Vengeance Is Mine (Book #1)
Defense of Innocents (Book #2)
Plea for Justice (Book #3)
Standalone:
The President's Man: Aaron Hardy Vol. 1-3
The President's Man 2: Aaron Hardy Vol. 4-6
Special Agent Cruz Crime Series
The First Agents

–

Patriot Assassin

By

Alex Ander

Continue reading for a preview
of the next book in the Aaron Hardy series...

Chapter 1: Surveillance

October 29th, 9:00 p.m.; New York City

Wearing a long-sleeved dark t-shirt under a black leather jacket, a pair of blue jeans and black five-inch tactical boots from 5.11 Tactical, Aaron Hardy hurried down 11th Street. The night was cool. A biting wind against his face reminded him that fall had come to the Northeast. Nights like these made him reminisce of his childhood, growing up in Northern Lower Michigan. He loved this time of the year. After enduring the hot and humid months of June, July and August, Hardy looked forward to the cold fresh air of autumn. He could match his clothing to the changing temperatures of fall much easier than he could during the stifling heat of summer. *You can only take off so many layers of clothing,* he thought, moving to his left to pass a meandering couple, who were in love and had no particular place to be this night.

As a young boy, he would have been sighting-in his hunting rifle right about now, eagerly waiting for the first day of deer season. Opening day was considered a holiday in his part of the state. He smiled, picturing his Marlin 336 lever-action rifle, chambered in .30-30 Winchester. The gun had been a gift from his father for his sixteenth birthday. Up to that point, Hardy had used his father's guns. The Marlin was his, however. Giving Hardy the rifle, his father had said to him, 'Son, it's time you had one of your own.' Hardy still owned that Marlin, vowing he would never sell it.

Hardy's jacket flared open, as the wind slipped inside it and sent a shiver up his spine. Fiddling with the zipper, he ran the pull-tab on the jacket to his chest, shielding his body from the cold. A voice in his head shattered the happy thoughts.

"He just turned right," said Charity, "onto 12th Street. It seems like he's picked up his pace a little."

"I'm on it." Hardy trotted to the corner of 11th Street and 5th Avenue. He grabbed the metal handrail and propelled his body forward down 5th Avenue, heading toward 12th Street. Slowing his pace, he waited for an update. Charity and Hardy were communicating through Hardy's wireless earpiece. She was in Washington D.C., tracking their target via the target's cell phone. With Charity acting as his eyes, Hardy could maintain a safe distance and not alert the man to Hardy's presence.

The target, Abdul Sayed, was a member of a terrorist cell and his skittish behavior this evening made Hardy nervous. Sayed had made several consecutive left turns, doubling-back over his route. Hardy knew the technique. He had used it many times to make sure no one was following him. *But, why now?* Hardy had been following him all over New York City for three days and not once had he attempted to disguise his routes.

During the day, Sayed worked at an office supply store, taking his lunch break at 12:30 p.m. every day. He would walk to a coffee shop and pick up food and coffee before proceeding to Washington Square Park, where he would eat his lunch; an hour after he left, he would be back to work. At five o'clock, he walked home to his apartment near Avenue of the Americas and Twenty-Third Street. He had stayed home the first two nights, but last night he went out for the evening, having dinner at a restaurant before spending an hour at a bookstore on Broadway. He left the bookstore and went home. His mannerisms had suggested he did not care who was following him. Tonight, however, was different.

Anxiety crept into Charity's voice. "I lost him."

"You what," Hardy shot back?

"I'm not sure what happened. His signal disappeared from my computer screen halfway down 12th Street."

Hardy ran along 5th Avenue. He turned right and came face to face with a group of people at the corner of 5th Avenue and 12th Street. He sidestepped them and dashed down 12th Street, scanning the street for Sayed. "What was his last location?"

Charity zoomed in on the map. "He was right in front of Goodmans."

Hardy slowed to a jog when he approached Goodman's Bar and Grill. Standing under the blue awning outside the establishment, he peered inside. "Are you sure this is the spot?"

"I'm positive. The computer doesn't lie."

"Yeah," he mumbled, "the computer doesn't lose targets either."

"Say again...I couldn't hear you."

"I'm going inside. Let me know if you get his signal back." He opened the door and walked into the restaurant. He passed through an open door, turned left and ascended a couple of steps, his eyes moving left and right. At the top of the stairs, he went left, analyzing every patron in the establishment. Absorbed in the search for Sayed, he was unaware of the approaching woman. Her head down, she was focused on a cell phone. The two collided and she recoiled, her arms flailing. The mobile device slipped from her hands, clattering as it slid across the floor.

Hardy took a long step forward and wrapped his arms around her waist. His left hand supported her upper back, while his right hand held the small of her back. Her head bobbing back before coming forward, she threw her hands upward and clutched his shoulders. Those who had not witnessed the accident would have thought the two were dancing, and Hardy had 'dipped' his partner.

The woman felt the power in the stranger's arms. A moment ago, she had braced for a rough landing. Now, feeling safe and secure in his grasp, she let her body relax. Her fingers maintained their vise-like grip on the muscular shoulders, while her eyes darted left and right, up and down. His hair was short and light brown in color. He had a square jaw that came to a slight point at his chin, which had a small dimple in the center. Settling on his eyes, she felt as if time was standing still. Never before had she seen such deep blue eyes. As the man brought her to a standing position, she found it impossible to turn away.

"I'm sorry, miss. Are you okay?" Hardy took a small step backward and glanced at her from head to toe. She was a few inches shorter, but the three-inch heels of her black thigh boots brought her even with his height. Under a long overcoat, she wore a black mini-skirt. The hem rose to the upper portion of her thighs. A tight, dark red sweater accentuated her rounded breasts. Long and straight bleached blonde hair fell to the middle of her back; the bangs stopped less than an inch above her well-manicured dark eyebrows, which curved slightly toward the bridge of her petite nose and the outer corner of her eye. She had a round face with hazel green eyes, narrowly spaced. Her full lips, colored to match her sweater, seemed to be permanently pursed.

The woman blinked her eyes a few times, shaking off the strange feeling. "Yes...I'm fine." Gazing into the man's eyes, she remembered why she was in this swanky bar in the first place. Sliding her hands down the strong arms, she cupped the back pockets of his jeans and drew his body closer. Manufacturing a seductive half-smile and tilting her head, she glanced at his lips before batting her eyelids. "I like it *rough*, anyway."

Hardy arched his back. *This isn't exactly what I had in mind tonight.* Peeling the smooth fingers from his backside, he picked up her phone and handed it to her. "You'll have to excuse me," he flashed a smile, "but I'm looking for someone."

She watched him walk away, eyeing his physical qualities from behind. Dragging out her words, she said, "If you don't find whoever it is you're looking for, I'd be happy to take her place."

Sayed's picture was back in the forefront of Hardy's mind, while he scanned the rest of the restaurant.

"What was that all about?" Charity had heard the exchange between Hardy and the woman. "Did you make a new friend?"

He ignored the question. "Have you found our man yet?"

"Still nothing," she replied.

Hardy had made it to the other end of the restaurant—no Sayed. He walked down a short flight of stairs. "He's not in the restaurant area. I'm going to check out the bathroom."

Entering men's room, he saw a man washing his hands. Hardy nodded his head and the man returned the gesture before drying his hands and leaving. Hardy peered under the stalls. They were empty, except for the last one. He unzipped his jacket and wrapped his fingers around his firearm; a Walther PPQ M2, chambered in nine millimeter.

Hardy pushed open the door to the first stall; it was empty. He repeated the process, until he came to the last one. The stall was occupied, but the door was ajar. His mental synapses were firing. *A man doesn't drop his pants without locking the door.* He drew his pistol and put it behind his back. He slowly pushed the door inward. His eyebrows shot upward. Staring back at him was a man sitting on the toilet, fully clothed. The man's head was down and cocked off to one side. Both of his hands were hanging at his sides. Hardy stretched out a hand and felt for a pulse under the man's chin. He was dead. Hardy examined the body; two bullet wounds in the chest and the left eye was missing, the result of a third bullet.

Holstering his pistol, he searched the man and stepped back. *What the hell happened here?* A few seconds later, Charity's high-pitched voice broke his concentration.

"Hardy, I've got him. Sayed is on the move again. He's heading east on 12th Street."

Hardy studied what was left of the man's face. "That's not possible. I'm looking at Sayed's corpse right now. Somebody killed him."

"I'm telling you his signal just appeared on my screen. He's getting away."

"All right, I'm on my way." Hardy exited the stall and ran toward the door. "Have Jameson send some agents to clean this mess up." He did not want this getting to the media, sending Sayed's friends into hiding.

On the street, Hardy glanced up and down 12th Street. Realizing Sayed was dead, he did not know whom he was trying to find. "Charity, what am I looking for? Where's the signal coming from?" Not getting a reply, he repeated the command. "Damn it, Charity, where the hell is it coming from?" His voice startled a couple who were entering the bar. The man hurried his female companion past Hardy and through the doors.

"It's not moving. The signal is stationary at the corner of 12th and University—west side of the street."

Hardy rushed to the corner of 12th Street and University, hoping his pace would not alert the person, or persons, who had taken Sayed's phone. Standing at the corner, he searched in all directions. Nothing seemed out of place. A man stood near a trash receptacle, his back to Hardy and his head down, looking at something in his hand. Hardy whispered. "Charity, dial the number to Sayed's phone. Let it ring once and hang up. Keep doing it until I say otherwise."

"Dialing now..."

Directly in front of Hardy, a muffled ringtone sounded once. The man near the trash container looked around. Hardy rushed forward, hearing the cell phone emit a single ring two more times. The man fished around in the trash before pulling out a cell phone. The mobile rang one time. Closing the distance, Hardy snatched the device from the man's hand.

"Hey, what the f—" the man noticed the pistol on Hardy's belt.

Hardy's eyes narrowed and his jaw muscles clenched. "Move along. This has nothing to do with you."

The man took several steps backward before turning around and scurrying away.

The phone rang again. "Charity, you can stop dialing. I've got the phone."

She had heard the verbal confrontation. "Is everything okay?"

He examined the phone. *How did this get in the trashcan?* He scanned the immediate area for anyone taking special interest in him. People were distracted by their cell phones, talking to others or rushing to their destination; nothing was suspicious. The person who had discarded the phone was gone.

"What happened? Hardy, are you okay?"

"I'll tell you when I get there." He turned the phone over in his hand. "I need a ride. Have Jameson set it up for me." Hardy took one more look around the area before walking back the way he had come. Had he glanced over his shoulder, he would have seen a figure slowly emerging from the shadows of a doorway, across University Place.

....

Go to <u>my author page</u> to continue reading <u>Patriot Assassin</u>.

Made in the USA
San Bernardino, CA
09 June 2019